SEEING LOVE

SAINTS PROTECTION & INVESTIGATIONS

MARYANN JORDAN

Cover design: Graphics by Stacy

Cover photography: Eric McKinney 612Covered

ISBN ebook: 978-0-9968010-5-8

ISBN print: 978-0-9968010-6-5

AUTHOR INFORMATION

I am an avid reader of romance novels, often joking that I cut my teeth on the historical romances. I have been reading and reviewing for years. In 2013, I finally gave into the characters in my head, screaming for their story to be told. From these musings, my first novel, Emma's Home, The Fairfield Series was born.

I was a high school counselor having worked in education for thirty years. I live in Virginia, having also lived in four states and two foreign countries. I have been married to a wonderfully patient man for over forty years. When writing, my dog or one of my two cats can generally be found in the same room if not on my lap.

Please take the time to leave a review of this book. Feel free to contact me, especially if you enjoyed my book. I love to hear from readers!

Facebook
Email
Website

Author's Note

Please remember that this is a work of fiction. I have lived in numerous states as well as overseas, but for the last thirty years have called Virginia my home. I often choose to use fictional city names with some geographical accuracies.

These fictionally named cities allow me to use my creativity and not feel constricted by attempting to accurately portray the areas.

It is my hope that my readers will allow me this creative license and understand my fictional world.

I also do quite a bit of research on my books and try to write on subjects with accuracy. There will always be points where creative license will be used in order to create scenes or plots.

All books have errors, no matter how many author, editors, proofers, and readers have looked at the manuscript. If the errors are minor and do not affect the story, please forgive and ignore. But, if you find errors that you deem necessary to report, please send me an email with your notations and do not try to report to Amazon.
Be kind to authors... we are human!
authormaryannjordan@gmail.com

1

PROLOGUE

The eager young boy and his smiling grandfather walked to the end of the pier and sat, side by side, as they readied their fishing poles. The Chesapeake Bay loomed before them, the early morning sun peeking behind. Bart Taggart loved the way the sunlight twinkled off the surface of the undulating water, creating never-ending patterns across the horizon. Glancing to the side, he realized his grandfather had already baited his fishing line and.

Bart's childish white-blond hair was now sandy in color and his slate-blue eyes were now the color of the water on a sunny day. He recently celebrated his eleventh birthday, but his size had him looming over his class-mates. Being with his father or grandfather made his size seem less noticeable—they were both large men them-selves. As much as he liked being with his dad, the morn-ings fishing with his grandfather had become their special tradition.

John Taggart, the CEO of his own business, was never too busy to spend time with his grandchildren.

Smiling up at the large man sitting next to him, Bart quickly tossed his line into the water. "Granddad?"

"Right here, Bartholomew," came the deep-voiced answer.

Bart covered his mouth with his hand and snickered. His grandfather was the only person to call him by his full name.

"Something funny, son?"

"You're the only one who calls me that," he answered honestly.

"Well, Bartholomew is your name. In fact, it was my father's name. Bartholomew. A good name. A strong name."

"Yeah, but I don't know anyone else with the same name," Bart replied. He thought of classmates named Bill, Tom, or even John, like his grandfather. But no other Bartholomews. "They all call me Bart."

"It's not unusual to shorten a name. Did you know my full name is Jonathan?"

Bart's eyes grew large, never realizing his grandfather had a nickname as well. Pleased, he ducked his head, smiling as he looked back down at his pole.

"Boy, I believe you wanted to ask me something," his grandfather reminded.

"Oh, yeah," he said. "Nonnie said there are mermaids in the ocean, and I wanted to know if you'd ever seen one. She said we might catch one today," he added with boyish enthusiasm, his eyes bright with excitement.

John snorted, shaking his head. "Son," he began carefully. "Your grandmother is a wonderful woman. I've loved her since the first time I laid eyes on her almost forty years ago. I'll never forget seeing her at one of my mother's garden parties. She was wearing a yellow dress, and her blonde hair made her look like an angel."

Bart was quiet as his grandfather reminisced. The idea of his grey-haired, slightly plump grandmother ever being a pretty, young girl seemed funny, but he loved the idea.

"I knew then she was the woman for me. She's a wonderful wife, a great mother, and" John leaned sideways, and shoulder bumped Bart, "She's a super grandmother, wouldn't you say?"

Bart nodded enthusiastically, remembering the cookie jar always being full at her house and her bedtime stories were never scary.

"But she's always been a bit...fanciful."

"Fanciful?" Bart asked, his face scrunched in question.

"Full of imagination. A bit of a dreamer."

"Oh," Bart said, disappointment now replacing the confusion in his expression. "There are no mermaids?"

"I've never seen a mermaid, Bart. I've never met anyone who has. I've never seen a photograph of a mermaid. Seen lots of people's drawings, but then that doesn't make it real, does it?"

Bart shook his head emphatically, wanting to please his grandfather more than really understanding.

"Son, I'll tell you what's real to me. If I can't feel it, touch it, see it, or experience it, then it's not real. And when it comes to people, you need to learn to judge a man by his actions and not just his words. I have to deal with fake people sometimes who will lie to get what they want."

Sitting quietly for a moment, Bart turned his face back up to his grandfather. "We aren't going to be able to see any of Nonnie's mermaids, are we?"

"'I'm afraid not, son, but your grandmother doesn't mean any harm."

"She's not a fake person?" his young mind tried to discern.

"No, no," John said, shaking his head. "There's no deceit in your grandmother at all. Nothing wrong with someone having an imagination, as long as there's no deceit. But in my business, I have to always look to see what someone's motives are. What their actions are. And that's how I determine what the truth is."

John's gaze was on his grandson as he quietly fished for a few minutes before Bart turned his face back up to the older man.

"Granddad, you love Nonnie, but you can't see that, so how do you know it's real?"

"Oh, son. Don't ever mistake that faith cannot also be truth. I have faith. Faith in God. Faith in love. But I don't believe in just telling someone you love them. It's got to be followed by actions. Deeds."

Bart's face continued to scrunch as he thought over his grandfather's words.

"Your grandmother shows me every day that she loves me, and I hope I do the same for her. I see God's presence in the world around me. Faith is just as real as truth."

Their conversation was interrupted by a nibble on Bart's line and for the next few minutes, the two were immersed in pulling in a fish before they decided to let it go back into the water. Bart watched it swim away, glad for the fish's chance to live.

His grandfather's voice broke into his musing. "Your name is synonymous with seeking the truth, did you know that?"

Bart's attention was immediately pulled from watching the water's rippling surface once more. "Huh?"

"Your name. St. Bartholomew was a follower of Jesus and known for always searching for the truth. Not a bad name to live up to, son."

"I didn't know that" he answered.

"Yes, indeed. Always search for the truth, Bart. It has served me well over the years," came the sage advice.

The two silently packed their tackle boxes and headed back up the lawn toward the mansion John and Arlene owned. They could already hear the sounds of Bart's cousins playing on the expansive back patio.

"Granddad? What should I say to Nonnie if she asks about the mermaids?"

"Did you see any?"

"Um...no, of course not. They're not real."

"All you need to say is that you didn't see any on this trip. Afterall, we don't want to make your grandmother feel bad, do we?"

Bart grinned, shaking his head. "No, I won't make her feel bad. But we know the truth, don't we, granddad?"

Patting his grandson on the back, John nodded benevolently. "Yes, Bartholomew, we do. We know what's real."

2

SEVENTEEN YEARS LATER

The early morning light filtered through the blinds, creating slatted patterns on the opposite wall. Bart slowly opened one eye, blinking, as he tried to remember where he was. Lifting his pounding head, he realized he was sprawled on a bed in an unfamiliar room, the sound of soft snores coming from his left. Turning his head toward the noise also caused him to face the window, the sunlight piercing his skull.

How much did I party last night? The sight of the woman sleeping next to him offered no answer to his question. He threw his large arm over his eyes to shade the light from continuing to stab his head. A huge man, his movement caused the bed to shake and for a moment he was afraid the woman would awaken. He hated the mornings after. No matter what had been discussed the night before—*this is only sex, I don't do relationships, it's only physical*—he could see the look in their eye the next morning. The look that screamed, *please stay.* Or worse, *please cuddle.* Or worst of all, *what do you mean you won't call?*

After years of practice, the former SEAL had developed his natural flirt down to a science, able to discern which women would be most conducive to a quick night of sex. But even with his immeasurable skills, he still tried to give a hasty goodbye with a wink as he let himself out of the door before the woman had a chance to offer to cook him breakfast.

As the mattress moved, he recognized the signs that his night's partner was awakening. Wanting nothing more than to roll over and sleep for a couple of hours, he sat up, throwing his long legs over the edge of the bed. Running his hand over his stubbled jaw and up through his hair, he fought the battle between wanting to run and wanting to sleep. *But only sleep if I were by myself in my own bed. Or with someone I cared about.*

Where did that come from? The thought of having someone to care about jolted Bart from his tired, hungover, sleepy state of mind. Sighing deeply, he knew why that thought crossed his consciousness. Jack Bryant, his boss and friend, recently married Bethany, a remarkable woman who fit into Jack's life perfectly. And Cam, his best friend and co-worker, now engaged to Miriam, another great girl. *Jesus—and my cousin, Sabrina, was now engaged to Jude, a former SEAL, who now worked for Jack.*

He realized his musings kept him sitting on the side of the bed too long when last's night fun sat up next to him, placing her hands on his back.

"Hey, baby," she cooed, running her long, blood-red fingernails over his skin. "What's this? I didn't even notice it last night." Her hand clasped the chain around his neck, holding a St. Bartholomew medallion.

A slash of irritation flew through him at the sight of her talons on the gift from his grandfather. He twisted as he stood quickly, effectively moving his body away from hers and the pendant from her clutches. Plastering on his famous, panty-melting smile, he greeted her as well.

Letting the sheet drop, she bounded to her knees on the side of the bed. His eyes dropped to her chest. *Funny, what gets me stirring at night has no effect in the light of the next morning.* Shoving that thought aside, he placed his hand over his heart, saying, "You're a tempting sight, but I've got to go. Maybe I'll call sometime."

Her eyes narrowed as she watched him finish dressing. "You're not going to call, are you? I know a brushoff when I hear one," she accused.

"Now don't be going and getting upset," he gently admonished, with another wink. "I'm a strictly one-night guy, and honestly...if I were to stick around, you'd be miserable."

Her seductive pout paired with her fantastic body would have most men writing her number down in their contact list. *But not me!* He just smiled and winked once more as he left her apartment.

Once inside his truck, he leaned his head back against the seat, scrubbing his hand over his face. Filled with an emotion he could not identify, he drove to his large home outside of Charlestown. Pulling into his driveway, he sat for a moment appreciating the view. His hand automatically reached up to finger his medallion, the memories of his grandfather pouring over him. *Gone, but not forgotten, granddad. Your advice...never forgotten.*

He headed through the house, up the stairs, and into the large master bathroom, stripping as the water in the shower became hot. Stepping underneath the spray, letting the water pound his tense muscles, he washed away the cloying perfume scent left over from last night.

Normally on a Sunday, he would hang with friends watching football, but today he felt uncharacteristically like staying home. Mowing the grass first before tackling a few indoor projects, he stayed busy, not willing his mind to focus on the growing sense of dissatisfaction with the recent hookups.

Across town, Faith Romani sat on her worn sofa, the early morning light between the buildings across the street tried to find its way into her small apartment. The tiny, tabletop Christmas tree with four antique, glass ornaments sat on the end table she had moved in front of the window. The only sign of the season in her apartment, but it gave her comfort, nonetheless.

Sleep had been elusive, and she finally gave up and fixed a cup of tea, settling in to let her mind wander. An art pad in her lap, she chewed on the end of her pencil. Closing her eyes, she allowed the feelings to flow through her mind, slowly taking on shapes and designs.

With the pencil clutched loosely in her hand, she began to sketch freeform, allowing the image to flow from deep inside of her. At first, the lines on the page meant nothing. Simple lines, curves, shadows. Half an hour later she held the pad at arm's length, staring at the image that came to life on the paper. A boy's face peered out at her. A slight smile curved his lips. His dark eyes seemed to be searching. For what...she had no idea.

As usual with these drawings, she set the pad aside so the images no longer stared at her, daring her to do something about them. Sucking in a deep breath, she slowly let the air out. It was times like this she missed her grandmother. Her *Babushka* would have understood...told her how to interpret her drawings.

Faith's father abandoned her and her mother soon after she was born. The stories her mother had told her depended on her mood. Sometimes it was because he moved back to his Russian homeland. Or he died a tragic death. Or he left to search for lost treasure. By the time Faith was ten years old, she knew the truth. Her grandmother finally told her that he was a man unused to being tied down, and the idea of a wife and child were foreign to him.

"Ah, dearie. Some men are like the wind. They blow into your life, never meaning to stay, but rush on by. Your mother fell in love with one of those."

Faith's mother, who never recovered from the emotional loss of abandonment, died of cancer when Faith was only twelve and her grandmother became her guardian. As much as she loved her mother, it was her grandmother that influenced her the most. *And understood me the most.*

"You have a gift, *Printsesa*," she would say, using her favorite nickname of princess. "Use it wisely, but guard it carefully. Others will not understand."

Closing her eyes, allowing the words of her grandmother to wash over her, she could almost smell the borsch, the soup that was often bubbling on the stove when she returned home from school. Blinking quickly, the loneliness of her existence rushed over her, but she refused to cry.

"Shed tears for the living, who exist in darkness. Not for the dead who have moved on to heaven," her grandmother would say.

Moving to her bedroom, she changed into running

clothes and headed out of the apartment, willing the pounding pavement to chase away the shadows in her mind. The art pad still lay on the coffee table, the image of the boy looking up from the page.

Bart drove to Cam's house to pick up his friend. They often rode to work together now that they lived in homes that were not far apart. He walked up the front porch knowing the wreath-covered door would probably swing open before he had a chance to knock.

"Good morning," sang the sweet-faced woman who welcomed him. Stepping inside, his gaze landed on the large Christmas tree in the living room, gold and silver decorations filling almost every space.

Cam's fiancé, a petite, dark-haired beauty, dressed in nursing scrubs, offered him a hug. She then stood back, eyeing him speculatively. "We missed you when we left the bar the other night. I'm assuming you went home with big-boobs? Oh, wait...that would make Saturday night just like every other Saturday night at Chuck's Bar."

"Now, now, Miriam," he laughed, seeing her dark eyes flashing at him. "You know I just like to have a little fun." Her gaze bore a hole in him as he threw up his hands in self-defense. Hearing his friend stirring in the kitchen, he called out, "Bro! A little help to fend off your tigress would be appreciated!"

A large, Hispanic man ambled toward the pair, pulling his fiancé back into his side. "She busting your chops over bailing on us the other night?"

"I didn't bail," Bart protested. "I just found myself diverted by a pair of—"

"Boobs!" Miriam interjected loudly with a huff.

"I was going to say blue eyes," Bart corrected. Giving his friend's fiancé a sweet pout, he said, "Come on, Miriam. You know I'm just a bit of a hound dog when it comes to the ladies."

Rolling her eyes, she answered, "Your little-boy expressions don't work on me, mister. One day, you're going to fall for someone, and I want to be around when it happens." Turning to walk back toward the kitchen, she stopped and looked over her shoulder. "And guess what? I hope you have to work like hell to get her interested!" With a wink at the two men, she left the room.

Bart looked over at Cam, a sheepish expression on his face. "She knows how to go for the jugular, doesn't she?" he joked.

Cam threw his head back with a laugh. The former undercover police detective looked at his friend and explained, "She just wants you to find what we've got, man."

Bart smiled at his friend, happy for what Cam had found. As the two walked toward the kitchen to grab the breakfast Miriam was dishing out, he could not help but wonder, *Is that kind of relationship in the cards for me?*

Driving through the security gates of Jack's compound an hour later, Bart parked outside the large log-cabin home. The Blue Ridge Mountains loomed in the background, the cedar, pine, and maple trees surrounding the house. Jack Bryant operated Saints Protection & Investigations, recruiting from former military and government agencies to form a unique security service. Coming from backgrounds including the CIA, FBI, DEA, SEALs, ATF, the alphabet soup took on the cases others did not want or needed assistance with. Some covert. The Saints would never officially be recognized as the ones who solved the crimes. That did not matter to them; not having to deal with the bureaucratic bullshit that each of them left behind, made the work interesting...and profitable.

"Where's Bethany's car?" Cam asked, glancing at the large SUVs and trucks around.

"Jack's got her parking in the garage now that she lives here." Laughing, Bart added, "He said it was because he was tired of scraping the frost off her windshield, but we know it's because he can't stand the idea of her not being completely protected."

The two men walked between the other vehicles parked in front and jogged up the wide front steps. Looking around, Bart appreciated the greenery draped over the porch banister, decorated with red bows. The front door held an enormous wreath. Upon entering, the scent of chocolate assaulted their senses. Quickly moving to the kitchen bar, where the other men stood, they looked over as Bethany pulled chocolate chip muffins from the oven.

"Damn, girl," Marc said appreciatively. "Those smell so good." The former CIA pilot was more at home in his small cabin than Jack's grandiose one, but he loved the treats Bethany baked. His culinary skills ran toward survivalist cuisine, and he never missed a chance for anything home cooked.

Other *hell yeahs* soon followed from the rest of the men. Bart glanced around, seeing the Saints now gathered. Luke, Chad, and Blaise sat on stools at the kitchen counter. The large, formidable group of men were reduced to a drooling mass around Bethany's cooking. The slim, natural beauty with her long, honey blonde hair pulled back into a braid hanging down her back, made homemade goodies for them once a week. Bart wondered if she had bewitched Jack by luring him with her baking skills. Looking at the man who was appreciatively staring at his wife and not the treats, Bart knew—Jack was in love with the woman.

His eyes moved to the large living room, the two-story stone fireplace on one wall and windows overlooking the mountains in the background on the other side. The Christmas tree Jack and Bethany decorated was taller than what Bart's grandparent's used to have, and he thought theirs had been the biggest.

"Damn, Jack, that tree is humongous," he laughed.

Jack, his taciturn expression morphed into a smile as he rubbed his dark beard, glancing at Bethany before turning to look at the tree that was now the center of attention. "After we decorated her Mountville cabins next door, we decided to start some traditions ourselves." With a wink toward her, he said, "We need to get our meeting started. You all can enjoy the muffins when they cool." He kissed Bethany before leading the men downstairs to their main work area.

Once settled around the large conference table, Jack began the meeting. The Saints had numbered eight, but now a new face joined the team. "You all know Jude from the work he completed in Virginia Beach with us last month. He's officially become a Saint employee and I'm assigning him to Monty and Marc for a while."

Everyone smiled at the former SEAL who had become engaged to Bart's cousin. They had recently moved to the Charlestown area so he could work for Jack. No longer sporting the SEAL haircut, his sandy curls gave him a youthful appearance, but his honed body spoke of one who worked out relentlessly.

"Luke will also offer him investigative skills during his initial employment. Jude, they can teach you methods that were learned from the FBI and CIA."

Jude nodded in appreciation, smiling at Bart who had been instrumental in his decision to work for the Saints.

"We've got a new assignment that will take precedence." Gaining the immediate attention of the group, Jack continued.

"We've been contacted by Ivan Krustas—"

Before Jack could speak further, a collective *what the hell* came from the men around the table. Jude's fiancé, Sabrina, had been kidnapped and the kidnapper tried to take her to Ivan, a member of the Russian mob operating out of the Norfolk area. Ivan, in an attempt to keep the Feds out of his businesses, had collaborated with them to turn over one of his nephews who had become involved in human trafficking. Ivan, having no desire to have anything to do with Sabrina, kept her safe until Jude and Bart came to rescue her. The kidnapper was handed over to the FBI and the group assumed that would be the last they would hear from Ivan Krustas.

Jack silenced the group with a stare. "His grandson was kidnapped about thirty hours ago and of course, the FBI are working the case. Ivan contacted me last night, wanting our assistance."

"Afraid of what the FBI will find out about his businesses?" Blaise asked. A veterinarian, with the looks of a Nordic Viking, had completed extensive work for the DEA before joining Jack. Trained to assess and question, his mercurial mood could shift from easygoing to unyielding investigator instantly. A muscle in his square jaw ticked as he leaned forward in his chair.

"It's his grandson," Chad admonished, shooting a frustrated look toward Blaise. A former explosive expert with the ATF, he usually saw the good in people, easily putting his life on the line.

Jack sucked in a deep breath, saying, "Probably a bit of both. He wants his grandson found but is afraid that the FBI might not give it the attention it needs because they will use the opportunity to spend more time delving into his businesses than working to find his grandson."

Monty, the dark-haired, debonair Saint, took over as Luke sent information to their tablets opened on the table. "I've been in contact with my former agency buddies and there's the possibility Ivan is right. Obviously, the FBI wants to find his grandson, but some agents are also chomping at the bit to dig more into the Krustas' holdings in Norfolk."

Jack carefully eyed the men around the table. All capable. All willing. His eyes landed on the large, blond, ex-SEAL. Something Ivan had told him this morning stuck in his mind, making his choice for the lead investigator on this assignment imperative. Not sure if it was the right decision to make, he had always relied on his gut instinct when in the Special Forces.

"Bart. You take the lead," Jack commanded.

Without hesitation, Bart nodded, glad for the vote of confidence. "You got it, sir," he replied, a smile on his lips. As much as he hated the Russian mob activities in the Hampton Roads area of Virginia, he appreciated the chance to assist Ivan Krustas since he had helped in keeping his cousin safe.

Glancing at Jude, Bart knew the young investigator

would love to be assigned to the mission as well since Sabrina was his fiancé, but Jack knew what he was doing. Jude needed more seasoning and working with Monty on the project would be perfect.

Luke, their former CIA computer expert, took over the presentation, his pen tapping on the table as the caffeine from his strong coffee kicked in. "Ivan lives in Virginia Beach, but his daughter and grandson live outside of Charlestown. The child was taken from his home at night while his mother was at a charity event."

"No security?"

"It appears when Ivan's son died several years ago and Ivan was embroiled in the investigations into his nephew's businesses, his daughter-in-law moved to Charlestown to escape the publicity. According to Ivan, she wanted a more normal upbringing for her son and kept a low profile in their new town. Her son went to a private school, and she lives in a gated community, but there is no special security."

"Any demands?" Bart asked.

Jack nodded, "Yeah. For a quarter of a million which Ivan paid last night." He caught the confused expressions of his men and leaning forward with his muscular arms on the table, continued. "All he got in return was a picture of his grandson holding a sign that said 'Thanks ,' and then he got another monetary demand. The missive said that Erik would be safe as long as the money kept coming."

"Damn, extortion!" Chad exuded, blowing out a sharp breath.

"Not the usual kidnapping modus operandi," Blaise commented, his calm statement belying his quick mind.

"Sounds personal," Bart added, voicing what the others were thinking.

"That's what I thought when I talked to him last night." Jack looked over at Bart and said, "It seems Ivan received a few threats before the kidnapping."

"He knew it could happen and didn't do more to protect his grandson?" Marc asked, his dark brows rose in question.

"The threats he received had nothing to do with his grandson," Jack responded. "The kidnapping came out of the blue."

Turning to look at Bart, he added, "We're all working this with you, and Monty will coordinate closely with his FBI contacts, but I want you to head to Charlestown this morning to talk to the family. Ivan is there at his daughter-in-law's house and since you have a history with the man, you would have a better insight into what we're looking at."

"What kind of timetable are we up against?" Bart asked.

"Time is of the essence. We want to find Ivan's grandson but, unlike most kidnappings and hostage situations, it seems that the kidnappers are willing to ride this out to financially cripple Ivan. The FBI is still very much in charge, and we haven't been called in to investigate by them. Our contract is with Ivan. He has a very specific assignment with us."

Holding Bart's gaze for a second longer than Bart was comfortable, Jack added, "Ivan told me that he has engaged the services of the local police's artist, to see if there was anything they could come up with."

Head cocked to the side, Bart asked, "Wouldn't that be more useful if there had been a witness?"

"Ivan's probably grasping at straws," Chad commented. "Looking for anything and anyone who had been seen in the area."

Nodding, Bart stood, saying goodbye to the group. The others stayed to continue delving into Ivan's business and life while Bart headed back up the stairs. Bethany met him as he passed the kitchen, handing him a plastic container. His eyes looked down at the proffered dish as she grinned, saying, "Your chocolate chip muffins to go."

Leaning over to kiss the top of her head, he said, "You're the best, Bethany. Thank you."

"Save your flattery for your hookups, big guy," she called after him as he winked at her, walking to the door.

As he drove through the security gate, chewing on a muffin, he appreciated his boss' wife. A strange emotion passed through his mind at the thought of the woman's bed he had left the other morning. *Dissatisfaction. Sure, sexually she'd been okay. She got off...I got off...what else is there?* Sighing, he wondered why he felt such disquiet. With a mental shake, he tried to focus on the mission at hand, but during his drive toward Charlestown, the idea of a special someone for him interrupted his planning.

3

———

Driving up to the security gate in front of the exclusive neighborhood, Bart was waved through after showing his identification to the guard. Jack had told him Ivan would take care of all the arrangements for him to have full access.

Following the street as it wound past new, multimillion-dollar homes, he wondered if this was one of the reasons Jack put him on point for the mission. Having grown up with wealthy parents and grandparents, he was accustomed to being comfortable in all types of social settings.

At the correct address, he noted the black sedans parked outside the home. His gaze roamed the neighboring houses, taking in the area. Perfectly manicured lawns leading to huge mansions, each exterior different from the next.

Folding his tall frame out of his extended-cab truck, he stretched before walking to the front door. He noted the presence of several dark-suited men wandering the perimeter of the yard, eyeing him suspiciously. Answering his knock, an elderly woman in a housekeeper's apron, her red-rimmed eyes partially hidden behind glasses, looked up. Introducing himself, she let him in and escorted him past several more men in dark suits, to the formal living room.

A young man Bart did not recognize stood near the fireplace. A huge Christmas tree, elegantly decorated, drew his eyes to the corner of the room. A few presents sat underneath, as though awaiting the child that would be coming down to open them in a week. The dark paneling of the room, along with the drawn heavy curtains, gave the room a gloomy countenance.

Sitting in a leather chair near the fireplace was Ivan Krustas. A distinguished older man, heavyset with a square jaw and eyes that did not appear to miss anything, he nonetheless looked very different than when Bart had met him in Norfolk a few months ago. At that time, Ivan was a man in charge—of his life and the situation with Bart's cousin. Now he looked...destroyed.

Ivan immediately stood, walking over with an outstretched hand. Bart took it, the shaky grip clasped in his hand. Instinctively, he thought, *This is a devastated man.*

"Mr. Taggart, we meet again."

"Mr. Krustas, please call me Bart. And I'm very sorry for the circumstances."

Grief passed through the older man's grey eyes as he offered Bart a seat. "You may call me Ivan as well. This," he said, pointing to the young man, "is one of my nephews, Dmitry."

Dmitry stepped forward, shaking Bart's outstretched hand. It was easy for Bart to see the family resemblance.

"Mrs. Dukakas?" Ivan called to the housekeeper. As

the woman appeared at the door, he instructed, "Would you please ask Constance to join us?"

The woman nodded quietly and left the room. Bart's eyes followed her. After she was out of earshot, he asked, "Was she here the night Erik was taken?"

Ivan's head nodded, each movement seeming to add age to his face. "Yes, she was the only one here. Her room is behind the kitchen. Actually, she has a small suite of rooms and has been with the family for many years." He gave a small smile, and added, "She was with us when my son was a teenager. And when Constance demanded to leave the Hampton Roads area, Mrs. Dukakas decided to follow her and Erik."

"I take it she did not hear anything that night?"

"No, no. She checked on Erik at about ten p.m. and he was sound asleep. She made sure the alarms in the house were set and then turned in. She said she watched television until about eleven before going to sleep. She awoke at two a.m. when Constance came home from her event and checked on Erik, finding his room empty."

"I've read the initial police report and, of course, we're working with the FBI as well."

"Humph," Ivan snorted. "They care about the case, but I also know the chance to delve into my businesses is of utmost importance to them. I fear they will use any excuse to focus on me rather than..." his voice cracked, "my grandson." Ivan pressed his palms to his eyes, stemming the flow of tears.

Bart respectfully waited for a moment to give the older man a chance to compose himself, watching carefully as Dmitry stood close to Ivan, placing his hand on his shoulder.

"I thought the loss of my son to a heart attack several

years ago would break me but this..." he said, looking directly at Bart through haunted eyes, "is the worst agony imaginable."

Ivan was offered a respite by the appearance of a beautiful woman entering the room. Her hair, normally coiffed, was pulled back into a ponytail. Designer clothes were replaced with yoga pants and a long-sleeved tunic that hung to her mid-thighs. Slippers encased her feet instead of heels. Her face was devoid of makeup as her red-rimmed eyes matched those of the housekeeper.

"I'll bring tea for everyone," Mrs. Dukakas said as she quietly left the room again.

Bart greeted Constance Krustas with a handshake and heartfelt condolences. Her eyes flared as she looked up at his face, but he knew his size could be intimidating. Wanting to make her more comfortable, he assisted her to sit on the sofa and he took the wingback chair facing her. Glancing at Ivan, he watched as the older man sat next to his daughter-in-law, placing his hand on her arm as he handed her a tissue. *Their relationship seems to be good,* he noted as Constance offered her father-in-law a watery nod.

"Mrs. Krustas, I've read the detective's report and have access to the FBI interviews. I want to make sure I understand the events from your and Ivan's perspectives." Receiving nods from the two, he continued. "Was there anything different about that night?"

Swallowing with difficulty, Constance shook her head. "No. I don't go out a lot. Not really. But I'm on a few charity boards and they usually have some evening events." Running her hand over her face, she took a shuddering breath and continued. "The police asked me if I noticed anything unusual, but I didn't."

"Did you drive yourself?"

"No, I had another charity board member give me a lift."

He caught a glimpse of blush on her cheeks as she twisted the handkerchief in her hand nervously. Pressing her, he asked, "Anyone special?"

Licking her lips, she nodded. "I...it was Roger Montague." Her eyes cut over to Ivan, but he just stared straight ahead. "We see each other occasionally. Just friends," she added quickly. "But he's been a good friend since I moved here."

Bart noticed as her eyes darted over to Ivan's once more. Ivan caught the movement and took Constance's hand. "You'll always be like a daughter to me, but I understand you'll want to date. I never expected you to stay a lonely widow."

She twisted in her seat and looked at Ivan. "It's not like that, honestly. I'm not romantically involved. He's just a friend and lives close by. He only gave me a ride that night."

Bart interrupted, saying, "He was aware Erik was home alone?"

She turned her face toward his, confusion clearly written there. "Yes, but then so would lots of others. I'm a single mother, and just about anyone who knew I was at the event would know he was here without me. But then, he wasn't alone."

"Yes, I understand that Mrs. Dukakas checked on him before turning in. In that case, the kidnapping would have had to happen between about ten p.m. and before you got home at two a.m."

She scrubbed her hand over her face once more, and

said, "I believe her. She's been with the family for over twenty years."

Ivan interjected his agreement. "Her mother and father worked for the family as well. Very reliable."

Bart nodded but appreciated the Saints would be doing their own checking on both the housekeeper and Constance's friend.

Her shoulders began to shake with silent sobs, and Ivan assisted her to stand. Walking with his daughter-in-law to the entrance of the room, he called for one of the guards. "Please escort her to her room and ask Mrs. Dukakas to take some tea up to her."

The suited man nodded and walked away with Constance leaning heavily on his arm. Just then, another man walked swiftly into the room. Bart recognized him instantly as Ivan's nephew from Norfolk. It appeared at the time he was Ivan's right-hand man and if the greeting between the two men was anything to judge, that relationship still served. Bart observed as Dmitry held back from the other two, his eyes darting between his brother and uncle.

Ivan pulled the newcomer into his embrace as the two patted each other on the back. "I'm glad you're here," Ivan said.

"I came as soon as I could," Anton replied.

Turning his gaze to Bart, Ivan said, "I know introductions were not made last summer, but this is my nephew, Anton."

Bart shook hands with Anton, noting his attire. While the man was clothed in expensive slacks and shirt, they appeared slightly wrinkled.

"You've been away?" Bart casually asked.

"Yes, yes," Anton nodded, holding on to Ivan's arm as

he escorted the man back to the sofa before taking a seat himself. "I've just come in from spending the week in California."

"Forgive me for sounding impertinent, but your cousin's son was kidnapped almost two days ago and you're just getting here?"

Bart caught a flash of irritation in Anton's eyes before being shuttered. Ivan interrupted, saying, "I asked him to stay. He was brokering a deal, and we had the police and FBI on the case. There was nothing Anton could have done if he had returned yesterday."

"I've read some, but I'd like to listen to your version of what happened a year ago with your operation."

Once more, Anton seemed perturbed by the question, but Ivan appeared to expect it. Heaving a sigh, he stood and walked over to the fireplace with his hands outstretched to the warmth. Measuring his words, he began, "My grandfather came to this country from Russia when war was decimating our land. Our country had been at war with someone for so many years that America seemed like the land of opportunity, even for a communist. He was a fisherman, off the coast of Alaska, when the crew decided to defect. Taken in by Americans on the coast, he made his way down to California. By the time he married and had a family, he moved across the country to Virginia."

Bart listened carefully even though everything Ivan said was in the FBI report.

"My father had three sons and we all became involved in the family business." At that, Ivan turned from the fireplace and pierced Bart with a stare. "I will not divulge our family business interests, but let's just say we were profitable."

Keeping his expression neutral, Bart was cognizant of extortion, fraud, money laundering, narcotics, plus a host of other nefarious dealings that constituted the family's businesses.

"As the oldest, I received the largest share of our family's interests. My brother, Mikhail, died in a business deal gone bad, but he had a son, Sergio. My other brother worked alongside me until he had a heart attack about three years ago. His sons are Anton, who followed in his father's footsteps and is now my right hand, and Dmitry, in graduate school learning accounting and finance. My son also had a heart attack early in life. It seems bad hearts are prominent in my family."

"Sergio is now in jail," Bart stated, knowing the situation but wanting to hear Ivan's explanation.

Anton stood, walked over to the polished oak credenza, and poured a tumbler of whiskey for Ivan. Handing it to him, he faced Bart. "I know this is necessary, but can I ask why the interest in our family?"

Bart considered standing but continued to sit...*for the moment.* Holding Anton's gaze, he said, "Doors and windows not broken; Constance's whereabouts were known; the only person in the house was an elderly housekeeper. We'd be negligent to not consider that Erik's kidnapping could have been someone close to the family."

At this, both Anton and Ivan visibly reared back. Blinking twice, Ivan made his way over to the sofa once more, closely followed by Anton. Ivan nodded, pinching his lips.

Bart added, "Sergio might be in prison, but his incarceration hardly means that he would not have those on the outside who would help him. Work for him."

"I won't go into all our family endeavors," Ivan

warned, but said, "Four years ago, I moved many of our family businesses, mostly into legitimate companies. I wanted to hand something to my grandson that he could take over without fear of being thrown into prison. Anton and Dmitry's father agreed and my son, along with my nephews, understood what we were doing. My other nephew, Sergio, never agreed and became a thorn in our side. I finally bought him out and gave him the money to start his own businesses."

Ivan stopped to stare at Bart once more. "I don't have to tell you what he got into."

Bart shook his head. "No, sir. The indictments and conviction told the story well enough."

Shaking his head, Anton said, "Stupid fuck. My cousin got into human trafficking, something our family would have never consented to."

"When the FBI and DEA came snooping into my affairs, I handed them Sergio. He became an embarrassment to the family. Always drunk at family gatherings. Whoring away his life right in front of his wife. Disgraceful."

"That must have been hard," Bart commented.

A glint of steel shown in Ivan's gaze. "Not at all, Mr. Taggart. I was not about to have my business interests, nor Anton, Dmitry, and Erik's legacy tainted and destroyed by a selfish prick, no matter if he was my nephew."

Bart nodded, taking in the information, and now adding Sergio at the top of his list. *The man may be in prison, but he would have no problem getting someone to do his dirty work. And how better to retaliate against his uncle than to kidnap his grandson and financially ruin him?*

"Tell me about the notes and the payout." Bart queried.

Ivan sighed again. "I received a frantic call from Constance about two-fifteen a.m. She had already called 911 but I made sure to make a few calls myself. I contacted Anton in California, my lawyer, and my head of security. I had my driver bring Dmitry and me here immediately and arrived about six a.m. By that time, I received the first email, saying Erik had been taken and I needed to have a quarter of a million dollars wired to an offshore bank account. Of course, I gave the email to the FBI when they arrived. I was advised not to pay until they could trace the account."

Anton erupted with a rude snort. "Those federal bastards didn't care about Erik. They were too interested in wanting to ascertain where Ivan was getting the money."

Bart watched the three men carefully as Ivan continued. He noted Dmitry quietly in the background offering no explanations, his face interestingly passive.

"My security people checked out what they could about the account, but it would be impossible for me to be able to see who actually got their hands on the money." Shaking his head, he looked directly at Bart. "It won't surprise you to know that money laundering has been a... family business...for a long time. I know it's possible to bury accounts so that someone can get to it, and we'll never know who they are."

"Is this something you asked Jack to work on?"

"Not at first, no. To be honest, I wasn't thinking as clearly as I normally do."

"That's understandable."

"Not if I want to outsmart the bastard who has my grandson," Ivan said emphatically.

"I don't know what Jack can do, but I'll talk to him this

afternoon when I report in." Bart saw the appreciation in Ivan's expression before continuing his questions. "You paid them, right? On time?"

"Yes, absolutely," Ivan confirmed. "Then nothing. There was no email telling me where he was. After about two hours another demand came in. They wanted another quarter of a million dollars."

Standing, Bart closed his notebook and placed it in the pocket of his jacket. "If you don't mind, I'd like to take a look at Erik's room."

Ivan leaned back heavily, as though the dissertation had taken everything out of him. Anton nodded toward the stairs. "If you go to the top of the stairs and back to the end of the hall, Erik's room is on the right."

Nodding, Bart turned and walked out of the room. He almost smiled but stilled it quickly. Not because he was happy, but because this was what he liked doing the best. He honestly wished Monty had come to do the interview since he was good at putting people at ease. *Me? Getting my hands dirty in an investigation is my forte!*

4

Faith walked around the room, looking at objects, noting their placement. No rhythm to the room. No symmetry. Books were scattered on the nightstand and desk but shared the space with toys. *Nine years old. Almost too old for certain toys, but too young to give them up completely.* She knew his laptop had been taken by the FBI, but it would have given her no clues anyway.

The curtains were closed but she crossed the room and held them back slightly. Down below, she could see the manicured lawn of the back yard, the swimming pool beyond the stone patio. Large pots held palm trees, surrounded by smaller pots of evergreens dotting the patio. *Palm trees?* She wondered how they grew in Virginia's mountainous regions but knew money could buy almost anything. The vista beyond held no interest, and she let the curtain drop back into place, plunging the room into faint shadows.

The walls were peppered with sports posters and a shelf held several little league trophies. She stepped into Erik's bathroom, wondering at the neatness found there.

A housekeeper would probably tidy it every day, but she noticed his toothbrush and toothpaste tossed casually on the marble counter. There was still a small glob of blue toothpaste in the sink bowl. His clothes were lying on the edge of the hamper in little bundles as though he had made a ball toss using the hamper as his basketball net. She turned off the bathroom light and made her way back toward the unmade bed.

Faith knelt on her knees by the side of the bed and laid her hands on the dark blue comforter. Closing her eyes, she allowed the feelings to flow through her.

He brushed his teeth, already in his pajamas. He's in bed with a book. Music. He's listening to some music. No more music. Sleep. Peaceful. Then—

Bart made his way down the plush carpeted hall, his footsteps muffled and the way lighted by soft wall sconces to the room indicated as Erik's. The door stood open; the space lit by what little sunlight filtered through the closed curtains. Starting to enter, he saw a woman kneeling in prayer. Not wanting to interrupt, he stopped at the doorway. *She must be another relative or employee.*

As his eyes became accustomed to the dim interior, he could tell she was a young woman. Her straight, ebony hair flowed down her back. It was hard to tell her height as she knelt but if her arms and hands were any indications, she was not a large woman. Her hands were delicate as they lay flat on the bed, her fingers splayed outward on the material. He heard no sounds coming from her and assumed her prayers were silent.

Uncertainty filled him. He was afraid she would startle

when she saw him standing in the doorway, but moving could create a noise that would frighten her. Caught in his indecision, his phone suddenly vibrated in his pocket, the sound reverberating in the eerily quiet room. He hustled to silence the phone, but the woman jumped from her kneel and whirled around, her hand on her chest.

Faith's heart pounded in fear at the shadow of a huge man filling the entire doorframe. Chest heaving, she said, "Who are you? What do you want?"

"I'm sorry, ma'am," Bart replied sincerely. "I didn't mean to interrupt your prayers."

"My...?" she halted, saying no more.

Knowing she could not see him and wanting to have a clearer vision of who he was speaking to, Bart leaned in and flipped the light switch. The overhead light immediately purged the darkness, causing both Bart and Faith to blink at the brightness.

Bart stared at the woman standing by the bed. Slightly older than he originally thought, her flawless complexion was complemented by the dark hair framing her face. Large, brown eyes, highlighted by thick lashes, stared back at him. Her hand, still over her heart, brought his eyes to her breasts. Not overly large, he suddenly could not imagine them being more perfect. Her slim waist and hips tapered to impossibly long legs, considering she stood a head shorter than him. Dressed in simple slacks and an emerald-green blouse, he wondered at her impact on him. Something about her drew him forward.

"You still haven't told me who you are," she accused softly. She was not sure she had ever seen such a large man...at least not this close. He filled the doorframe, his head just underneath the top. Blond hair, slightly tousled. More than a little stubble on his jaw. He was wearing a dark, tailored suit evidently made especially for his bulk.

Bart found himself uncharacteristically dumbstruck. Beauty was something he saw, and bedded, on a regular basis. *But her eyes...as though they can see right into me.*

Shaking himself, he quickly stepped forward with his hand extended. "I beg your pardon. Bart Taggart. I'm investigating the kidnapping at Mr. Krustas' request. And you are?"

Her breathing had slowed back to normal as she placed her much smaller hand into his. Leaning back to look into his face, she realized once more how tall he was as he towered over her five foot, six inches. His hand was astonishingly gentle as it held her. She saw his questioning gaze as his mouth quirked up in a smile.

"Oh," she exclaimed, pulling her hand back as she blushed. "My name is Faith. Faith Romani. I'm a...um... sketch artist. I do some work for the local police."

Cocking his head to the side, he observed her closely. "There are no witnesses to the crime that I know of, so how exactly are you going to sketch anyone?"

Just then, Anton showed up at the door. "Oh, good. You two have met. Uncle Ivan wants to brief the two of you."

Lifting his arm to the side, Bart motioned, "After you, miss." Walking behind her, he could not help but notice her body as her clothes showcased it perfectly. He followed her down the stairs and into the living room.

Ivan was standing by the decorated mantel, Dmitry at his side. Nodding toward the pair as they walked toward him, Ivan said, "Good, good. The two of you will work well together and I know we'll make progress now."

Before Bart could question either Ivan or Faith further about her involvement, Ivan ushered them to the sofa.

"Bart, you're here because I know you will focus on my grandson and not be distracted by what my companies are involved in. You will be able to be objective when looking at my main competitors. Faith, you're here because of your special gifts."

"Special gifts?" Bart questioned.

"I'm also a psychologist," Faith said softly, but with conviction. "Mr. Krustas is hoping that I'll be able to get a handle on what type of personality we're dealing with."

Bart turned and looked at the woman sitting on the other end of the sofa. Her eyes held his gaze, but something was off. He just was not sure what it was. "Do you work for the FBI?"

"No," she replied honestly. "I would have to go through their training to be an FBI profiler. I have a master's degree in psychology and a minor in art." Seeing his incredulous expression, she explained, "I know it seems to be a strange combination but they both interested me. I've worked with the local police as a sketch artist and use my background in psychology to get an idea of what type of person we'll be checking into."

Bart nodded, carefully considering her words. *Everything sounds normal, so why do I get a weird feeling she's not telling me everything?*

Ivan interjected, "Anton is gathering the information that I have asked him to compile for you. Would the two of you be able to come back in two hours, once he's ready?"

Before Bart could agree, Mrs. Dukakas appeared at the door, saying, "Excuse me, Mr. Krustas, the doctor is here for Constance."

The weight that momentarily lifted from Ivan was firmly back on his shoulders. Looking over at Bart and Faith, he offered his apologies. "I'll see you in about two hours. The FBI will have another report for us, and Anton will have the information you'll need." Walking over to grasp Bart's hand, he added, "Please keep me informed about anything you discover. I'll be traveling back and forth to Norfolk but will mostly be here. Anton will be taking care of many of our businesses back in Norfolk."

With that, he left the room and Mrs. Dukakas said, "I'll show you out now."

As Bart and Faith left the mansion, they walked silently back down the driveway past the vigilant guards. Arriving at her small car, Bart noticed the old model vehicle. Not wanting to leave her side yet, he placed his hand on her arm.

"Would you like to get some coffee?" he asked, turning on his famous charm.

She looked up at his grin and hesitated. *He looks like he never gets turned down.*

Bart noticed her reticence and pressed his point. "We can share information," he enticed.

Offering a small smile, she agreed. "There's a coffee shop about a mile from here," she commented.

"You can ride with me, and I'll bring you back," he said, already placing his hand on her shoulder to guide her to his truck.

"No, thank you," she declared. "I'll drive and you can follow." With that, she opened her car door, tossing her bag into the passenger seat.

Bart realized it made sense for a woman to be cautious, especially with a large stranger. *But damn, it feels odd.* He could not remember the last time a woman refused to take him up on an offer. Hustling over to his truck, he pulled out behind her and followed her through the neighborhood and to a small shopping center with a little café.

Parking behind her, he jogged to her side to offer his hand in assisting her from her car. She placed her hand in his as she alighted from the vehicle. She felt him squeeze her fingers before letting go, noting the sparks tingling long after the release. Wiggling her fingers, she wondered why this man had such a strong effect on her.

Entering the café, the warm interior was inviting, and they found a small booth toward the back. Once the coffee was ordered, they sat, both analyzing each other. Unbeknownst to her, he also felt the tingle from their touch. Unused to such reactions, he wondered about the beautiful woman sitting across from him.

"So...um...are you with the FBI?" she asked, wanting to break the awkward silence. She wrapped her hands around the hot cup, hoping its warmth would thaw her freezing fingers.

"No," he answered. "I work for a private investigation company that Mr. Krustas has contracted."

"Oh," Faith replied, not sure what working for a private investigation company entailed.

Bart grinned as he leaned back in his seat, stretching his long legs to either side of hers. "And you? How does one become a psychologist and artist?"

Smiling in return as she relaxed a little, she answered, "I was always interested in people. And art was a way for me to express myself. I only work part-time for the sheriff's department. They call me in when they need me. I also teach art part-time at the local elementary school."

" Part-time?"

Sighing heavily as she absentmindedly twirled a lock of ebony hair, she nodded. "With budget cuts, the arts often are on the chopping block when the school systems have to cut costs. I work three days a week at the elementary school teaching art and then I'm on call for the police department."

Bart quickly estimated what her income would be with the two part-time jobs and was curious how she managed to make a living. His eyes dropped to her clothes. Neat, clean, but not new.

She watched his eyes assess her and wondered what he thought. She noticed the woman behind the counter strip Bart with her eyes and the waitress had freshened their coffee twice already, trying desperately to get his attention. She noticed his quick grin and wink at the waitress and wondered if he realized how many hearts probably broke every day when he would smile and then walk away. *Oh yeah. I definitely get a feeling about him!*

Drawn to her like a moth to the light, Bart wanted to know more about her. She appeared immune to his charm, but that only made her more attractive to him. "Tell me more about yourself."

Giving a shrug, she admitted, "There's not much to tell. I was raised in the Charlestown area by my mom and grandmother. They've both passed now." She twisted the napkin on the table, her nerves taut. *Why does he make me nervous? It's hard to clear my mind and think with his overpowering, testosterone, devilishly handsome presence opposite of me!* A giggle erupted as she thought of her description of him.

Bart wondered what she was thinking that would make her laugh, unintentionally drawing focus to her perfect lips. Quirking his eyebrow, he noticed her blush. "Are you all right?"

"Yes," she said, clearing her throat. "I...um...sorry. I just had a silly thought." *He must think I'm an idiot!* Determined to redeem herself, she quickly asked, "And you? What does an independent investigator do?"

Knowing she was attempting to lead the conversation away from whatever had made her laugh, he played along. He leaned back again, managing to move his leg so that it touched hers.

She attempted to shift her leg over but found them trapped between his.

Before she could protest, he said, "I was a SEAL, then did a year with Border Patrol when I was medically discharged. Found that I hated the red tape that went along with our assignments. When I heard about Saints Protection & Investigation, I knew it was perfect." Seeing the question in her eyes, he said, "We take on cases and are able to work...outside of the agency regulations."

Unsure exactly what he meant, the twinkle in his blue eyes told her he enjoyed his job immensely. Unable to think of anything else to say, she just nodded, turning her cup up to finish the coffee dregs in the bottom.

Bart wondered about her silent response. *Usually, women practically swoon when I tell them I was a SEAL.* He was unsure if he should be insulted or relieved.

Their coffee finished, they stood, Bart tossing a few bills on the table for the tip. He looked over and winked at the waitress again, who was still eying him as though he was the last cookie before a diet. Rolling her eyes, Faith proceeded him out of the door. His long legs quickly caught up to her before she reached her car.

"You okay?" he asked, true concern on his face.

Realizing the stupidity of being irritated at him for flirting with the waitress when they were doing nothing more than having a business lunch, she smiled and nodded.

"I still don't quite understand why Mr. Krustas hired you since there are no witnesses," Bart said.

She wondered how much to say. Glancing up into his face, his easy-going expression made her feel accepted. *Maybe, just maybe, he'll be understanding.*

"I don't just draw what other people describe. I...feel things and see images in my head. Then I draw them as well. Sometimes it can help."

Bart's expression was one of confusion as he cocked his head to the side. "I'm afraid I don't understand what you mean."

"Sometimes when I'm around someone or something where strong emotions have been involved, I...I don't know. I...just get images in my head and draw them. Sometimes they've been helpful. The FBI has used me a couple of times for something local, but that's completely off the record."

She watched in fascination as a myriad of emotions crossed Bart's handsome face—confusion, dawning realization, then morphing into pure anger.

"You...you're psychic?" he barked out. "You're shittin' me. Seriously? You dig around a crime scene, *see* things, draw them down, and jerk some poor unsuspecting family who's grieving, to pay for your *services*? Damnit! And here I thought you were legitimate!" he yelled.

Rearing back away from his rage, she tried to still her quivering while shaking her head. "No, no, you've got it all wrong!"

"Oh, I've got your number, sweetheart," he growled. "I

dealt with a slick-shit, fake medium a few months ago who was trying to rook my grandmother and cousin." He whirled around, pacing furiously, his large frame menacing. Stalking back to her, he stopped only when his large boots were directly in front of her small pumps. Leaning down over her, using his size to intimidate, he said, "Well, your little scheme ends here, dearie. You won't be getting rich off anyone else!" He refused to focus on her quivering chin and tears that formed on her lashes. "I'm officially calling our partnership quits right now. I'm telling Krustas you're a phony and I've got no problem talking to our FBI and police contacts as well."

With his angry face inches from hers, he growled one more time. "Consider yourself officially out of business!" Pushing away, he whirled around and stalked to his truck, hopping inside and squealing out the parking lot, leaving Faith shaking in his retreat.

5

Bart drove around for half an hour, furious with Faith's deception, Krustas' gullibility, and for allowing himself to become interested in a pair of dark, soulful eyes. *Goddamnit!* His mind rolled back to the previous summer when Cecil Nastelli, a con-artist disguised as a medium, was stealing millions from lonely, wealthy widows by pretending to speak to their dead husbands. Nastelli would then tell them their husbands wanted them to invest in bogus companies, all of which he owned.

Bart's grandmother was being scammed and he worked with his cousin and her fiancé, Jude, to catch the swindler.

His mind continued to roll through Faith's explanation. *She gets feelings. She gets images and then draws them. What a crock of shit! She visits crime scenes for her images and then plays on the emotions of poor, unsuspecting people. I wonder how much she gets paid?* He thought back to when he broke into Nastelli's expensive condo when looking for evidence. *I'll bet she lives grand also!*

He finally found himself back in his neighborhood, determined his first order of business was to shut Miss Faith down. *Faith! Jesus, she's even given herself a name that would fit her scam!* As soon as he hit his driveway, he called Jack.

"Yeah," Jack answered.

"Bro, you're not going to believe what I found out about that profiler Krustas hired. She's a phony. Claims to be a psychic! Says she gets feelings and images that she draws. Hell, she visits crime scenes to get her *visions!*"

Bart was met with silence on the other end. "Jack? You still there?"

"I'm here."

"Okay, man," Bart said. "You don't seem too outraged by this."

He heard a deep sigh from his boss, before Jack said, "Look, I appreciate this is hard for you to swallow, especially in light of what happened last summer. Did she actually say she was psychic? Did she use that word?"

Bart thought for a second before answering honestly. "No, but what the hell does it matter what she calls herself? She's still scamming people and I'm not going to work with her. If Krustas wants to throw his money at a fake that's his business, but she's not getting me to do her investigating just so she can draw some bogus picture that has everyone claiming she did anything." By this time, he was virtually yelling and growing more frustrated that Jack did not share his indignation. "Okay, Jack, you want to tell me what the hell is going on?"

"All I know is that when Krustas called to ask for our help, he also said he had asked someone to assist. He used to know her grandmother and said the women in this family have the ability to see things. I know you don't believe, and you don't have to, but Krustas has hired her, and you have to, at least, pretend to work with her."

"You have got to be kidding?" Bart said, leaning back heavily against his truck headrest. "I do all the work and she gets to claim the glory of solving the case by psychic means."

"Since when do we care who gets the glory?" Jack challenged him. Not hearing an answer from Bart, he continued. "We solve cases and who gets the glory doesn't matter. FBI. CIA. DEA. Hell, the local police department."

"I hear you, but I'm still telling Krustas what he's gotten himself into."

Jack chuckled. "Go ahead, but I think you'll be surprised."

"Boss, I gotta tell you, this whole conversation is shocking the shit outta me," Bart confessed.

"I'm not telling you to believe her. I am telling you that you have to work with her because, right now, that's what our client wants. But you also have to not work against her. You prove she's a phony in the meantime...that's fine. But your job is to assist Ivan Krustas, not discredit Ms. Romani. Got that?"

"Yes, sir," Bart answered, frustration burning in him.

"Now what else do you have for me?"

"I need you to check out Sarah Dukakas. She's Ivan's housekeeper and was alone with Erik that night. They say she's been with the family for years, including her parents. I figure Luke can dig up her finances. Also, a man named Roger Montague. Erik's mom was out with him at a charity event that night."

"What about Sergio?"

"Yeah, I was going to get to him. I got a bad feeling that, even from prison, he's involved somehow. Ivan didn't want to believe it, but I think I convinced him and Anton that Sergio can still be a threat."

"You talking to Ivan this afternoon?"

"Yeah. I'm going to talk to him about the psychic medium he's hired."

"Just remember, you're on the job regardless of who he's pulled in."

"Got it," Bart replied, disconnecting before tossing the phone to the console before running his hand over his face. *Jesus, what have I gotten myself into?* The more he thought about how she duped him with her innocent, doe-eyed appearance, the angrier he got. *My job might not be to discredit you, but I sure as shit will work to do just that!*

Faith drove to her apartment, angry tears streaming down her face. *Oh, grandma. This is why I never told anyone what I saw when I was little. No one understands.* She could not get the vision of Bart's furious rant against her out of her mind. His accusations stung as his words sliced through her. *Asshole! Who does he think he is?* Pulling in a ragged breath, she parked her old car, leaning her head on the steering wheel for a moment before walking up the stairs to her apartment. Dropping her bag and kicking off her shoes, she walked the few steps to the worn sofa and plopped down. As she looked around at her meager surroundings, his words echoed. *You won't be getting rich off anyone else.* She would have laughed if the situation were not so ridiculous. *Rich? What does he think I do?*

Thirty minutes passed while she lay back on the sofa,

trying to quell her racing thoughts. The images of his handsome face twisted in anger—in rage—were stuck in her mind. Pulling out her phone, she googled the name, Taggart. The first thing that popped up was an article about Arlene Taggart and other wealthy widows in Virginia Beach being taken in by a swindler who was caught before the women lost any money. *Great. Just great. Arlene Taggart must be the grandmother he mentioned.*

Grabbing her art pad, she closed her eyes, willing her mind to focus. Tucking her hair behind her ears, she quickly began sketching, allowing her pencil to flow over the paper, freely drawing lines, circles, shapes, shades. Bart's angry face rose from the page, his rage palpable in the portrait. She was panting by the time it was finished and tears of frustration came again.

Tossing the pad on the sofa, she rose and moved toward the kitchen, which was no more than a row of cabinets ending with a sink next to a stove and refrigerator, both the avocado color of a long-ago era. Eating a quick meal, she rinsed out the dishes, stacking them back onto the drying rack. *I've never felt so alone. Not even after grandma died. Oh, Babushka, I miss you.*

Walking back to the sofa, she picked up the art pad turning to a clean page. This time, her pencil flowed without anger or frustration. Slow strokes crossing the paper. Another image began to take shape. Another image of Bart appeared, but this time with the flirty, crooked smile he flashed. *Funny, he would wink at the waitress but didn't pay any attention to her. But to me? This smile would come out constantly. For a while he focused on me...and it felt... special. Damn!*

Sighing deeply, she turned off the lights and walked back down to her car. It was a little early, but she wanted to make sure she got there in time. She would have to tell Mr. Krustas that she would be unable to work for him.

As she headed down the road, she was restless as the image of a small boy, smiling in a windowless room filled her mind once more.

Bart arrived at Constance's house early for their meeting. Mrs. Dukakas opened the door to him, and said, "Mr. Anton Krustas will meet with you in the study, but he isn't here right now."

"Actually, I wanted to talk to Mr. Ivan Krustas."

A small smile crossed her face as she nodded and turned toward the dining room. Bart walked behind her, seeing Ivan sitting alone, at the end of the table. Ivan looked up and nodded toward the housekeeper.

"Can you bring Mr. Taggart some refreshment, please."

"No, no, thank you," Bart assured Mrs. Dukakas. "I'll just take some coffee if it's not too much trouble."

The older woman patted his arm, saying, "You're a good man to help us. Have a seat and I'll take care of you."

He watched her walk out of the room before sitting down, facing Ivan. The haggard look on Ivan's face suddenly halted Bart's words. He wanted to demand that Krustas admit Faith was a phony, but the words choked in his throat.

Ivan spoke after a moment of watching Bart silently struggle. "You're a man on a mission this afternoon but, for some reason, you're hesitating to say what's on your mind." He set his fork down on his plate, pushing it back before pinning Bart with a stare. "My grandson is missing, and I don't have time to beat around the bush...or have someone else do so."

Duly chastised, Bart nodded. "I want to understand what you hope to gain from employing Ms. Romani. Do you know her? Did she approach you? What did she promise you? Did she talk about finding Erik using some kind of gift of sight?"

The moment was broken as Mrs. Dukakas brought in more coffee. Ivan glanced up at his housekeeper and said, "Mr. Taggart is wondering about Faith. I'm not sure he has any."

Bart looked between the two, seeing a fleeting smile at the inside joke they shared. Mrs. Dukakas left the room and Bart looked back for an explanation from Ivan.

"Bart, I knew Ms. Romani's grandmother. She and I grew up near each other. We were from the same heritage. We may claim Russia as our ancestor's country, but our heritage is of Russian gypsies. You are a man who looks for truth in facts. We appreciate there are many truths found in faith."

"I do have faith, Ivan," he countered. "Faith in family, faith in God."

"Faith in love?" Ivan asked.

"Yes," Bart answered without hesitation. He looked past Ivan's shoulder, lost in thoughts of his grandfather. Drawing himself up, he shared, "My grandfather taught me to have faith in family, God, and yes, in love. I've never found it myself, but I saw it every day with him and my grandmother and between my parents. But when I was a SEAL on a mission or investigating crimes, I needed facts. Substantial evidence. Not some mumbo jumbo."

Ivan leaned back in his chair, carefully considering the young man in front of him. "There's a world of difference between the swindler Cecil Nastelli, who your grand-mother dealt with last summer, and Faith Romani."

"Oh, yeah? What's the difference?"

Ivan stood, picked up his coffee, and motioned for Bart to follow him. The two men made their way to the comfortable study, sitting back down in easy chairs.

"For years, there have been those, particularly women, who have what can be called second sight. Yes, many have exploited it, calling themselves psychic and charging money for their gift. Others use it cautiously. For good."

"And you think that's what Ms. Romani is doing? Hell, Ivan, be reasonable. She goes to crime scenes, gathers clues, and then claims to have seen the images she draws."

"Her grandmother had the gift. It skips a generation and Faith has it also." Ivan watched the look of disbelief mixed with disgust cross Bart's face. "But, regardless of your opinions, I want Ms. Romani on the case. If you do not think you can accommodate, then I'll be forced to negotiate with your boss for another investigator."

Bart stiffened at the insinuation he could not do his job. "That won't be necessary," he stated forcefully.

Just then, the housekeeper walked to the doorway. "Ms. Romani is here."

"Send her in and call for Anton as well."

Bart was not happy, but as he stood to greet Faith when she appeared in the hall, Ivan leaned over, whispering, "And for the record, she did not contact me. I contacted her. And she refuses any money I have offered."

Bart jerked his head around but did not have a chance to question Ivan further since Faith was walking into the room.

"My dear, join us."

Bart's gaze stayed on her as she walked toward him

cautiously, the look of a mouse approaching a cat on her face. Her long hair pulled back away from her face in a simple headband, its length still flowing down her back. *She refuses any money Ivan has offered. She doesn't dress expensively, so what's her game? Does she dress down to gain pity?*

As she crossed the room, her timidity lessened with each step. By the time she sat in the seat Ivan had indicated, her spine was steel, and she pierced Bart with her glare. *I am not going to be intimidated!*

"I'm glad you're here," Ivan spoke, breaking the pointed silence. "Anton will be joining us in just a few minutes. Dmitry was sent back to the university since his presence is not needed at this time. I know Jack has given Bart information on my possible enemies; I will have Anton brief you from our family's perspective."

Faith's gaze shifted between the two men in the room. "Do you still want me involved?" she asked, sure that Bart had already painted her as a fraud to Ivan.

"Of course," Ivan said. He sat down next to her, reaching out to grasp her cold hands. "Bart and I have discussed his concerns. They are not shared by me," he promised.

"I...I don't know what to say—"

"Faith, I knew your grandmother. We grew up in the same neighborhood. She was beautiful...fun...and special."

Her eyes held his as he continued to speak. "I knew her gift. I perceived it passed to you. Whatever it is...whatever you can do, I want you to do it. If it is using your psychology and knowledge of people or any insight you may have...I just need to know you will assist in bringing Erik home to me."

Tears pricked the back of her eyes as she blinked quickly. Glancing over at Bart, she lifted her chin, saying, "What about you? Can we work together?"

She watched as a muscle in his jaw tightened, but his words confirmed, "Yes. All that matters is finding Erik."

6

As the four sat down in the study, Bart made sure to sit next to Anton and across from Faith and Ivan. He wanted immediate access to what Anton was divulging, but also to keep an eye on Faith. She looked up at him but, instead of seeing soulful eyes, all he could see was deceit, then hurt, before she glanced down at her hands, gently rubbing her fingers over her chewed thumbnail. *Is she nervous?* Anton's voice brought him back to the task at hand and he admonished himself for focusing on Faith. *Get in the game, man. She's secondary to what's in those files.*

"Ivan and I have compiled as much information as we could about who we think may have a hand in this. To be honest, Ivan feels like some of this may not be necessary but, we cannot leave any stone unturned."

Bart had spent most of his time after getting off the phone with Jack pouring over the information that Luke sent to him and was anxious to see what Anton would offer.

"We do a lot of business and have been around for a

very long time," Anton began. "There are a few newcomers who have tried to nudge their way in...or blast their way in, and we have prevailed. The money is substantial, and the stakes are high. Any of these three would profit greatly by knocking Krustas down."

Bart understood what was at stake. If the Krustas empire crashed, the chaos would resemble vultures on a carcass. And Anton was about to reveal the top three vultures.

"Miguel Escobar runs a gang that has the backing of a local gang in Richmond and national backing of MS13 . Drugs, whores, pussy clubs...uh, sorry," Anton said, his eyes looking across the table at Faith.

"It's fine," she said, but Bart noted a blush rise from her modest neckline to the top of her forehead.

"Mostly drugs and some extortion," Anton finished.

"What exactly would crippling Ivan do for them?" Bart asked.

"My family controls the warehouse area in Norfolk. Getting rid of us would allow someone else to do that. It would make for easier shipping of drugs, humans, goods...whatever they wanted to smuggle."

Faith jerked her gaze around to Ivan, surprise and silent questioning in her expression. Ivan noticed and as he turned toward her, he gave a small smile. "This shocks you, my dear?"

With a quick shake of her head, she turned her eyes back to Anton, her naïveté surprising her. She glanced over, seeing Bart watching her like a hawk. Lifting her chin slightly, she adopted a blank expression as she turned her attention back to Anton.

"Miguel's group is ruthless and, frankly, they're at the top of our list."

Bart interjected, "You share this with the FBI?"

"Of course," Anton growled. "Nothing's as important to us as finding Erik."

"The questions have to be asked," Ivan admonished his nephew. Turning back to Bart, he confessed, "Yes, we shared our concerns with the FBI but, as you can imagine, they were excited to get insights into our businesses. That is one of the reasons I went to Jack to find a private investigation firm that had the resources to dig into these people.

Anton nodded, sighed deeply, and continued. "There is another Russian family. Volkov. They're newcomers and by that, I mean new to this country. No background to guide them. No elder at the helm. Gavrill Volkov is their head."

"Have you had dealings with them?" Bart asked.

"They landed on our shores about five years ago and have tried to muscle into our territory. Each year they become a little more ruthless. Sergio tried to integrate them into our businesses, and we actually wondered if my cousin was working for them before going to prison."

Bart glanced down at the photographs in front of him, but the faces were already familiar. He had purposely not divulged that the Saints had already sent him compiled dossiers on these gangs. So far, his impressions were on target with Anton and Ivan's assessments.

"The last true threat comes from the Maldonis."

At this, Ivan scoffed, then looked up at the eyes facing him. "They are not high on my list. Yes, they would love to take over my territory and businesses, but they are an old family. Italian. Luciano Maldoni is their head. He is my age and runs his family as I do. His sons and nephews may handle his interests, but Luciano is still very much in charge. I would never consider a strike against the family of an enemy, especially not with a child. Luciano would feel the same."

"But there are many under him who may not feel the same. No longer respecting the ways of the old," Faith said. Her eyes stayed on the picture of Luciano Maldoni, her fingers resting lightly on the paper. "The ways of the old are dying."

The three men watched her carefully, two with interest and one with disgust.

"Yes, well, we can't condemn or dismiss anyone based on feelings, so I suggest we get to the rest of the business at hand," Bart growled. He watched as her gaze lifted to his, held for a moment and then moved away. *Jesus, how's this going to work,* he thought in anger once more.

Within the hour, Bart headed down to the conference room at the Saint's compound underneath Jack's large home. At a quick glance, he saw the rest of the Saints already there.

"Whatcha got for me, boss?"

"Monty's arranged with one of his FBI cohorts for you and Ms. Romani to talk to the men on Ivan's list."

Monty took over the explanation. "When Jack said you were coming, I arranged for Mitchell Evans to do a video conference with us." With a few taps on his keyboard, Luke pulled up the image of the FBI agent onto the screen. The dark-haired FBI agent smiled at them.

After introductions had been made, Mitch began, "It's good to meet you. Hated like hell to lose Monty but, after hearing a bit about your organization, I can understand why he left." He looked down at the papers in front of him and continued. "Krustas' concerns are legitimate. While the Bureau is taking the kidnapping seriously and working around the clock to find Erik, there are some other agents that are using the opportunity to delve deeply into organized crime in Virginia. Not only Krustas, but the other three organizations he mentioned to you are under scrutiny now."

"What does this mean for us?" Monty asked, looking between his neat notes on his tablet and the screen. Organized and efficient, he typed as quickly as Mitch spoke.

"I was in contact as soon as we got Ivan's suspicions and have arranged for Bart and Ms. Romani to meet with each of those organizations."

Bart's eyes immediately jerked to the screen. "Ms. Romani too? What the hell? She's not an investigator."

"Yes, but Krustas wants her involved to see if there are any impressions she gets with these men," Mitch replied.

"So, what?" Bart almost yelled, his hair standing on end as he ran his hand through it fiercely. "You're asking me to take an untrained, unarmed woman into not just one den of thieves, but into three of them? Jesus, what a disaster!"

"No harm will come to you, I assure you. These organizations have agreed to an interview because they're under pressure from us to cooperate. I've personally talked with Escobar, Volkov, and Maldoni. None of them are happy, but they know your purpose is about Erik, not their businesses. They agreed because you're independent and Ms. Romani is going as a profiler."

Bart looked around at the other faces of the trusted Saints, seeing their expressions of doubt as well. It did not seem to sit well with any of them, taking an innocent woman into these kinds of meetings.

Before he had a chance to argue further, Mitch continued, "Look, I've had the opportunity to see Ms. Romani at work twice with the Charlestown police. She listens intently and has a way of drawing not only what someone is saying, but also adding an element that's...that's...hell, I don't know. As if she can really see inside of someone."

Scoffing, Bart shook his head. *Great, now the FBI contact is enamored with her. She's certainly spun her web... but not over me!*

The highway lines passed along that afternoon, the sound of the engine the only noise breaking the silence in the cab of Bart's truck. He and Faith had left Charlestown behind, driving first to Richmond to meet with Miguel Escobar. Bart comprehended Miguel had agreed to a meeting only to try to exonerate himself of the kidnapping and to keep the DEA and FBI from digging too deeply into his businesses.

He wanted to ignore the woman sitting beside him but found his gaze continually straying to the side. *When was the last time I tried to ignore a woman in my truck?*

She faced the front, occasionally twisting her head to look out her side window. By now he had her profile memorized. Her complexion was difficult to describe...not olive tan and not pale, but a curious mixture of both. He wondered about her father, who had never been mentioned. Her large, dark eyes had not looked at him since they started the trip.

Bart thought back to what Jack said to him earlier. *Work with her, but if you prove her a phony in the process, that's fine.* A smile crossed his face for the first time since he accepted this case. The chance to find Erik and prove her false at the same time appealed to him.

Faith had spent the last thirty minutes trying to keep her eyes off the wall of angry testosterone sitting next to her. His large truck cab felt too small, as his presence seemed to take up all the space. *Why am I doing this to myself? How am I going to function if the only thing I feel is negative vibes pouring off him? I'm not psychic—I just get feelings. Oh, Babushka...I should have never given into the first time I noticed I was different.*

She tucked an errant strand of hair behind her ear and wiggled slightly in the seat to stretch her back. The tension building in her neck had morphed into a full-blown headache, but she did not dare ask him to stop for water to take an aspirin.

She became aware of him looking at her and for the first time during the trip, she turned her gaze toward the driver, surprised he was smiling.

Bart's glance revealed she was finally looking at him, a confused expression on her face. Clearing his throat, he said, "I just thought that even if I don't believe in your psychic abilities, there's no reason why we can't work well together on this. After all, we want to find Erik."

She slowly nodded her head but was still reticent. "What changed your mind? About working with me?"

"To be honest, Ivan and my boss have an agreement, and it behooves us to do whatever we can to make sure we investigate without personal distractions."

Personal distractions? She knew he was talking about his distrust, but the idea of him being interested in her as a woman had her blushing. *Yeah, me and every woman within flirting distance and that sucks! He may be an arrogant jerk, but he was still a hot one, something her body noticed. But if all he sees of me is a fraud, then forget him!* Forcing her thoughts from his muscular, rock-hard body, back to the matter at hand, she said, "Agreed. I can keep my personal opinion about you from interfering if you can."

For a second, Bart's smile faltered. *Her personal opinion about me? What the hell is wrong with me?* Quickly recovering, he plastered his famous smile back on his face, determined to easily charm his way into her good graces.

"Tell me what you thought of Ivan and Anton's lists," he prompted.

Unsure of Bart's true motives, she decided to plunge ahead and give her opinion. "All of them have a lot to gain by financially crippling the Krustas empire." She rubbed her aching head. "But to take a child is very different from a business decision."

Bart glanced to the side, watching her pinched face. "Do you have a headache? Do you need to stop?"

"I...I have some aspirin but can't swallow pills without water."

He saw the sign for an exit up ahead and moved the truck into the right-hand lane. She discerned what he was doing and hurriedly objected, "We don't have to stop. I can deal."

"No need to," he said, easily pulling into a convenience store parking lot. "I'll grab a couple of waters," and was out of the vehicle before she could protest again.

Within a minute, he returned, handing her a plastic bag. Peering down inside, she saw a water bottle, two sodas, a bag of peanuts and a package of Skittles.

"What didn't you buy?" she joked.

Giving a shrug, he said, "It dawned on me that you might need the caffeine, protein from the nuts, or maybe a sugar rush."

Returning his smile, she twisted the cap off the water and quickly washed down the aspirin. Handing him the bag, she noted he grabbed a soda and opened the bag of peanuts before placing them in the console between them. She took the Skittles, saying, "You have no idea how much I love these!" as he pulled back out onto the highway.

The beginnings of conversation eased her headache as much as the aspirin and she continued her thoughts on the case. "I also have to say that I wonder if Ivan is throwing us toward his known enemies just to keep us from looking too hard at his businesses as well."

At that, Bart jerked his gaze to hers. He had had the same thought, but never expected her to think that much less say it.

She caught his surprised expression. "What? You think because Ivan asked me to be involved, I won't consider all the possibilities?"

"Yeah, I guess that's exactly what I thought," he admitted.

"I don't want it to be someone in his organization," she continued, "because I know how much it would hurt him. But then, to be honest, I don't have any background in this kind of criminal case." Giving a self-deprecating shrug, she added, "The local police have used me when they needed an artist. There's an FBI agent in the area that noticed me when I was working on a victim's drawing, and he has used me a couple of times also."

"Hmmph," Bart groused. *I'll bet you caught the eye of Mitch!* Forcing his thoughts away from her beauty, he smiled once more. "I'm sure you were a big help. This FBI agent married?"

"Married? I...I don't know." Her confused gaze turned toward him. "Why would that matter?"

He grimaced, not liking the answer himself. *Why do I care if some FBI agent has the hots for her?* "No reason," he casually remarked. "Tell me about the way you've used your *gifts* for the police."

She heard his sarcastic manner when speaking of her gifts but refused to show him it bothered her. "Same as most police artists, I suppose. If there's a victim or witness that can describe a suspect, then I sit with them and draw what they tell me."

"Just what they tell you?" he prodded.

"No, I make it all up and just draw clowns!" she bit back angry that, within a minute, she lost her resolve to not be perturbed. Sucking in a deep breath, she said, "Let's focus on Erik and what we need to do now that we're in Richmond and forget about you interrogating me."

A feeling of regret flew through Bart, who had come to enjoy the sound of her voice. *Damn, why is this so hard?* He felt like the rope in a game of tug-of-war, his emotions pulled this way and that when it came to Faith. The reality of her being unpretentious warred with the conviction that she was a fraud.

Before he had time to finish those thoughts, they were driving through a rundown neighborhood. The brick buildings on either side of the road had a few shops on the first floors, but some of the upper windows were broken out and graffiti covered many of the alleyways. A few older people shuffled along the sidewalks, but the area was mostly vacant. Following the directions, he pulled up to a bar on the first floor of one of the buildings.

Parking was easy—no one else was on the street. The desolate area gave validity to his fears.

"I've got a bad feeling about this," Bart admitted. Alone, the deserted area, old storefronts boarded up, and the few people hanging around with a look of desperation would have made him cautious, but not afraid. *With a woman? Jesus, what a disaster!* Cursing Mitch, he thought, *An old bar? Could he not have insisted on a neutral location?*

"Faith, I think having you on this trip was a mistake. I can't guarantee your safety and I'm sure as hell not leaving you out here alone."

Her heart hammered with fright from what she was seeing. Realizing the scene resembled a TV detective show, one where a secondary character might get killed, she looked around dubiously. She glanced over at Bart, instantly seeing his Hollywood looks and knew he would be the main character in the show and would be walking away unharmed at the end. *Where does that leave me? As a secondary character or the kickass heroine?* Taking a deep breath, she refused to give in to the fear, but knew she was no kickass. "It's okay. I've got this. Miguel agreed to this meeting, and he knows it behooves him to talk to us, even if he doesn't want to talk to the FBI."

Bart had to agree but made her promise to stay in the truck until he could make his way around. Assisting her down, he kept one hand on her back while the other hand was ready to draw his weapon if necessary. She hated to admit it, but the feel of his hand on her back was comforting. Unfamiliar, but not unwelcome.

Approaching the door with a board over the broken window, it immediately swung open, and they were escorted into a poorly lit bar. Giving his eyes a second to adjust, Bart quickly scanned the room for potential danger. The long, narrow room was empty of patrons, but sitting at a table to the side was a Hispanic man with three others standing behind him.

Faith felt Bart's hand continue to be on her lower back as he guided her to the only occupied table in the dirty room. The seated man's coal black eyes stared at them as they approached, his expression unsmiling. Tattoos covered his arm from his shoulder to his fingers. The wife-beater shirt he wore exposed tattoos that crossed his neck and appeared to disappear down his back as well. She refused to look away as his gaze trailed from her head down to her toes and back again, gradually appraising. When they landed and stayed on her breasts, she could feel Bart's fingers flex. Trying to still her racing heart, she stopped when Bart did, allowing him to take the lead.

Bart was willing to play Miguel's game up to a certain point. *Little man wants to be the lord of his manor and stay silent, works for me.* Stopping a few feet away, he held the gang leader's stare refusing to back down.

With a barely perceptible nod of his head, Miguel indicated for them to sit. He cast his eyes back to Faith, saying, "Who's the *perra*?"

Bart felt Faith's leg quiver next to his and he grinned slowly. "Don't know that you want to insult a Fed by calling her a bitch to her face," he said casually, knowing the lie would make Miguel back down. *Or at least, I hope it does. Now if Faith will just cooperate.*

"You brought the law in here?" Miguel growled, leaning forward.

"Don't worry," Bart said. "She's a psychologist that works for the FBI. She's here just to observe and ask some questions of her own."

Hoping Miguel took the bait, he leaned back casually

in his seat. He wanted to look at Faith to make sure she was holding up all right but did not dare take his eyes off the men in front of him.

Miguel's eyes cut back and forth between Bart and Faith, not saying anything for a moment. Slowly he nodded and leaned back as well. "Sure. I ain't got no info about Krustas' kid so I don't care who you brought."

Bart could sense the slow release of air from Faith and knew her tension was at an all-time high. "What can you tell us?"

"I only heard about it yesterday. Krustas and me, we don't run in the same circles, if you know what I mean."

Bart kept his expression neutral but thought, *No shit, Sherlock. You and Krustas are both involved in criminal acts, but that was where the similarities ended!*

"How did you hear?" Bart prodded.

"Got me a bro at the beach. It hit the news that next morning and he called."

"Why would he call you? What interest would you have in an old man's grandson?"

Gold teeth flashed from Miguel's smile. "That old man owns prime real estate. Lots of people be interested in that."

"What would your interest be?"

"Waterfront, man. Waterfront. It's the name of the game now. You want to get anywhere in today's market, you gotta use the water. The old man gets out, then his cut is up for grabs and the strongest man'll win. And I plan on being the strongest man around."

"You use the James River from here. Any reason you need to expand?"

"Always looking to expand."

Bart knew Miguel was not going to answer any more

direct questions about his business, so he took a different angle.

"Why did you think the kidnapping of Krustas' grandson would make his real estate, as you call it, interesting?"

Miguel leaned forward, laying his arms on the table, piercing Bart with his gaze. "You see this place? When you drove in?" Not waiting for Bart's answer, he continued. "Grew up on the streets of Richmond. Got beat into a gang when I was only eleven. But I was smart. I worked and I planned. I made Pres of this club, I wanted to take it as far as I could go and that wasn't going to be sticking here being the king-of-the dump. I made friends."

Leaning back, still smiling, he said, "Don't trust you. You may be wired, but I gotta feeling you're not. Still..." he paused, spreading his hands wide, "it's no secret I made deals with those bigger. Now I'm still king, but my empire's growing. So, yeah, any news about the competition is something I'm going to keep track of."

There was a momentary silence as the two men sat, holding each other's gazes, until a soft voice broke through the testosterone tension.

"What did you feel when you heard that a child had been taken from his home?"

7

The room became silent as five pairs of eyes landed on Faith. The air in the room changed drastically. Bart's hand on her knee flexed, squeezing automatically. She heard the sudden intake of air from the man sitting across from her. Keeping her eyes on his face, she willed him to speak. *Come on, Miguel. Talk to me.*

Miguel dropped his eyes to his hands still resting on the table. A shadow passed across his expression, and he exhaled slowly. "I was surprised."

"But how did you feel?" she prodded carefully. Emotions hung heavy in the room. The muscles in the back of her neck began to twinge as a bead of sweat trailed a path down her back. Little particles of light hovered at the edges of her vision as she struggled to make sense of what she was experiencing.

"Not right, taking a kid," Miguel finally answered, his expression hard.

Bart wanted to look at Faith but did not want to break the spell that her soft, melodic voice spun.

"Do you have children?" she asked, seeing an image of two small children playing on the street.

Miguel's voice softened, instinctively matching hers. "Yeah." He added, "Got a couple...you know how it is."

She did not understand what he meant, but Bart knew he was referring to several illegitimate children.

"I got a couple with my main woman, but I treat 'em all the same."

"It's hard to imagine what type of man would take a child," she said.

Miguel's expression hardened once more as he growled, "Fuckin' coward."

Faith wanted to close her eyes to allow her mind to process the emotions, but she was afraid. *These are not men you turn your back on...or close your eyes in front of.* Instead, she studied him, seeing him as a child. Alone. Scared.

Standing suddenly, he said, "Meeting's over. I talked. You can tell the Feds I didn't do shit to Krustas." With that, he turned and walked toward the back of the bar and disappeared through a door. One of the men went with him while the other two looked at Bart and Faith.

Bart, glad the meeting was over, stood and offered his hand to Faith, wanting to get her out of the viper's den. She placed her hand in his and allowed him to escort her out the front door. The bright light was blinding as they stepped outside.

Her natural reaction was to slow down so she could focus, but Bart's hand on her back propelled her toward his truck. Opening the door, he boosted her in before jogging around to pull himself up. She started to question him but found his gaze was darting around, on guard for trouble. Slumping down in the comfortable seat, she willed the truck to start and let out a long breath when the engine rumbled to life.

Neither spoke for several minutes as Bart expertly maneuvered them down a few streets and back to where civilization was stirring. Bart pulled out his phone and called Jack. "We're out. Yeah. Yeah. Nothing to report right now. Tonight." With that, he disconnected and continued to drive.

Faith wanted to hear what the next step should be but decided to keep her silence and let Bart take the lead. Glancing to the side, he seemed to be deep in thought, and she settled back as the truck merged onto the main highway heading to the Hampton Roads area.

Thoughts of what they experienced floated through her mind...the bar, the fear, the men. She could feel the violence in the room emanating from the men across the table. Fights. Rape. Torture. Death. Shivering, she wrapped her arms around her middle, tightly pulling in.

Without saying a word, Bart reached over and turned on the heat. A small smile curved the edge of her mouth as the warmth in the cab of the truck began to chase away her chills. Her mind now slipped to the way he protectively escorted her inside the meeting room. How he kept his hand on her knee, constantly assuring her he would protect her. *He can't possibly hate me as much as he acted when we first began the trip.* Crossing her arms across her chest, she tried to stop her body from reacting when he did something nice. She reminded herself that his not-easily-forgotten words had cut into her, and the smile slipped from her face. Sighing heavily at the inner battle, she hit her head against the headrest.

A few quiet miles down the road her mind was slowly

settling when suddenly his voice broke the silence. "What are you thinking?"

She jerked her head around, but he was staring straight ahead at the road, making it difficult to see the expression on his face. Not knowing exactly what he was asking, she hesitated. "Thinking? About...?"

"Miguel. The meeting," he answered curtly.

She stared out of her passenger window at the trees flying by as the truck churned down the miles.

Bart said, softer this time, "Faith, I really want to know what you thought."

"Why?" she could not help but ask.

He sighed heavily, knowing she was cautious considering he had done nothing but trash-talk her since finding out about her. Guilt ate at the corners of his consciousness. *Granddad would have been furious to know I'd spoken to a woman like that, even if he hadn't believed her story.* "I'd like to hear what you're thinking. I can feel your mind whirling ever since we got back in the truck. I've been running things through my mind and I...well, we're supposed to be working on this together."

The snort coming from her side of the truck cab let him know what she thought about his suggestion. The silence fell once more between them, this time thick and choking.

Closing her eyes and breathing deeply to clear her thoughts, she realized by keeping quiet she was doing to Bart what he had done to her and she no longer wanted to continue the battle. "I was thinking there was violence in that room."

Bart fought the urge to give her a *duh*-look and continued his silence to see what else she would say.

"Miguel is hungry for more than what he has. He wants power and thinks the respect he craves will come with gaining more. He's not above taking advantage of whatever opportunity that comes his way and if Krustas falls, he would be all over moving into the Norfolk waterfront."

"But?" Bart prodded, knowing there was more she was feeling.

She fell silent again, turning to look at him. "Why are you asking? You think I'm a fraud making all this up."

He finally responded, "Look, you're a trained psychologist and seem to have a good grasp of people and motives. I don't doubt your training. I don't actually doubt your instincts. I just doubt your psychic abilities."

In an instant he knew he had said the wrong thing as she exploded, "I never claimed to be psychic! Those are your words and I'm sick and tired of you throwing them at me! You decided I was a fraud. You decided that I was untrustworthy. All based on your background and prejudices. Throw in that medium that tried to scam your grandmother and now you've made up your mind about me without even learning anything about me.".

"How did you know exactly what happened with my grandmother?" he growled.

"Gee, I don't know. Maybe I am psychic," she bit back. After a moment of tension, she sarcastically added, "Actually, I googled it, and the article came up about what happened last summer."

"You googled my grandmother?" he asked, his head snapping around. "Why the hell would you do that?"

"Maybe to find out why you're such a prick to me!"

"It's none of your business," he pronounced.

"Oh yeah? And you haven't tried to check me out?"

Starting to lie and deny it, he clamped his lips shut instead. The conversation died at that point, each retreating to their own mental corners. Bart flipped on the radio and, finding a country music station, turned the sound up secretly hoping she hated country music.

Faith leaned back in her seat once more, closing her eyes to the world. Choking back a smile, she began to relax. She loved country music.

Bart looked over at Faith, sleeping beside him, angry at his desire to know her more, warring with the desire to prove her false. *It's true, she never claimed to be a psychic. But images? Impressions? What is she trying to gain from this if Krustas isn't paying her?*

He thought back to the meeting with Miguel. *Why did she ask how he felt when he heard a child had been kidnapped? She kept focusing on Miguel's feelings when I wanted to know the facts.*

Rubbing his hand over his face, he turned his gaze back to the road. They entered the Norfolk area, and he knew there was nothing else they could do this evening.

Time was of the essence with Erik still missing. Mitch had set up a meeting for them tomorrow morning with the Volkov head and then in the afternoon with the Maldoni family. He was surprised the groups had agreed to meet but Mitch had been persuasive.

She stirred in the seat next to him, stretching her legs and arms out in front of her. "Where are we?"

"You were out for about an hour. We're in the Hampton Roads area now."

"Where are we going to spend the night?" she asked. "I know your grandmother and parents live here, so you can just drop me off at a hotel if you want."

He chuckled and said, "Love my grandmother, but I won't stay there tonight." Seeing her curious expression out of the corner of his eyes, he continued, "Nonnie loves to talk and well...I'd like to process the case tonight instead of answering her million questions about how Jude and Sabrina are settling in, how my job is going, and when I'm going to bring home a nice young lady of my own."

Smiling, she commented, "She sounds delightful."

"Oh, don't get me wrong. She's really a darling."

Sighing, she admitted, "I miss having a grandmother."

"I'm sorry, Faith. I..." Feeling like an ass, his voice trailed off, unsure what else to say.

"It's okay. I was luckier than most to have had her for so long." Not wanting to devolve into silence again, she said, "So what are we doing tonight?"

Uncharacteristically, Bart hesitated. "I...well, there's a nice Bed & Breakfast Inn on the cape in Virginia Beach, not too far from where I was stationed as a SEAL. I thought we could stay there tonight unless you want something else."

"No, no, that's fine," she admitted. "The sea air and a walk on the beach might be just the thing for me."

"The weather's chilly tonight."

Smiling at him, she said, "No worries. I'll be fine." She recognized he had a natural protectiveness, regardless of what he may have thought about her.

They drove the last few miles, finally in a peaceful silence, each to their own thoughts but no longer filling the truck cab with animosity. Pulling into the driveway of the B&B, Faith peered out of the window at the charming three-story Cape Cod style house. Checking in, the grey-haired owner smiled at the two, greeting them warmly. Her twinkling eyes moved between them when he asked for two rooms, but her friendly smile never wavered. The comfortable home was decorated with every Christmas ornament imaginable. A nativity set was placed on the sideboard near the door. The front porch was covered with evergreens. A tree stood tall and proud in the living room. Little Christmas knick-knacks perched on shelves, tabletops, and cabinets with lights hung around each window.

Bart noticed Faith's eyes jumped around to all of the decorations, her face glowing with childlike enthusiasm.

Walking to the top of the stairs, the owner opened a door on the left and Faith looked into the beautifully appointed bedroom. White paneling surrounded a queen-sized bed, with a pale-yellow comforter, taking up most of one side of the room facing the windows offering an ocean view framed with fluttering yellow curtains. A small matching dresser and blue brocade chair completed the room.

"I hope this will be all right for you?" the proprietress, Mrs. Carswell, asked.

"Oh, the room is lovely!" Faith exclaimed. "I have no view outside my little efficiency apartment except for the brick wall of the building next door."

"Well, then you should be very happy here." Turning to Bart, the woman said, "You will be right next door with the same view. The bathroom is across the hall and break-fast will be served at eight a.m."

Thanking her, Bart took his key and checked out his

room. It was a copy of Faith's except decorated with various blues as the color scheme and it sported a desk.

"I thought we could go out and grab something to eat in about an hour if you would like?" he asked.

Smiling back at him again, Faith nodded. "I'm going to take a walk down to the water. I'll be back in plenty of time."

Bart watched from his window as she made her way down the boarded path from the back of the property to the sandy beach. Grabbing his cell, he called Jack.

"What have you got for me?" he asked.

Jack chuckled, "Miguel thought you weren't wired but then he didn't expect what we had rigged, did he? I've got Cam, Luke, and Blaise still here going over the video feed and checking out his men."

"He wants to play with the big boys but he's still a small shit," Bart growled.

"From what we could tell, Faith held her own well," Cam added.

Bart knew his best friend was curious about how things were going, but Bart's mind was whirling, and he refused to agree or disagree at this stage. He glanced out his window, seeing her walking with her pants legs rolled up, holding her shoes in her hands, and dipping her toes into the cold water. "Yeah, she did. Kept her cool. Did exactly what I asked."

"I'm still investigating her for you. So far, I've found nothing," Luke added. "She lives frugally, works as a part-time art teacher in one of the elementary schools in the area and comes in to do police sketches when they call."

Bart thought back to what she had said about her tiny apartment. *That doesn't sound like someone telling fortunes and stealing from unsuspecting ones. What's her angle? Is she just a talented artist and thinks she has a special psychic gift?*

"Keep looking. Before I trust anything that comes out of her mouth, I want to make damn sure she's honest."

For a few more minutes, the five men continued to conference until Bart saw Faith walking back up the path.

"Gotta go. I'll report in tomorrow after we check out Volkov and Maldoni."

By the time he quickly cleaned up in the bathroom, Faith was coming up the stairs. Her long, ebony hair was windblown, and her cheeks were rosy from the breeze. Admitting to himself she might not be the swindler he originally thought she was, he was still uncertain about her purported gifts.

After taming her long hair, she asked him where they would eat dinner. "I don't have any clothes for today other than what I'm wearing," she mentioned, her voice trying to sound casual.

He immediately understood her reticence. *Nowhere fancy.* He appreciated her unspoken request not to go somewhere expensive, especially since it would have been on the Saint's tab.

"I know a little seafood shack," he said. "At least I hope it's still there."

The two of them walked the few blocks to a small restaurant at the end of the beach cove. The neon sign glared brightly against the weather-beaten wooden structure. Being a weekday evening, it was not crowded, and Bart winked at the hostess as she showed them to a corner booth.

Faith looked over at her partner, once more amazed at how his body was showcased no matter what he wore. His shoulders and biceps appeared huge as the material of his sweater stretched over his muscles. It had been impossible to ignore the way his jeans stretched over his large thighs and his butt...*oh, my God—that butt!* Wiggling in her seat, she determined to push these thoughts out of her mind. She had not missed the wink. *Such a flirt...with everyone but me,* she thought ruefully. Shaking her head, she wondered why she wanted him to notice her. *It's not like I'm interested in the big jerk.* As soon as the thought popped into her head, she knew she was lying to herself. *Yeah, I am interested. And he's not such a jerk when he's being nice. But me? That'll never happen. I refuse to be another notch on his bedpost!*

By the time the food came, the bland topics of conversation had been exhausted and Faith was tired of pretending the elephant was not in the room. Looking at the handsome, yet irritating, man sitting across from her, distractingly pushing his hand through his hair once more, she decided to plunge in.

"Bart, we're here together and we haven't mentioned the case one single time. I know your brain is on the mission, but I'd like to be involved as well." Seeing him about to speak, she threw her hands up in defense. "And I mean talk about the case. Not argue about what perceived notions you have about me that are false. Can we do that?"

Sheepishly he looked over at the woman sitting across from him. The thought of the many women he picked up over the years, not wanting to talk at all but just get back to their place for some quick down and dirty, flashed through his mind. Some wanted more than the night he offered, but he could not remember the last time he had dinner with a woman, and they only talked. With no thought of sex afterward.

His silence embarrassed her. "Fine, forget I said anything," she huffed.

Jolted out of his musings, he said, "No, no. I'm sorry. I was lost in thought. I'd like to talk about the case." He saw her eyeing him warily. "I promise, no arguing tonight."

Nodding, she said, "You wondered what I thought earlier."

"Yeah, I did. I was questioning him about what he knew about the kidnapping and when he knew about it. I was...well, looking for facts."

She smiled, saying, "And I asked about how he felt."

"Why that question?"

"I wanted to see his expression. I'd been watching this man, filled with the desire to scratch out more of a living as a small-time gang leader by trying to entice the national gangs to notice him. He wants the waterfront. He'd benefit if Ivan lost his business. We all know that."

"But you wanted to know what he felt?" Bart prodded incredulously.

Her eyes held his, feeling the intensity of his gaze. "Yes, exactly. I wanted to see his expression when he was forced to feel and not think."

"What did you see?"

"I saw a man who may have virtually no scruples, and yet I didn't get the feeling he would have ordered the kidnapping of a child for business reasons."

"Business reasons?"

"Yes. There are sexual predator kidnappers, those who plan on using or selling their victims. But kidnapping for money is seen, in their eyes, as a business deal. You know, *you have something I want, so I will take something precious of yours until you give me what I ask for.*" Her eyes continued to hold his as she said quickly, "Bart, I'm only giving you my opinion based on his body language and how he spoke. His body language was open—he splayed his hands wide on the table. His eyes flashed irritation but not guilt." Faith did not mention that, for a moment, the image of violence faded in her mind as she pictured Miguel as a child.

Bart nodded, for the first time understanding she was extremely in tune with people's expressions and mannerisms. Not only as an artist but as a psychologist. "What about someone in his organization?"

Giving a shrug, she admitted, "I have nothing to base that on, but with you looking more at facts, I could see that being a possibility."

He nodded, "Yeah, I've got the Saints working on that with the FBI." The waitress came around to offer them a refill and Bart shook his head after Faith did.

She could not help but notice this time his eyes never strayed over to the pretty waitress. *He must be really concentrating on the case for him to not even flirt with her!* Suppressing a smile as he paid the bill, they walked back toward the B&B.

The evening was chilly and Bart noticed her shiver slightly. The desire to put his arm around her and pull her into his warmth was overwhelming, but he forced his hands to stay at his side. *She's a partner in this case, that's all. And not a trusted partner...at least not yet* he told himself, trying to hold on to his distrust.

Reaching their rooms, they stood in the hall outside of their bedrooms for a moment, nervously avoiding eye contact.

Faith leaned back to look up into his face, his strong jaw now covered in stubble. "Thank you, Bart." Seeing the question in his eyes, she said, "For talking with me."

Looking down at the stunning woman in front of him, he battled the desire to take her in his arms and kiss her pink lips. *What the hell is happening to me? How the hell did I go from wanting to prove her false and denounce her to Krustas to wanting to kiss away the shadows I see in her eyes?*

Before he could find an answer to that question, she gave a sad smile as she opened her bedroom door and then closed it behind her with a soft click.

8

Faith lay in the cozy bed, the sound of waves crashing in the background. She huddled under the thick comforter but refused to close the window all the way. It had been many years since she had been to the beach, and she did not want to waste a moment of hearing the surf.

She had stayed awake for an hour after they returned from dinner, sitting in the comfortable chair next to the open window. Pulling out her art pad, she closed her eyes, focusing on the images forming in her mind. Beginning to draw, she allowed the reflections to flow to her fingers. Lines, shapes, and forms. And once more the drawing of a boy, this time sitting on a bed with his head down reading a book, filled the page.

"Auugh," she growled. The image never moved beyond that drawing. Something unusual about the child hovered at the edges of her consciousness but never broke through.

Turning the page, she closed her eyes and allowed the

meeting with Miguel to take over her mind. Putting pencil to pad again, she began to draw and the image of the gang leader at the table took shape. The details came into view, from his gold-capped teeth to the tattoos on his arms. Even though in their meeting his eyes were full of enmity, what came through in her drawing was the look of bleakness. *Something truly bothered him about a child being taken.*

As she continued to draw, the figures of the men standing behind him stayed hazy and she realized she had missed the opportunity to study them. No matter how hard she tried, she could not make them clearer, and they stayed fuzzy shadows behind Miguel. *I must do better tomorrow!*

Frustrated, she turned the page and began drawing again. This time, she knew almost immediately where the art was going. Strong jaw. Hair, slightly on the longish side, brushed to the side with spiky pieces sticking up where his hand often ran through it. Deep-set eyes that always seemed to be looking at her as though trying to figure out a complicated puzzle.

By the time she laid the pencil down, the image of Bart rose from the page to stare at her. *I wish...*

Flipping the art pad closed, she silenced the wishes that crept into her mind whenever she thought of him. *Perhaps it will be impossible to find a man that believes in me.* Remembering Mitch, the handsome FBI agent, she smiled. *Well, he believes in me...but there's no spark there.* Sighing, she wondered why the spark was felt with the man who did not think she was true. She slipped out of her clothes, folding her pants and blouse neatly over the back of the chair. Pulling a simple nightgown over her head, she was glad for the long sleeves as she felt the chill in the room and slipped under covers.

Now, an hour later, she rolled over and her mind wandered to the man sleeping in the room next to hers. The tall, gorgeous, blue-eyed, virile man. *Oh, Babushka, you told me it would be hard to deal with my gifts. But does it have to keep me alone? What would I give to be one of the women he crooks his finger at and go running?* Snorting, she turned over, pulling the covers up to her ears. *Yeah? I wouldn't know what to do with someone like him.*

The sound of the surf finally lulled her to sleep, her twisted thoughts eventually giving in to the peace of the night.

In the next room Bart sat up for hours poring over the files from Luke, adding what little he had gained from Miguel. The words from Faith continued to trail through his mind. *"I didn't get the feeling he would have ordered the kidnapping of a child."* Bart closed the files and stripped off his shirt and pants, leaving on his boxers as he slipped between the sheets. As much as he wanted to deny it, her words echoed his own thoughts. *But the men under Miguel? That's a different story.*

The next morning, Bart knocked on Faith's door and was surprised when it opened, showing her completely dressed with her overnight case packed.

"You ready?" incredulity creeping into his words.

Her blue eyes twinkling, she laughed. "I'm not very high maintenance as you can see. It doesn't take me long to get ready in the mornings!"

He stepped back and gallantly waved her to pass in front of him as they made their way to the breakfast area. He noticed her body beautifully hidden beneath a light blue turtleneck, showing no skin and, yet, as seductive as the skimpiest costume. No longer fighting his attraction, he told himself it was only physical. *But if it was, then I'd have already tried to get her in bed. No, I couldn't do that with a partner in an investigation,* his thoughts battled. As he followed her downstairs, he admitted to himself that she was different and that made her all the more endearing. . .and frustrating, because he could not trust her yet.

Mrs. Carswell escorted them to a glassed-in side porch, filled with a small table covered with a light blue tablecloth. The dainty white dishes gleamed against the blue background. Bart felt like a bull in a china shop, afraid to move for fear of knocking something over.

Faith noticed the furniture was not made for someone of Bart's stature and could not hold her giggle in. Pretending to glare, he gave in to his chuckles as well.

Sitting across from her, he did indeed notice she was not high maintenance. Not in her appearance, which included simple makeup on a flawless complexion and her long hair pulled back in a neat ponytail. Her mannerisms also bespoke of someone used to fending for herself. She jumped up to pour the coffee so that Mrs. Carswell would not have to keep coming in to wait on them.

They talked like old friends, the animosity and distrust seeming to fade away. The more time he spent with her, the less she seemed what he feared...and appeared to be what he liked.

Within the hour, they were back on the road for the short drive to meet with Gavrill Volkov.

"This one's going to be different," Bart warned. "Miguel's mostly into drugs and maybe guns, but Volkov, like Krustas, is a higher functioning organization. What all they're into, you don't want to know."

"I still don't understand how Mitch managed to organize a meeting with these...um...men," Faith said, tucking an errant tendril of hair behind her ear.

Irritated at the mention of the FBI agent, he tried to ignore the way her long, slender fingers moved through her hair, stunned with the realization he had never noticed those little innocent movements a woman would make. Most of the women he associated with had their practiced flirtations down to a fine science. *Crossing legs to make their skirts ride up higher. Swirling their tongue around the straw in a drink. Throwing their head back when they laughed to make their tits stick out, their neck exposed, and their hair hang longer down their back—*

"Are you all right?"

Startled, Bart jerked in the driver's seat. "Yeah, sure. Just had my mind on the case," he lied. Falling silent again, he thought about his friend's wives and fiancés... beautiful women with no pretentions. Glancing back to his partner, he had to admit that she was a lot like them.

"How do you want me to do it?" Faith asked.

Almost choking on the idea of how he would like to do her, he whipped his head around to hers, jerking the wheel at the same time. A car honking had him pulling back into his lane quickly.

"Don't do that!" he grunted angrily.

"Do what?" she asked, surprise in her eyes.

"Distract me while I'm driving."

"You really are a jerk, you know," she groused. "All I

wanted to know was how you want me to handle the meeting today. I thought I would let you tell me what I needed to do but, if you're going to be such a prick, forget about it. I'll ask whatever I want, whenever I want!"

Running his hand down over his face in frustration, he drove silently for a few more minutes, angry with her for being such a contradiction in his mind. Slowly, the irritation dissipated and the realization that it was his problem, not hers, hit him. Looking over sheepishly, he admitted, "I'm sorry, Faith." At her look of doubt, he added, "No, really. I'm sorry for biting your head off."

"Accepted," she sighed, sadness lacing her voice.

He heard the melancholy in her single word answer. He suddenly wanted to wipe the sorrow from her face but had no idea what to do. Looking up, he realized they were almost to the meeting place. *What the hell is wrong with me? She was trying to focus on the mission, and I keep wanting to focus on her.*

"Listen, you were right to be asking about the meeting." Looking at the time, he pulled to the side of the road and parked the truck. Twisting his body around to face her, he continued, "The FBI is looking into every possible clue to find Erik, but some of these men will be stonewalling because it's in their interest not to give the FBI a chance to dig deeply into their activities."

"It's as though Erik's kidnapping is actually hurting them as much as it could help them?"

"Absolutely. But we're not an agency. We're an independent investigation service that's less threatening. We're only looking for information about Erik and don't care what their illegal activities are."

"Aren't they afraid we'll find out what they're doing and turn that information over to the FBI?"

"The Feds already know what these organizations are doing and there's no way they're going to say anything to us about it. We go in, get them talking about Krustas and...well, I guess it gives you a chance to see what impressions you get."

At that, she sought his eyes looking for indignation. She saw none...only a glimmer of...*belief? No way!*

"But don't worry, I'll make sure you're safe," he assured, reaching his hand out to cup her cheek only to catch himself, dropping his hand down onto the console instead. *Get a grip, man. She's not here for you to paw her.* But he knew the fight to keep from touching her was real. *Can't say I believe her completely...but something about this woman makes me want to understand her. Protect her.* And he had to admit...*possess her.*

Turning back around, he restarted the truck and drove the last mile to the Volkov meeting.

———

They pulled up to the chain-link gate at the front of a warehouse area in Portsmouth. Faith gazed wide-eyed at the two guards that stepped to Bart's window and then jumped when she realized another man was at her side. She gave a half-hearted smile to the one standing a foot away from her, but no return smile was forthcoming. *I guess the mob doesn't smile.* Turning her head back toward Bart, she watched as he lowered his window to identify himself. The men's guns were obvious and had the desired effect of frightening her.

Nodded through, the gate swung open, and they drove a few hundred feet on a crumbling asphalt drive surrounded with huge metal warehouses, toward an older brick building with more guards wandering around the front. The area was different from Miguel's—while not neat in appearance, it was visibly more guarded.

Parking, Bart looked over at her, noticing the obvious nervousness pouring off her. Without thinking, he reached over and squeezed her leg, saying, "We got this, babe."

She realized the endearment slipped out, easy for a practiced flirt, but he did nothing to retract his words. The awareness of his hand on her sent a warm tingling from her leg to the rest of her body. A little gasp escaped at the unfamiliar excitement.

He glanced sideways, assuming she was still nervous. "Honestly, we'll be fine. They're not going to touch us."

Glad that he misinterpreted the gasp as unease, she simply nodded and slid out of the passenger side, meeting him at the front of the vehicle. One of the suited and armed goons next to the front door moved ahead of them and another one fell in step behind.

This time, instead of being led into a dingy bar, they moved through a well-lit, tiled corridor into a large conference room. At a quick glance, they saw a large metal and glass table in the middle of the room, that also included other pieces of modern furniture. No one was in the room as they were escorted to the table and shown where to sit.

Bart held Faith's chair for her, then settled in next to her. They were alone in the room once the two men left. After a silent moment, she turned to Bart, asking, "Why are we waiting?"

"Power play," he answered back. Seeing her unspoken question, he added, "They think it insults us to make us wait. It's a show of power that they won't bend to our schedule."

"Jerks," she whispered, as he chuckled at her response.

The few minutes stretched interminably until finally the door opened and in walked six men. Three sat down opposite of them, leaving the other three to position themselves around the room. Faith's eyes darted around furiously, trying to see who was where and not making the same mistake as before when she virtually ignored Miguel's men. They were all dressed in dark suits and, for an instant, she wondered if it was some mafia dress code. Her heart was pounding when she realized Bart's gaze was firmly on the man directly in front of them. Determined to play it as cool as Bart, she forced her breathing to slow and kept her eyes on the main man for now.

He looked to be in his forties, black hair with splashes of grey throughout. He was not tall…in fact, his whole being appeared very short and squatty. She could not help but notice dark, beady eyes peering from his square head as they jerked from her to Bart and back again.

"Taggart?" the man asked.

Nodding, Bart said, "Yes. Gavrill Volkov?"

Sneering, Gavrill also nodded. "I'm not happy about being coerced into this farce of a meeting, but having a chat with you is better than turning my whole organization over to the Feds to pore through."

"You know they're doing that anyway, don't you?" Bart asked.

Gavrill's eyes flashed dangerously as his lips pursed. "Well, the sooner you can help prove my organization didn't do shit to Krustas then the sooner we can end this."

"Then let's get to it. You tell me what you know about

Krustas' grandson and how you came about your information."

Gavrill tore his eyes from Bart over to Faith for a moment then slid them back. "I got the news about Krustas the morning after it happened."

Bart noticed that his words were almost identical to Miguel's, but he remained quiet.

Gavrill held Bart's gaze as though daring him to look away first, but neither man gave in. Dark eyes narrowing, he continued, "My second came to tell me."

"Why would your second in command wake you up with this news?"

"Anything to do with my...competitors would be of interest to me."

"Forgive me, but I don't understand why a personal matter of Mr. Krustas would have been that necessary to you," Faith interjected softly.

Gavrill's gaze went back to hers and stared for a long moment. "We may be competitors, but we come from the same homeland. What affects one of my countrymen, affects me as well."

"But you're not from the same homeland, are you?" Bart asked, drawing a hiss from Gavrill.

"I see you've done your homework." With a sneer, he added, "Yes, I'm in fact from Croatia while Krustas is from," he chuckled derisively, "Mother Russia."

"In light of that, why would you have been so interested, Mr. Volkov?" Faith asked again. She peered deeply into his eyes, watching them dart around as he tapped his hands on the table.

"Krustas is old. His time of ruling his businesses is almost over. Since his nephew, Sergio, is now out of the picture, then it shouldn't be too hard to move in. Take advantage." His eyes landed back on hers, "It cannot possibly be a surprise to you that this is a ruthless business. I'd be a fool to not take advantage of every opportunity afforded." His eyes moved back to Bart's as he added, "And I assure you that I am no fool."

"And the news? Besides making a business decision, what did you feel when you learned that a child had been taken?" Faith asked.

Gavrill's head turned slowly as his gaze landed on hers. And stayed. Not moving. He blinked several times as though trying to discern her purpose. Finally, he answered, "Feel? You don't feel anything when making a business decision."

"But besides being a businessman, you're also a man," she stated, knowing she was treading into dangerous waters. "You have children, perhaps? Or friends with children?"

"What game are you playing at?" he growled, eliciting the slightest response from Bart, who stiffened at the tone.

Faith shrugged her shoulders delicately. "No game, I assure you. I'm just trying to see the man behind the business." She felt no softness. Nor peace. Nor sadness. The temperature of the room seemed to drop the longer it took him to answer.

"I am the business," was his answer, each word punctuated succinctly.

Bart moved in to question more. "How well do you know Sergio? After all, when he was going against Ivan's wishes, he must have been seen as a very profitable ally."

Gavrill's expression flashed life before going back to being hard and cold. He sat stoically for a moment, appearing to weigh his words carefully. "When Sergio was arrested, there was no link between the two of us. Why do you think that would be different now that he's behind bars?"

"You've had no contact with Sergio since he's been in?"

Gavrill's stone face held for a moment before he growled, "I won't repeat my answers."

"You didn't actually answer my question the first time around," Bart pointed out. *Asshole!* "You answered with a question of your own, so I'll repeat—do you have a relationship with Sergio?"

"No," came the curt response.

He's lying, Bart thought.

Faith considered Gavrill intently, *He's lying.*

Faith lifted her eyes to the men standing behind Gavrill, but they held nothing but cold. Black cold. The two men sitting on either side of him, introduced as his brothers, held the same expression. She wanted to close her eyes for a moment to see if an image would form in her mind, but she did not dare. A shiver ran over her as the presence of pure evil rushed through her. She felt Bart's hand on her leg once more, offering a reassuring squeeze.

Bart continued to press Gavrill for details about Erik's kidnapping but received nothing. Gavrill glanced at Faith to see if she had more questions, but she shook her head slightly.

As they were escorted back to their vehicle, Bart kept his hand on the small of Faith's back, guiding her as well as providing a modicum of comfort. It was obvious she had never been around men like Miguel or Gavrill and the need to protect was overwhelming.

They stayed silent as they drove back through the security gate. Faith turned and said, "What—"

"God, I'm hungry. I forgot we didn't even eat breakfast.

Want to grab some food and then we can talk about everything?" Bart said, then mouthed, *Truck is bugged.*

Her eyes opened wide as her mouth hung open in surprise. She watched as he nodded his head toward her, indicating that she should speak. "Um...yeah...we could... eat," she stammered.

Taking over for her, he kept up a rambling conversation, sprinkling it occasionally with non-secure comments about Gavrill. Throughout it all, Faith sat quietly, feeling lost. Pulling up to a diner, they got out. Walking over to her, he said, "Go on in and grab a table. I've got to make a call to have my truck swept for possible bugs."

He looked down, her large eyes peering into his. "It'll be okay, I promise." Giving her a little nudge, he watched as she entered the restaurant, then he moved to the side, pulling out his phone.

"Jack? Gotta get my truck de-bugged."

"Volkov?"

"Yeah. I can't be sure, but I'd bet while we were inside his men worked my truck over."

"Mitch is there in Virginia Beach. He was going to meet with you after you have a chance to interview Maldoni. I'll send him a message to catch up with you."

Great. Just great. "Thanks, boss," Bart added, hating the idea of Mitch Evans having a chance to be around Faith again. *What the hell am I thinking?* he admonished himself. *I certainly don't care who she sees...or scams.* That idea caused an unfamiliar feeling of guilt. *Nothing she's done has indicated that she's anything other than what she said—a psychologist who's gifted at reading people and with the ability to transfer that to her art.*

Scrubbing his hand over his face, he shoved his phone back into his pocket in frustration. He had never had a woman put him on such edge. She was such a paradox; he wanted to denounce her one moment, protect her the next. And if the tingling when he touched her was any indication? *That's not all I'd like to do.* The last thought had him shaking his head in frustration. *What the hell am I thinking?*

Walking into the diner, the hostess immediately puffed out her chest, glancing down to make sure her cleavage was showing before greeting him enthusiastically. Bart noticed this—he rarely missed the preening that women did when he was near and always reciprocated with a smile and a wink. His eyes landed on the dark-haired woman in the back who saw him walk in and greeted him with a pure smile. Glancing back to the hostess, it slammed into him how Faith's genuine smile struck him in a way that had the hostess' greeting leaving him empty.

He pushed past the eager woman in a hurry to move closer to Faith, feeling the daggers in his back. Chuckling, he slid into the vinyl padded booth opposite her.

She cocked her head to the side, wondering why he had such a big smile on his face. "Are you all right? Is the truck bugged?" she whispered.

"Yeah, I'm fine and Jack's having someone check the truck for us. We have time to eat before they come."

"Oh," she said, not able to think of anything else to say. She fiddled with the napkin for a moment until the waitress came and took their order.

"Okay, now we should be safe enough to talk some." He saw her hesitate and hurried to add, "It's okay, Faith. I want you to feel free to tell me any of your impressions. I promise I want to hear them."

He saw the uncertain expression on her face and

running his hand over his scruffy jaw, added, "I haven't apologized for what I said when we first met."

Her eyes narrowed as they jumped to his face. Cocking her head, she waited to see what else he would say. *It seems apologies do not come easily to him. Well, suck it up, 'cause I've been waiting for one!*

"I made assumptions about you...false assumptions it seems. Instead of finding out more about you, I thought the worst." He held her gaze and admitted, "I really am sorry, Faith. I do want to hear about your impressions."

With that assurance, she nodded slowly, taking in his words. "Well, I was honestly frightened at the level of violence coming from Gavrill." She lifted her gaze to his, seeing nothing but true interest, and explained. "Usually, with the police, or even the few times I worked with an FBI agent to interview a witness, victim, or possible suspect, the strongest emotion I get is anger or fear. The violence comes as a flash, like..." she struggled how to explain, before saying, "like a lightning bolt. But with Gavrill, it felt black. Deep. Pervasive, not sharp. The room was thick with violence that had nothing to do with anger."

Bart stared at her, hearing for the first time how descriptive she was in her words. While he knew the same thing to be true about Gavrill, it was fascinating to hear how she interpreted the emotions in the room, giving an insight into their thoughts. "What about Miguel?"

They were interrupted when the waitress brought their food, both diving into the cheeseburgers and greasy fries.

"Well," she began between chews, "It was a different feeling of violence. With Miguel, the room was filled with lots of lightning." She wondered if Bart was going to mock her but found him listening intently. "Just as much violence, but more anger. Quick. Sharp. Reactionary."

Chewing methodically, he nodded. "I see what you mean. It makes sense. Did you get a sense of whether or not either one of them may have taken Erik?"

"With Miguel, no, I didn't," but then she added quickly, "but that doesn't mean he didn't, Bart. Remember, I'm just reading people and am in tune with the emotions, body language. I'm not psychic. I can't say he wasn't in charge of taking Erik. Or, for that matter, it could be someone in his gang."

They continued to eat silently for a few minutes, each to their own thoughts. Glancing to the side, she could not help but smile. "I don't think you paid enough attention to the hostess when you came in."

"Huh? Who?" he asked, stunned out of his musings as his gaze followed her nod. "Oh," he said, actually embarrassed at the unwarranted attention. "I guess it was hard to focus on that when I wanted to get over to you."

He watched as her eyes warmed at his words. *I don't know what the hell I'm doing anymore.* His phone vibrated and he growled as he saw who it was from. "Stay here and finish eating. I'm stepping outside while someone from the FBI checks the truck."

She watched as he folded his tall frame out of the booth and immediately missed the warmth his long legs provided when they surrounded hers. Glancing down at the table, she realized he had finished his burger, and she was full. After taking a quick trip to the restroom, she stopped by the table and paid by cash. *Bart has picked up the tab for all the expenses, this is the least I can do.*

She pulled on her coat as she walked through the door

and looked to the left at Bart and another familiar man, talking next to the truck.

"Mitch!" she greeted while waving.

Dressed in dark jeans paired with a grey blazer, the tall, dark-haired FBI agent looked at her in surprise, then grinned a huge grin while calling out, "Well, if it isn't the gorgeous girl herself." Jerking his eyes back to Bart before she was in earshot, he said, "And I thought you said she wasn't around!"

9

———

Bart stood to the side, irritation oozing from every pore, as Mitch greeted Faith with a hug. He glared as she smiled up at the FBI agent, finding himself wanting to punch the man out. *He may be physically fit, but I've got at least three inches and forty pounds on him.* Blinking, Bart wondered where the hell the thought of taking out an agent came from. *Jealousy? No way!*

"How're things going?" Mitch asked, barely letting Faith step out of his arm's reach.

"Good, I suppose," she answered, her gaze sliding over to Bart. "I've never been around anyone like Miguel or Gavrill before. I have to confess it really throws me."

"Got any impressions yet?"

Shaking her head, she said, "I was telling Bart that I wasn't getting any vibes of guilt about Erik, but that could have been because of the severe viciousness I felt in their presence."

Mitch nodded thoughtfully, rubbing his chin. "The level of crime or devious experience from someone might inhibit your ability to get a good read. Interesting."

Bart rolled his eyes behind Mitch's back, figuring the agent was interested in Faith...and not just her gift. Forced to admit to himself that he was jealous, he interrupted. "The FBI got anything?" Bart asked, unable to keep the snark out of his voice.

Mitch turned toward him, his grin replaced by an expression of frustration. "We've got many Amber Alert sightings, and it's keeping my man-power tied up. We're not grateful for the possibilities," he added quickly, "but so far none of them have panned out."

Bart, empathizing with Mitch who had obviously been working around the clock, nodded sympathetically. Looking to Faith, he said, "Come on Faith, we need to get going."

She flashed a confused look at Bart, knowing they had over an hour to make it to the meeting with the Maldonis. His normally easy-going expression was replaced with a tight grimace and a tick in his jaw. He was definitely irritated and acting strangely.

Mitch gave her another hug and, as he walked away, tossed a comment toward Bart over his shoulder. "Make sure to take care of her, bro. She's special."

Once inside his truck cab, he noticed Faith shaking her head. "I'm not, you know."

"You're not what?"

"Special...at least not in the way he thinks I am. I know he and some of the others keep hoping I'll be able to point to someone and say, 'you're guilty,' but I don't work that way." She turned and faced him, looking deeply into his steel blue eyes. "I'm just tuned into people, that's all." Over the last two days, she had come to respect Bart for his investigative abilities and craved his respect in return. *As long as he thinks I'm some kind of phony, I'll never earn that from him.*

"You're wrong, Faith," Bart said. Her expression fell, and he quickly added, "You are special."

Her eyes sought his, sharply searching. And finding... sincerity.

Approaching the gated neighborhood, Faith asked, "Did Mitch find anything?"

Bart nodded. "Yeah. He took care of it."

She wanted to ask more about the device Volkov's men put on the truck, but Bart appeared preoccupied, and she decided to keep quiet. She perused the scenery as the vehicle moved through the old neighborhood of stately homes, many surrounded with their own security gates and tall trees.

Pulling up to an exquisite home, completely decorated for the holidays, Bart identified himself at the security box located on one of the brick pillars next to the ornate metal gate which immediately swung open. Parking in the driveway circle in front of the house, he looked over seeing her wide-eyed expression. It dawned on him he had no idea where she lived. He grew up in a neighborhood similar to this one, although less secure. His grandmother currently lived in an expensive gated community. His earlier assumption she lived well was proving to be false.

"Ready?" he asked.

Jolted out of her astonishment, she jumped. "Yes. Sorry, I've just never seen a house this large before. This is bigger than Constance's."

He peered at her closely but ascertained nothing in her expression other than blatant amazement. He escorted her to the wreathed front door, where a manservant answered and led them through a garnished entry foyer to a comfortable room to the left. The room, decorated in warm tones of browns and taupe with splashes of green, held overstuffed furniture, family photos, knickknacks, and much to Faith's surprise, a few toys. And of course, a huge Christmas tree, with some brightly wrapped presents already underneath.

An elderly gentleman, his silver hair neatly combed back, rose to greet them. As with their other experiences, there were a couple of other men in the room as well, suits tailored and their appearance as neat as Luciano Maldoni's.

"Mr. Taggart. Ms. Romani," Luciano greeted as he stepped forward to shake their hands. "Please sit down and make yourself comfortable."

Instead of standing behind Luciano, the two men in suits sat in chairs as well, creating an atmosphere of guests in a home, instead of one of anger and intimidation. Bart wondered if it was all for show, to put them off a possible scent of guilt.

"I appreciate you taking the time to talk to us. As you know, we're trying to gather information about Ivan Krustas' grandson."

Luciano's face distorted in anger, saying, "Anyone who would take a child is not a fucking man." Moving his gaze to Faith's, he apologized. "I'm sorry, Ms. Romani, but this makes me very angry. I am a businessman. Some may not like the businesses I run, but nonetheless I am ultimately a businessman. I run my companies and my family's interests the way I would expect anyone to do so. I buy and sell goods. When I give my word, it is solid."

Bart knew most of the goods the Maldoni family dealt in were illegal, and wondered if there really was honor among thieves, but moved ahead with the questions. "When did you first hear about the kidnapping of Erik Krustas?"

Luciano held Bart's gaze, never wavering. "The next morning. I pay some of my employees well to scour the news—local, national, and worldwide—to let me know of anything that might affect my businesses. My oldest son alerted me." He indicated the man to his left, who nodded in response.

"What was your reaction?" Faith asked, watching the participants closely.

"I was incensed," Luciano bit out. "I actually called Ivan to tell him that he would have my support if needed."

"But wouldn't your family's businesses possibly profit by Ivan's losing focus on his business?" Bart queried.

The steely-eyed gaze of Luciano captured Bart as he leaned in and said, "Mr. Taggart. Business is business. Family is everything."

Faith felt warmth, something lacking in the last two interviews. *Anger? Yes. But guilt?*

Suddenly, the sound of laughter rang through the hall as two children being chased by a young woman rushed into the room.

"Papa, papa," they giggled and then stopped suddenly as they realized their grandfather was entertaining guests.

"Excuse us," the young woman gushed, blushing at the intrusion.

First giving the children a stern face, Luciano then broke into a smile and opened his arms wide, scooping the errant ones into a hug. Looking over at Bart and Faith, he said, "If anything ever happened to my grandchildren, I would leave no stone unturned. And when I found the man responsible..." his expression turned hard, "even God would not mind what they would suffer at my hands."

Faith turned her gaze to the two men sitting with them, now knowing they were his sons. Both men appeared at ease, the oldest with an open expression as though there was nothing to hide. The younger seemed distracted, occasionally fiddling with his necktie or cuff-links. Trying to discern if he was nervous, she simply could not get a read on him with the other distractions in the room.

The children finally left, and Bart continued his questions for several more minutes. With the noise of the children gone, Faith focused on the younger son once more. *Definitely ill at ease. What are you hiding?* She was startled when Bart touched her arm as he was rising from his seat.

Luciano walked them to the front door and lifted Faith's hand, kissing her knuckles. Cocking his head to the side, he commented, "You have an old soul, my dear. I get the feeling there is more to you than just an investigator."

Not knowing how to respond, she simply gifted him with one of her smiles and received one in return. Bart stepped forward, ushering her back to the truck. Once more inside, she mouthed, *Are we bugged?*

Shaking his head, Bart said, "No, that's not Maldoni's style." As he drove out of the gated community, he noted the time. Rubbing his hand over his jaw, he added, "Look, it's later than I thought it would be. It's going to be late when we get home."

His phone vibrated. "Yeah, boss?" he answered.

"Don't head back yet. I want you to meet with Ivan in the morning. He'll be at his place in Norfolk."

"Something come up?"

"Yeah, the next demand came in."

"Are we meeting with just Ivan?" he queried.

"No. FBI will be all over it, but you'll have a familiar face. Mitch will be there. We'll process the video and audio leads you have from your two meetings today. When you return tomorrow, we'll all be up to speed."

Trying not to show his irritation at Faith spending more time with Mitch, he agreed before disconnecting. "Looks like we need to find a place to stay tonight again."

"What choices do we have?" she asked, twisting to look at him.

"Well, we can see if the B&B has rooms available tonight. We could discuss our thoughts and get a good night's sleep, before driving back in the morning."

She turned away from him, a small smile curving the edges of her mouth. *He must not hate me now to want to spend more time with me.* Feeling his earlier apology was sincere, she no longer saw him as an ogre. The thought of being with him longer made her smile widen. Nodding, she said, "I'd love to."

To Bart's relief and Faith's joy, Mrs. Carswell greeted them like old friends and offered them the same rooms they had the night before. She even told them about a nearby bar that had music on Friday nights and was well known for their chicken wings. Thanking her for the information, Bart paid for the rooms and then leaned down to grab their overnight bags.

"No need to show us up," he called out, heading toward the stairs. "We can find our way."

Faith followed him and moved into her room, immediately going over to open the window to hear the surf. Twisting around, she glanced over her shoulder and said, "I'm going to go back down to the beach for a few minutes before we head to dinner."

Once more, he watched from his window as she made her way down the wooden plank to walk on the beach. The wind from the ocean blew her hair away from her face, the silky ebony strands whipping around her shoulders. She looked...lonely.

Calling Jack, he discovered his good luck that most of the Saints were still at the compound reviewing the material.

"How's she doing?" Jack asked, knowing Bart had been unable to speak earlier.

"We're going to grab a bite to eat and I'll find out more about what she thought."

"You're starting to believe her?" Cam asked.

Sitting down on the bed facing the window, Bart watched as she walked along the shore. "I don't know," he answered honestly. "I'll admit that a lot of my preconceived notions about her don't seem to be true. I don't believe she has any kind of *gifts* or psychic abilities, but she seems to be very in tune with people. I go for the facts, and she goes for the emotions."

Luke piped up, "Just so you know, I still haven't found out anything negative about Faith. I'll send over what I do have on her. How do you want it?"

"Send it to my email," Bart said, watching her turn and walk back toward the house. "I'll talk to you tomorrow after meeting with Ivan."

He met her at the door as she came up the stairs, her appearance the same as the evening before. Red cheeks and windblown hair. Dark eyes twinkling. *And beautiful.*

Arriving at the bar, they found it was crowded but managed to snag a bar top table. As tall as he was, it took little effort to wave down a waitress...and as handsome as he was, it took little time for the perky blonde in short shorts and a cut-off top to make her way over to him.

The waitress managed to place herself in between their stools, giving her attention to Bart and her back to Faith. Recognizing the maneuver, Bart felt an unusual sense of irritation. "Miss, you need to step back so that you can take the lady's order first."

Chastised, the waitress moved but gave a grim-lipped smile to Faith. The orders placed, the woman moved away, tossing her hair over her shoulder as a sign of indignation.

Faith peered up at Bart and asked, "Does that happen a lot?"

He cocked his head, unsure of her question.

"You know, having women throw themselves at you. Try to catch your eye. Ignore anyone else you might be with?"

Bart squirmed uncomfortably as he thought of his answer, having the grace to be embarrassed. Hearing her giggle had him jerking his gaze back to her.

"It's okay, Bart. I have a feeling it happens all the time and you just take it for granted. And you didn't have to reprimand her on my account," Faith said. "It's not like we're on a date."

"But she didn't know that" he replied. "If we had been on a date, it wouldn't have been acceptable for her to cut you off. Even if we're not on a date, a good server would know that it is commonly expected to serve the woman first."

They were silent for a moment before Bart confessed, "I admit, in the past, I didn't give it much thought." Seeing her questioning gaze, he shrugged as he explained, "Women coming on to me. I've always been a big man, and I worked out. I could play football in college and then be in the Navy and then SEAL training."

"No doubt about it, Bart. You've got a body women love," she said honestly.

Her candor caught him off guard, realizing her comment was not being used to get him into bed.

With their wings and beer delivered, they continued the light conversation while eating. He occasionally looked around and saw other men eyeing Faith, feeling a jolt of unfamiliar jealousy. She no longer seemed the threat he originally assumed and, staring at her innocent beauty, he could not help but think, *Could this be the woman for me?*

As his eyes moved back to her face, he leaned over and wiped a dab of barbecue sauce from her cheek. She blushed as she laughed, trying to wipe her cheek in case there was more.

"I got it all," he said, smiling at her blush. Flustered, she was adorable.

Normally one for enjoying a loud bar, Bart found himself wanting to spend more alone time with Faith. Assisting her down from the tall stool, they made their way out of the crowd and walked back toward the inn.

"Can we walk on the beach?" she asked, her eyes bright as the wind gently lifted and blew her hair.

Grabbing her hand, assisting her over a few rough patches in the sidewalk, he led her along the boardwalk until they came to the beach. The sun had long set in the early winter sky, but the water caught the lights from the buildings behind them.

Sighing, she said, "It's been ages since I've been to the ocean. That's why I wanted to walk on the beach. Even though it's cold now, it's so peaceful."

Bart looked over the waves, watching the undulating current glisten with the neon lights' reflections. "I used to go fishing with my grandfather," Bart said. "He was a busy CEO of his own company, but almost never worked on weekends, saying they were for family."

She smiled up at him, encouraging him to continue to speak while secretly loving that he had not let go of her hand. *He might not fully trust me, nor me him, but I can't deny that he is changing. Even if he doesn't quite realize it yet.*

"About once a month, granddad and I would walk down to the little dock at the back of their property and fish."

"He sounds like a remarkable man."

"Yeah, he was. I haven't thought about those fishing trips in a long time." He noticed she shivered when the wind blew, and this time did not hesitate to put his arm around her. "Um...is this okay?" he asked, unsure of his actions.

She nodded, glad for his warmth. The few blocks to the Bed and Breakfast were over too quickly, but both knew they needed to get a good night's sleep. Walking up the stairs, they hesitated at their doors.

"Well, goodnight, Faith," he said softly.

"Sleep well, Bart," she replied before walking into her room, once more closing her door with a soft click.

She sat in the chair by the open window again, trying to clear her mind so she could draw the images from the day. The black eyes of Gavrill's men, his square jaw set in anger, Luciano's youngest son picking imaginary lint from his jacket as he avoided looking at anyone. All the images rushed through her mind, creating a hodge-podge of drawings in her art pad. And before she went to bed, she allowed herself one more drawing. This time of the handsome man walking on the beach with her, sharing stories of his childhood. Tossing the art pad on the other side of the bed, it was the last drawing that left a smile on her face as she fell deep into sleep.

10

The next morning, sitting at the same breakfast table, once more afraid of breaking the chair, Bart looked over at Faith. Sleep had eluded him, as his mind had been a convoluted mixture of the case, the interviews, and the beautiful woman in the next room. She, on the other hand, appeared rested and fresh.

"Are we making any progress?" she asked, her expression worried.

"Yeah. Jack's group has been working on the surveillance tapes from our three interviews. The FBI has them as well and everyone is trying to garner more information. Ivan has another demand for money and, even though the FBI is all over that as well, Ivan wants to meet with us also."

"I thought something would come from the interviews. I...I just don't know. To be honest, the violence coming from Miguel and Gavrill was overwhelming. It was the only thing I could feel."

"And Maldoni?"

He watched as she bit her bottom lip nervously before lifting her gaze to his.

"The domestic scene appeared sweet," she began.

"Sweet? That's all—"

"I wasn't finished," she admonished, before continuing. "A little too sweet. Almost as though it were staged. Luciano, welcoming us into his home. His sons sitting nearby. The children running into the room."

Bart leaned back, smiling. "You picked up on that also?"

"Oh yeah. But to be honest again, I didn't get a strong guilty emotion from Luciano. But his youngest son? Nervousness poured off him."

I didn't even notice that, he admitted to himself.

They finished breakfast, said goodbye to Mrs. Carswell, and drove over to Ivan's home. Like Luciano, Ivan lived at the end of a long road in a gated neighborhood, populated by families craving privacy. His property covered five acres and appeared well fortified.

By the time they made it to his house, Faith's mouth unashamedly hung open. "Oh, my God. People really live like this?" Remembering what Bart said about his grandfather's mansion, she blushed. "I'm sorry. I didn't mean to make you self-conscious."

"It's fine. My grandparents did live in a house this large and the house I grew up in wasn't much smaller. But you'll see my house now is very normal."

Did he just insinuate I might see his house? Before having a chance to process that, they saw a line of large, black SUVS.

"The FBI is here, seeing what Ivan needs to do for the drop," Bart informed her.

"Do you think the kidnappers will let Erik go this time?"

"I don't know," Bart shrugged. "Best case scenario? Yes, and the only thing wasted was a couple of days of us questioning some very scary...uh...men that will give the FBI more info to pore over."

Stopped by a guard before being signaled to drive on, they eventually parked as close to the front of the house as possible. Walking through the front door, they had to move through the swarm of dark-suited FBI. The starkness of their appearance was in sharp contrast to the bright Christmas decorations adorning the room. Seeing Mitch over to the side, they made their way to him.

Bart noticed Mitch eyeing Faith as he shook her hand and had the flash memory of the waitress cutting Faith out of the equation with her body. *Damn, this is what it feels like?*

"As you heard, Ivan got another demand. It's for another quarter of a million dollars," Mitch informed them.

As the men continued to talk while moving into the den to meet with Ivan, Faith held back, overcome with emotions. Lightheaded, she quietly slipped into another room—one less crowded. Images hovered at the edges of her mind but were hazy. Looking around, the room she escaped into sported French doors leading to an outdoor patio. Stepping outside, a blast of wind hit her, sending her hair flying wildly around her face, but helped to clear her mind. She tried to bring the images back to the forefront of her mind, but they were gone. Sighing deeply, she turned to walk back inside and ran into a wall. Stumbling backward, her arms were grabbed.

"Faith? Are you all right?" Bart asked, steadying her.

"Sorry," she exclaimed. "I needed some fresh air and came outside." Part of her wanted to tell him about the images flying through her head, but she decided against it. *I don't have anything firm...and he wouldn't believe me anyway.*

Offering a small smile, she allowed him to escort her back inside the house. "Are you done already?"

"Yeah, I talked to Ivan and the FBI in charge. They're working out the details of making the drop. I let Mitch know Jack had the surveillance tapes from our meetings and Monty had sent them to him. If you're ready, we can go."

"I'd like to see Ivan quickly if that's possible."

Bart maneuvered her among the agents crawling around as they approached Ivan. The older man smiled when he saw her.

"My dear, do you have anything for me?"

She stumbled at his words, feeling like a failure. "I'm sorry, Mr. Krustas. There is nothing definite yet." She wanted to offer him comfort by telling him she could see Erik smiling while sitting on a bed, reading a book. *But that was yesterday's image...nothing today.*

He smiled and patted her cheek. "Maybe this payment will do it this time. I pray they'll send him back to me after this."

Tears hit the back of her eyes as she tried to speak over the lump in her throat. He looked devastated; her heart ached for him as she was filled with a powerful image of despair. With a final goodbye, she stepped away, allowing Bart to move her toward the front door. Her mind swirled with the image of the boy in a room, on his bed, reading.

The trees on the side of the highway once again flew by as Bart and Faith drove back toward Charlestown. This time, the trip was much friendlier than the one two days earlier.

The country music station was softly playing in the background when she suddenly reached over to turn up the volume. "I love this song!" she exclaimed.

Bart lifted his eyebrow, remembering his previous attempt at irritating her, but kept silent. He watched as she looked over at him, an expression of victory on her face. *Minx!* "You like country music?" he asked, trying to sound nonchalant.

"Yep," she declared. She decided not to torture him about the other day, keeping quiet instead while grinning widely.

Moving to a safer topic, she twisted around to look at him and asked, "Did you grow up in Virginia Beach?"

Nodding, he replied, "Yeah. My great-grandfather made his living in the shipbuilding industry during WWII and that's been the family business ever since."

"But not for you," she stated, rather than asked.

"Shipbuilding wasn't in my blood, but the ocean was. I joined the Navy after college and trained to become a SEAL."

Not wanting to touch on a sensitive subject, she queried cautiously, "You were injured?"

Heaving a sigh, he nodded. "The last mission I was on, I blew out my knee. I'm strong but, as big as I am, knees can be a weak joint."

"You sound...I don't know...almost irritated with yourself."

"Yeah well, I can't even have a good war-injury story. I was carrying a bunch of shit and then a buddy got hit. Not bad, but he couldn't travel fast, and I was the closest."

His story stopped, but her mind quickly put together the pieces. "Oh, my God! You carried him, didn't you?" The silence filled the truck for a moment, and she began to wonder if he was going to continue at all.

Finally, he nodded. "Yeah. I picked him up and got him to our transport. Right near the end, I stepped into some kind of hole and went down. Tore my knee to shit and almost dumped my team member."

"Was...did he...?"

"Live? Yeah. He's still a SEAL. Feels guilty as hell and every so often I remind him that he, at least, owes me a beer when we get together," he laughed.

She decided that she liked hearing the sound of his laughter. "Then you went to work for the investigative company?"

He shook his head, saying, "No. I did a year with Border Patrol. I was interested in what they had to offer and liked the work." Giving a little shrug, he said, "But with the SEALs, we could usually do what we needed to do to get the job done. With the BP, our hands were often tied with a lot of bureaucratic bullshit. Then I made a trip to visit a former SEAL buddy and happened to meet Jack. Found out about his business and I was all in. Turned in my resignation and moved to Charlestown."

A comfortable silence ensued as each returned to their own thoughts. After several miles had passed, she asked, "What about your family?"

"Mom and dad still live in the house where I grew up in Virginia Beach."

"The mansion?" she joked.

Glancing over at her smiling face, he could not hold the smile back either. "Yeah, the mansion." Her face did not seem to hold any envy, and he continued. "My brother's an accountant with the family firm and my sister is an engineer."

"You were the wayward son?"

"I'm the black sheep—the only one who did not go into the business." He laughed again, saying, "Nah, it's all good. Mom and dad, hell, even granddad, were proud of me being a SEAL and what I'm doing now."

"Are you going to go visit them for Christmas?" she asked, curiosity and envy warring.

"Probably," he answered. "At least for a day, just to see everyone. My parents'll have a big meal with all the trimmings, and we'll head to Nonnie's for some early presents to open. My whole family will be there, so I'll probably go to spend Christmas Eve night and Christmas morning with them."

He said the words casually but was instantly aware of the quiet in the truck. Not angry quiet. Not pouting quiet. He had heard a lot of that from women over the years to recognize it easily. No, this was a sad quiet. A grieving quiet. *Jesus, I'm an idiot*, he berated himself. *She has no family to spend the holidays with.*

She broke the silence first, saying, "You seem close to your grandmother, and you mentioned your grandfather in past tense. Is he...um...?"

"He died about five years ago and I swear, when I'm at Nonnie's house, I can still hear his laughter booming through the halls." He sobered thinking about his grandmother. "She's never recovered from his death."

"I don't think people recover, Bart. They just learn how to live with grief."

"Is that what you do?"

This time, the silence hung heavily, each to their own thoughts. Finally, she nodded. "Yes, I suppose it is. I live with the grief of my lost family." Sighing deeply, she admitted, "But sometimes it's a lonely place to be."

Suddenly, Bart wanted to know about her. Their conversation had been all about him and he realized, for the first time, he truly knew nothing about her...and desired to.

Looking over, their gazes locked for a second. His eyes dropped down to her mouth. The smooth, pink, plump flesh drove him crazy, and he wanted to taste it more than his next breath. Her tongue darted out to lick her lips and his cock jumped to life.

Sucking in a deep breath, he said, "Tell me about yourself?"

"Me?" she said, surprised at the question. "What's to tell?" She sat silent for a moment, the peaceful truce between them slowly fading. "After all, I'm sure you've been checking me out. Have your co-workers discovered my hidden secrets yet?" She did not want to be bitter but could hear the sharp tone of her voice and winced. Lifting her hand, she nibbled on her thumbnail while looking out of her side window. *Wow, we're almost to Richmond.* She realized the miles had passed quickly as she had gotten to know him.

Bart's fingers tightened on the steering wheel. He wanted to dispute her accusation that he had been investigating her but could not lie. He had looked over the documents Luke sent to him. He knew her bank account balance...for the past two years. Very little money had been deposited from her police work and teaching job. She lived in an old apartment in an ancient building in downtown Charlestown...and not in a safe area. He finally came to the absolute decision that she was not a swindler, scammer, medium for hire, or any of the other unsavory names he had called her.

Glancing to the side, he saw the sadness in her eyes as she stared forward, purposefully keeping her eyes from moving to his. Even though he had apologized before, he knew his earlier words had stung. He wanted to take his spiteful comments back, but the words caught in his throat. Somehow, they seemed trite, a reminder he had not believed her in the beginning.

Looking at the clock, he knew he only had her undivided attention for about another hour or so and wanted to make the most of it. Glancing at her stoic face, he knew if he did not take a chance to make it all right, then she might never want to be around him again once they got back home.

"No, really," he said, tentatively. "I'd like to hear about you." Grasping at straws, he prodded, "Tell me about your grandmother."

The silence continued for several more minutes, leading him to believe she was no longer speaking to him.

"Babushka was my savior," she began tentatively. After a moment, she continued. "My father left soon after I was born, and my mother never recovered." Giving a derisive snort, she said, "My mother's hold on reality was...tenuous at best. Growing up, she would sometimes tell me my father went to fight in a war. Or went looking for treasure. Or whatever seemed to flit through her mind that made it easier for her to deal with the fact that he left her. It was my grandmother who stepped in and finally told me the truth. She said the truth was always better than make-believe anyway."

Bart was startled at this pronouncement. *Truth? She believes that fully in truth?* In the ensuing silence, he realized whatever gift Faith believed she had was real to her. *That doesn't make her a liar if she believes it. Like Nonnie and her mermaids.* "And what was the truth?" he asked softly.

She stayed quiet for a second too long, nibbling on her thumbnail once more before adding, "My dad was not the type of man who wanted to be tied down. Certainly not to a squalling baby."

Hurt stabbed his heart as he realized all the love he experienced as a child was a foreign concept to her. Another few silent moments had passed before he prodded again, "You said your mother never recovered?"

"She remained sweet, but a little...um...out of it for the rest of her life." There was another pause as she sighed heavily before adding, "She died of cancer when I was twelve and Babushka became my guardian. As hard as that was, in some ways, it was better. My grandmother was fun-loving and taught me much more about life than my mother ."

"She sounds amazing," he said honestly.

Faith pondered how much more to tell him. How much more of her story would he be able to handle without becoming angry again? He must have noticed her hesitation because he asked about her drawings.

Her head jerked around as she peered closely at him. "Seriously? You're not just going to use this as an opportunity to slam me again?"

"No, no," he promised. "Really, I'd like to hear about it. I can't promise to...um...believe it the way you do, but I'd like to try to understand."

This time, the quiet in the truck cab lasted for several miles. He wondered if he should have pushed—*maybe she doubts that I will keep my mouth shut.* He was about to tell her not to worry about it when she began to speak.

She sat for a moment, silent in her indecision. *Should I give him another chance?* The cold of loneliness crept over her, and she longed for the warmth of human understanding. Glancing at his face, anger and doubt no longer appeared, but were replaced with interest. *How can I expect to be given another chance if I'm not willing to give back?* Deciding to open up, she prayed it was the right decision.

"I always loved to draw. I think it was my escape sometimes. I would read a book and think of how I saw the characters and spend hours drawing them. I would wake up at night from either a dream or a nightmare and have to draw what I had seen. The first time I ever had something different happen to me, I was at school, and we were in an art class. I had drawn a picture of the boy sitting next to me in detail—his striped shirt, his red hair, everything. Except he was lying on his back in the classroom. About an hour later, he fell to the floor just like in my drawing. I didn't know it at the time, but he had epilepsy and had had a seizure. When the teacher found my drawing from earlier in the day, she wanted to know how I knew he was going to become ill. I had no idea, but she never treated me the same after that. In fact, I know she told the other teachers because they all avoided me."

Bart stayed silent, his mind searching for a reason. *Dogs can tell if a person is about to have a seizure, so maybe there was a scent she smelled.* The idea sounded ridiculous to him, but as usual, his mind desired a logical explanation.

"Another time, I drew our neighbor's dog chained to a tall pole in an unfamiliar yard that had an old metal swing set in the back. Later that day, our neighbors came to ask if we had seen their dog because it had gotten loose. We hadn't, but I showed my grandmother my drawing. She recognized the swing set from a yard several blocks away. She told the neighbors she had seen their dog and when they went to look, they found him."

"What did the neighbors say about your drawing?" he asked, afraid that, as a child, she had suffered again.

"We never told them." Thick, soupy silence formed around them. Finally, slicing through, she admitted, "That was when Babushka told me about my gift."

11

―――――

F aith heard the sharp intake of breath and knew Bart was reacting to the words *her gift*. She wanted to turn and look at him, see his expression, peer into his eyes to see his look of disbelief. Or anger. But she kept looking straight ahead at the highway. *I'm such a coward!* There had been several minutes of silence in the car while they had talked, but nothing like this one. *I guess that ends our conversation,* she thought ruefully.

The stillness was suddenly broken. "Tell me about your gift," Bart encouraged. Catching her glare, he said, "Please. I want to try to understand how you see things."

For a moment she sat quietly, pondering his words. *He wants to know how I see things which means he wants to view things through the eyes of a nutcase.* Sighing, she had to admit to herself he did not actually say that. *Maybe...oh hell, what's the worst that can happen?*

"My grandmother told me that for as long as family stories have been told, our family had women that could feel things that were unseen." Turning her head toward him, she added, "She never said fortune-telling, or psychics, or mediums, or any of the other words used to talk about some who pretend to predict the future or talk with the deceased."

"Okay," he acknowledged. Taking his eyes off the road for a second, he caught her struggling with the words.

"I mean, probably down through history I'm sure there were some Romani women who were accused of witchcraft or heresy or whatever and probably burned at the stake!" she huffed. "But Babushka never said that was what she did or what I did."

Another mile had passed in silence before she spoke again. "She said the gift was in women and always skipped a generation and that was why my mom didn't have it."

"Were you frightened? Did the uh...things...uh...scare you?"

Emitting a small chuckle, she questioned, "Things?" She watched as he grimaced, running his hand through his hair and decided to take pity on him. "No, I was never scared. I confess, it was odd sometimes to feel something strongly and I didn't know if it was real or not. But I usually drew whatever I was feeling."

She stared at the inner struggle playing on his face as a myriad of emotions came through in his expressions.

"My Babushka told me to be cautious. She said others would not understand and most people run from things they do not understand."

Once more the cab was silent as both thought on what she was saying. For her, she knew finally talking about it would either push him away irrevocably or he would finally accept she was not what he feared. She knew if she were honest with herself, her heart already hoped he would accept her. *Oh, why does my heart have to be involved?* Her chest constricted as she waited to hear what he was going to say, for his next words would decide if she would be able to trust him.

Bart rolled her words around in his head, realizing his first assessment of her was based on a judgmental bias. *Granddad, you always told me to search for truth, but I condemned her before learning the facts.* He thought of the lonely little girl, shunned by her classmates, dealing with something she could not understand.

"I'm sorry, Faith," he said, his words sounded too simplistic, but could not seem to find other words to express his regret.

She closed her eyes as her head hung down. For so long she had been alone, knowing that a large part of who she was would not fit into many people's worlds. She had no idea how she might fit into his world, but hearing his honest apology touched her heart. She knew she could forgive him and know that he truly was a good person.

He glanced to the side, seeing her bowed head and reached across the console to touch her arm. "I'm truly sorry. I judged you before I found out anything about you and that's not me. That's really not me. My...my grandfather would not be proud of me for condemning you before I learned the truth."

The silence, lasting for a moment, was broken when he shook his head, snorting. "In fact, it was my grandfather who always told me that my name stood for *searching for truth.*"

"Your name?" she asked in confusion.

"Yeah. Bartholomew. St. Bartholomew."

She kept her head lowered but opened her eyes. His large, tan hand was lying on top of her small, pale, clenched ones. Sucking in a shaky breath, she lifted her head and gifted him with a smile. "Thank you. I know you don't have to understand or even believe me, but thank you for no longer condemning me."

The air in the truck cab seemed lighter as the tires continued to churn up the miles. Taking it a step further, he gazed at her again and asked, "When did you start working for the police department as an artist?"

"After high school, I went to the college in Charlestown, so I could live with my grandmother. I love psychology and art both, I double majored. When I got out, I went to work for the school system. The job was supposed to be full time, but they cut their art program back to part time. I worked as a waitress to help pay the bills. I had a scholarship to help with my master's program."

It did not escape his notice that while he grew up with a large, loving family that was very wealthy, she was struggling to pay for essentials. He rubbed his hand through his hair once more, making the ends stick up at odd angles.

She watched him, her fingers twitching to run through his hair herself, before slipping down to cup his strong, stubbled jaw. Giving herself a mental shake, she pushed thoughts of her hands on him away.

He saw the glazed look in her eye and, cocking his head, said, "Are you all right?"

Jerking, she blushed adorably again. "Yes, yes. Sorry, my mind wandered." *And I hope you can't tell where it wandered!*

"But about my police work, I got the job when I answered an ad in the newspaper for a police artist. I applied for the job and was called back for a trial run. I was interviewing an elderly woman who had been assaulted. I listened carefully, but the emotion continued to push its way in. Her anger. Rage. And fear. I felt completely in tune with her. I drew her description, but everything came out in the drawing. When I was finished, one of the detectives recognized the man in my picture. They brought him in for a line-up and the woman identified him immediately. They allowed me to see him as well. It was weird to recognize the man that I had drawn so precisely." She gave a little shrug and said "I was hired right then. It's not what I expected to do, but it helps with the bills, and I found that I liked it. And, as Babushka always said, if I use my gift for good, then that was why God gave it to me."

He looked at her profile, staring out of the window. Her dark eyes were matched by dark circles underneath in stark contrast to her pale complexion. She nibbled on her thumbnail, her nerves so taut he could feel them radiate throughout the truck.

"What about the FBI? How did you get to know Mitch?"

"There was a bank robbery in town and the FBI took over the investigation. I was called in to do sketches from the witnesses. Once more, there was such anger and fear. Most artists draw while the person is describing, but I don't do it that way. I listen. I feel. And as they are talking, an image comes into my mind. When the witness finishes, I draw the image. I know it may sound risky, as though they would just agree to whatever I was drawing, but each time, I nailed it. They caught all three men. Mitch had been in on the interviews I was doing when sketching. He liked what he saw."

I'll bet he did! Bart thought, the now familiar stab of jealousy hitting him once more.

"Since he's with the local office, whenever the FBI needs an artist, he calls me."

A more comfortable silence enveloped the truck cab as each settled in with their thoughts. He turned the information over and over in his mind, finding that so far what she said made perfect sense. *But...* "Can I ask another question?"

She heard the cautiousness in his voice and twisted to face him this time. "Absolutely," she stated.

"What about when you draw but haven't talked to someone...or seen anything? Like with the dog or the boy with the seizures?"

"Yeah, that's the harder part to explain. It's what my Babushka told me was the gift and she also said it could be a curse."

Faith twisted a strand of hair around her finger as she thought how best to explain what she could not understand herself. "All I know is sometimes I get strong images in my head. It doesn't happen often...it's not like I walk around every day having some kind of premonition. Like the day I drew the boy on the floor, I simply saw him on the floor in my mind. And with the dog, the same thing happened. I saw an image of him chained to a tall fence in a backyard with a swing set."

Seeing tears fill her eyes as honesty poured off her, he knew that no matter if it made sense to him or not, she was real. Her ability was real. He wanted to find out more, but they had made it to Charlestown. He glanced at the clock on the dashboard. "I really want to keep talking to you, but I gotta call Jack and see what we need to do."

Giving a little nod, she replied, "Of course. The drop-off should have happened by now, shouldn't it?"

"Yeah, but it may be a bit before we hear about Erik."

Calling Jack, he found out that Ivan had indeed made the drop, but there was no word of Erik's return at this time.

"What do you want us to do, boss?"

Jack replied, "You can take Ms. Romani home and then come here. We'll meet as soon as you get in."

"I should be there in about thirty to forty minutes." With that, he disconnected before turning to Faith. "I guess you surmised we don't know anything yet."

She nodded, sadness filling her eyes. Looking up, she said, "I can't imagine the devastation Ivan and his family are living through right now. Especially Erik's mother. It... it just makes my heart hurt." Sighing again, she glanced out the window and added, "Oh, I forgot to tell you where to go. I live off Broadland Street. There are some apartments above the old shop buildings."

He already knew where she lived but did not let on. And he knew what a crappy area of town she lived in. Turning onto her street, he saw the three and four-story, century-old buildings. Poor streetlights. No security lighting. Parking near her building, he grabbed her arm as she prepared to hop out of his truck.

"Stay," he commanded before he stepped out of his side. By the time he hustled around, he could see her face, the hard expression clearly showing through the window.

"You did not just tell me to *stay*, did you?" she asked, her eyes snapping.

"I'm not about to have you go in alone."

Looking around, she wondered aloud, "Why not? I'm in and out of here all the time."

Without answering her, he grabbed her overnight case and assisted her out of the truck. As they approached the door, he reached for the security pad. "What's the code?"

A slight giggle had him turn, seeing the corners of her lips lift up. She reached around him and gave the door handle a push. As it swung open, she watched as his face morphed from surprise to anger.

"You've got to be kidding me," he bit out.

"What?" she asked, pushing past him and entering into the dingy hallway. "That security panel hasn't worked since I've been here." She turned awkwardly tucking a loose strand of hair behind her ear, wondering how to end their odd partnership. Taking a deep breath, she stuck out her hand as she looked into his eyes, and said, "Well, thank yo—"

"Not leaving you here, Faith. I'm walking you to your door."

"Oh, you don't have t—"

"Non-negotiable, babe," he answered.

Cocking her hip, she tapped her foot impatiently. "Really? Alpha much, are we?"

Chuckling, he said, "I'd think you'd know the answer to that by now."

Not to be deterred, she continued. "And *babe*? Now you're talking to me like I'm a waitress or a bartender. What's next? Your little wink?"

"Stop busting my balls and show me the way to your apartment."

Glaring, she whirled around, heading to the stairs. Stomping up to the second floor, she walked down another dingy hall coming to her door. "We're here. Do you want to come in and check for the boogie man also?"

His answer was to take the key from her hand and unlock her door himself. Stepping inside, he flipped on the lights. Her apartment illuminated to reveal a tiny, but warm, interior. The kitchen was immediately on the right, the short bar with stools as the only eating area. The living room was barely big enough to hold a worn sofa, coffee table, end table, and one other chair. The small, flat screen TV was mounted on the wall opposite the sofa with bookshelves underneath. There were two open doors near the kitchen, and he could see one was the bathroom and the other led to a minuscule bedroom.

The end table held a small, three-foot tree, decorated with what looked to be antique, glass ornaments. His words came slamming back to him. *I accused her of getting rich by scamming others.*

Dropping his chin to his chest, he felt his body being shoved to the side as she stepped in around him.

"Smee? Smee? Come on out sweetie."

Bart's eyes jerked open as an orange cat with a white face walked in from the bedroom. He watched Faith move to the kitchen and stoop to refill the food dish as the cat swirled between her legs before eagerly diving in.

She looked up, saying, "I felt bad staying one extra night, but I knew I left enough food."

The comfort of their early conversations passed and now an awkward silence descended. Her eyes glanced over at her little Christmas tree, proudly displaying the old ornaments handed down from her grandmother.

"Well, I guess this is goodbye. I'm sorry I wasn't more helpful with the interviews. I know that Mr. Krustas...and even Mitch, hoped I would be able to get a feeling that one of the people we talked to would strike something in me about Erik, but..." her voice trailed off.

He reached out, taking her small hand in his much larger one. At first, it was nothing more than a simple clasp—like any two people standing too close, unsure of what came next. But he didn't let go.

Instead, he stepped closer until the toes of his boots nearly touched her shoes. She tilted her head slightly, her face just beneath his chin, her breath catching as his gaze dropped to her lips.

He lowered his head slowly, giving her time to pull away if she wanted. His breath brushed across her skin, warm and unsteady, and he paused just before their mouths met. A question lingered in his eyes.

"Yes," she whispered.

That was all he needed. His lips met hers. Slow at first, almost tentative, before the kiss deepened. He drew her closer, one hand firm at her back as she melted against him, her fingers curling into his shirt.

The world narrowed to the space between them.

Her breath hitched as the kiss grew more intense, their movements no longer uncertain. She leaned into him, rising onto her toes, as though trying to get closer still. For a moment, nothing existed beyond the warmth of his mouth and the steady strength of his arms around her.

He shifted, brushing his lips along her jaw, then to her ear, sending a shiver through her. When his mouth moved to her neck, lingering just long enough to make her pulse race, she tightened her hold on him, silently urging him closer.

And for a heartbeat, he almost lost himself in it. But something inside him pulled tight. He stilled.

Slowly, reluctantly, he lifted his head, the heat between them still crackling in the air. When she opened her eyes, she found him watching her—something unreadable in his expression.

Not distance. Not quite regret. But something that made her chest tighten all the same.

Throwing caution to the wind, she held onto his

massive shoulders, pulling him down so he could continue his trail of kisses as low as he would. Slowly, she felt his lips leave her body, the cold seeping in where the fire had been burning. Opening her eyes, she saw him staring at her, regret in his expression. *Regret? Oh, my God, he regrets this.*

Trying hard to still her rapid heartbeat, she loosened her hold on him, steeling herself for his dismissal.

"I've got to go," he said, knowing the Saints expected him, but wanting nothing more than to lay her down and continue to explore her mouth...and everything else about her.

"Of course," she replied, mistaking his need to leave. Masking her hurt, she chastised herself. *I'm such an idiot. He might accept who I am now, but I know what kind of relationship he has with other women and that's not for me.* The cool reality forced its way in, and she sucked in a shaky breath. "You're right. I'm sorry." She stepped back, brushing her hair away from her face with her hand. Sucking in her swollen lips, she could still feel them tingling from his assault.

Pulling her back into his arms, he pressed her face against his chest. Holding her body protectively again, he kissed the top of her head. Then, using two fingers under her chin, he lifted her face up to peer into her eyes. "I don't regret this. I hope you don't either."

Forcing a smile, she shook her head. "No regrets."

"I don't know when I'll be able to see you again. I have no idea what Jack is going to want me to do. Whether or not Erik has been returned and I'm off that case and assigned to another one, or still working the case to find him with the FBI."

Nodding, she was not sure if he was being truthful or

if his words were a not-so-clever attempt to imply he did not want to see her again. She assured him, "I know. It's okay, really it is. Tomorrow's a school day for me anyway."

As she closed the door behind him, throwing the deadbolt, she leaned her back against the wooden door and pressed her fingers to her lips. It had been a while since she had been kissed...and never by anyone as talented as Bart. Giving her head a little shake, she made her way over to the sofa, petting Smee as he jumped into her lap. Looking down at the sleek, orange cat, she said, "I guess that was a taste of what I'll never have, Smee." Leaning her head back, she wondered what it would be like to be kissed like that...by him...every day.

12

Bart drove the twenty minutes to Jack's place, his mind a whirl of contradictions. Two days ago, he wanted nothing more than to prove Faith false. Tonight, if he had not been pressed for time, he would have pursued her...for more than sex. Pulling through the security gate at the compound, he called upon his SEAL training to force his mind to clear.

Jogging up the front steps to the large log cabin, he could not help but compare the seasonal decorations to what Faith had in her tiny apartment. He lifted his hand to knock when the door opened. Bethany greeted him with a huge smile. "They're all downstairs," she informed him, offering him a welcoming hug.

Kissing the top of her head, he stalked down the hall to the hidden entrance to the compound's hub. Rounding the corner at the bottom of the stairs, he walked into the large conference room. A quick glance told him everyone was present. And their grim expressions told him Erik had not been returned.

He took a seat, nodding at their collective greetings and pulled out his tablet to check the latest information.

"The drop-off payment was completed exactly as ordered. The FBI is tracing the electronic transfer, but it appears an extensive security program was set up to immediately block tracing the money as it maneuvered quickly between accounts," Monty reported.

"As soon as it landed in one account, it moved to another?" Blaise asked, brushing cat fur off his pants.

Luke, tapping furiously on his keyboard, added, "Yeah. Shit, it's genius," he added.

Chad, sitting next to Blaise, glanced over at him. "Seriously? Have I ever seen you without fur?"

Blaise glared back. "Sue me. I'm a vet for Christ's sakes. I'd take my animals over most people any day, even if they do leave a little fur on me."

Marc interrupted, "There's no way we're dealing with a kidnapper who's just wanting money. This is about revenge. This is about wanting to force Krustas out of the picture."

Monty added, "We've dug into Vera Dukakas, long-time housekeeper for the Krustas family. So far, she's exactly what Ivan said. Her parents came over from Russia and worked for Ivan as a gardener and nanny. Vera has been with the family for almost thirty-five years. Nothing turns up on her emails, phones, accounts, or her comings and goings from the house. She recently had some money deposited into her bank account, but when the FBI questioned her, she said Anton had given her a bonus." Before the others could ask, he added, "Anton confirmed, saying it was a bonus for her dedication and a tax break for him."

"Hmph," Blaise groused. "Probably an illegal tax break."

"What about Roger Montague?" Chad asked.

Monty replied, "He's a lawyer in Charlestown and has a firm in Richmond as well. He's divorced, good credentials, no unusual blips on his records either. On the board of numerous community service organizations and has escorted Constance Krustas several times. There's been no rumors of a relationship, other than what she presented." Monty stopped and grinned at this point. "Now, I did a little more digging and found he had lost heavily in the stock market drop last year and is just now starting to make a come back."

The group mulled over the information on the two persons involved the night of the kidnapping.

"Bart, you've been with Ivan's three largest competitors...and the most ruthless ones. We've all read your reports, but what are your insights?" Jack asked.

Bart slowly rubbed a hand over his face, a gesture that bespoke of his fatigue and frustration. "I don't like making assumptions, but Escobar's operation just doesn't seem like it has the money or, quite frankly, the brains to run this."

Chad looked up from his notes. "What about the MS13 he's trying to get in bed with?"

"It's not their MO. None of this is their MO. I got the feeling Escobar is more reactionary, although, I confess he's doing a lot of planning in moving his gang up in the organization."

"What about the Maldonis?"

Bart leaned back in his seat, answering, "It fits their MO, but old Luciano is a family man at heart." He saw the questioning expressions from around the table and explained, "Yeah, I know he's a ruthless bastard with his organization but, honest to God, I don't see him ordering a child to be kidnapped." He looked thoughtful for a second and then added, "But I'd like to have his youngest son checked out."

Luke nodded and immediately added him to their list.

"What makes you say that?" Chad inquired, curious about the inner workings of a crime family.

"He seemed evasive, disinterested...even when his father was speaking. It was actually Faith who mentioned that for a patriarchal family, for the youngest son to act aloof in the presence of his father was unusual."

Jack nodded. "Good info. What about the Volkovs?" Jack asked.

"They'd be the most obvious ones. Ruthless. Vicious. Jesus, he's a cold motherfucker."

Cam studied his best friend and prodded, "But..."

Bart shook his head in derision. "It's almost too obvious. Like someone wanted the finger to be pointed right at him."

"Sooo," Marc began. "What did the psychic have to say about all of this? Who does she see as the guilty party?"

"She's not a psychic," Bart growled, his eyes snapping in anger.

Marc threw up his hands in defense. "Hey bro, we all know that."

"No, what I mean is that she never claimed to be psychic," Bart added, running his hand through his already tousled hair, closing his eyes for a moment gathering his thoughts. Realizing the room was silent, he opened his eyes and saw everyone looking at him.

Heaving a deep sigh, he knew an explanation was necessary. "I...I misjudged her."

"Seriously?" Jude asked, incredulously. "Don't tell me

she snowed you?" Thoughts of helping Bart last summer against the con-artist ran through his mind.

"No, no, it's not like that," Bart answered, uncharacteristically floundering for the right explanation. He scanned the men sitting at the table, seeing expressions ranging from confusion, surprise, uncertainty, to knowing smiles coming from Cam and Jack. *How the hell do I explain what I don't even understand?*

Leaning forward, he placed his forearms on the table and said, "Faith Romani never claimed to be a medium, psychic, or any kind of seer. The fact is she is trained in both psychology and art—two things that she really loves. I watched her closely and she's very in tune with people. She got into their feelings while I was looking for facts. She's a gifted police artist and, as she explained to me, she doesn't just draw what they say, but listens to the victim or witness carefully, gets an image in her head from what they tell her and then draws that, so far, she's been successful at it. She doesn't sell herself out and she's definitely not a scammer."

"Why did Ivan want her on the case?" Marc prodded.

"Besides working with victims, she also...gets images in her head. Damn, this sounds psycho, I know, but it has to do with the women in her family having a gift of...of..."

"Of sight?" Cam asked.

Bart jerked his eyes around to his friend, seeing confirmation not condemnation in his eyes.

Cam continued, "My folks believe strongly in things that are out of our ability to see or feel or touch. I was brought up to believe there are things that cannot be explained by logic or facts. It's part of my heritage. Maybe Faith has this ability."

Jack sat back, rubbing his thick beard thoughtfully.

"Bart, it sounds like you had a chance to get to know her. How does this sight work and was she able to use it in this case?"

Sighing, he replied, "Honestly? I was a prick to her for the first thirty-six hours we were together. And not much better after that. I didn't trust her. Didn't want her on the case. And generally made her life difficult." He snorted, "But damn if she didn't stick right there doing her job. We finally talked on the way home when I finally realized she wasn't trying to scam anyone. Unfortunately, we ran out of time, and I had to leave her to get here. She had a chance to explain her methods in police artistry, but as to her... um...other abilities...I don't know how they work. Well, other than that she has no control. She can't just summon up the ability to find someone or any shit like that."

"I still don't make the connection to Ivan," Marc continued.

"It seems Ivan knew her grandmother from when they were much younger. Her grandmother ha this gift and Ivan wanted Faith to try to see if there was anything she could do."

"But since she wasn't able to gain any insight into Erik's disappearance, it was all a waste, wasn't it?" Blaise pointed out.

"No," Bart replied, realizing his voice betrayed his emotions. Trying to play it off with a shrug, he said, "I mean, she had some good observations from our interviews."

Looking around, this time, he saw a few of his friends trying to hide smiles and a couple of them outright grinning. "Damn, guys. It's not like I'm involved with her or anything. I probably won't even see her again." *That's a lie.* Shrugging, he continued, "I'm just admitting that I had preconceived prejudices and now I know she's not like that."

"Well, she's an awfully pretty police artist," Monty noted, his wry grin crossing his face.

Several chuckles broke out, and Bart was unable to hide his grin as well until Monty added, "I'll let my friend, Mitch, know she's available."

Bart growled, opening the door for the laughs to come his way.

Jack allowed the joking to continue for a moment, knowing they all needed an escape when doing the intense work they did, before pulling them back to the task at hand.

"At this point, we've fulfilled Ivan's contractual request. The FBI is in charge of this investigation, but I appreciate you all are invested as well. Luke will still be working on the money tracking angle. Bart, you, and Monty will stay in contact with the FBI through Mitch to see if there is anything we can do to assist. Check your tablets and you'll find other assignments for the rest of you."

"Jack, this doesn't feel right," Bart complained. "Erik's not back yet and—"

Throwing up his hand to halt Bart's tirade, Jack said, "Not every mission is successful. Doesn't feel good, but it's a fact. Ivan wanted his interests protected, afraid the FBI would spend more time snooping around than investigating. We've done our job. The intel you provided to the FBI with your interview is giving them more to work with. But, you're not off this. You and Monty, along with Luke, want to keep digging? Go for it."

"And if you and the pretty artist need to work together some more, then..." Cam added, a smirk on his face as the others chuckled again.

Jesus, Bart thought. *I'm so fucked.*

Faith walked around the classroom, looking at the children as they worked with pastels. Their giggles kept her smiling as she bent over to observe their work. She glanced up when the classroom teacher stood from her desk and pointed to the door. Faith nodded, knowing the teacher was leaving for a break. She preferred it when she had an actual art classroom, and the children would come to her. The room was filled with the supplies needed for whatever creation or plan she had for the day. Now, with budget cuts, that room was turned into a fifth-grade classroom, and she was relegated to hauling her supplies with her on a large rolling cart to each room on her schedule. Today, the fourth-grade class was exuberantly working on their drawings using their individual art pads and pastels.

She had been on her feet for most of the day and decided to sit on the stool near the front of the room, still eyeing the children, but giving her tired feet a rest. One of the boys sat near the window, his head bent over as he diligently worked. The sunlight coming in cast a glow and a shadow on him creating an ethereal look as she watched the play of light. He looked up as he finished his drawing, catching her eye, and smiled. A wide smile, filled with the oversized teeth that ten-year-olds seem to have before their bodies catch up to their faces.

She gasped as a vision filled her mind. Closing her eyes, she saw another dark-haired boy, the one she had seen in her other visions, sitting on a bed again but, this time, there was a light coming from a lamp illuminating him as his head was bent over reading a book.

"Miss Romani?" a voice broke through, snapping her back to reality as her eyes blinked open.

Looking around, she saw the children staring at her. "Are you all right?" one girl asked. "You look like my sister right before she's gonna puke."

The giggles from the students forced her to smile as she smoothed her hair from her face. "Yes, yes, I'm fine," she assured, glancing at the classroom clock, grateful it was time for the art class to end. Hustling them through the cleanup process, she smiled as the classroom teacher came back in and then Faith rolled her cart down the hall. She and the music teacher had a large closet as their office. The space barely held their carts full of art and music supplies and had room for a small desk and chair.

Sitting down gratefully, she pulled her pad from her large bag, opening it immediately and grabbing a charcoal pencil. Closing her eyes, she pulled the image of the boy back to the forefront of her mind, and upon opening them again, began to draw.

When she finished, she stared at the picture for a long time. The dark-haired boy was sitting cross-legged on a bed, covered with a dark bedspread. A book was open on his lap and one hand was resting on the page. There was no window on the wall behind him, but a light shone down from somewhere off the page, illuminating the book on the bed as well as the side of his face. His focus was on what he was reading, and a slight curve of his lip could be seen.

She lay the pad down on the desk, leaning her head on her hands. *What does this mean? Is this real or a figment of my tired, overactive imagination?* When Ivan first called her, he begged her to come and see if she could get any images of where Erik was. She wanted to say no, but he sounded so heartbroken and afraid. She agreed to go, but only to see if there was anything to be gained from being around others who might know something.

I was unprepared. Too much violence clogging every thought. She had hoped that she would use her gift by being suddenly overwhelmed with an image of someone taking Erik but had been unprepared for the emotions that flooded her when in the presence of those they talked to.

Self-doubt filled her being as she stared at the drawing. *It could be any child. It could be the boy from the class. Maybe I'm drawing what I think might be happening but isn't really happening. Aughh!* She slapped her hand down on the art pad, her fingers poised to scrunch the paper into a wad. Her breath came in short spurts and once more she felt the loss of her grandmother acutely.

Babushka. I don't know what I'm doing. I can't possibly pin Ivan's hopes that Erik is still alive by these drawings. That would be too cruel.

Her heartbeat slowed down as she allowed the calm of memories of her grandmother to wash over her. She could hear her say, *"Accept the gift and believe in yourself."* Warmth washed over her as she opened her eyes and peered down at the image.

She wondered if she should give them to Bart. *Would he want them or believe them?* They had made such progress in burying his misconceptions...*if he saw these drawings, would it send him right back to ranting about her pretending to be a psychic?*

Sitting in the tiny room, she realized she was too much of a coward. The memory of the kiss they shared filled her mind, pushing aside all possibilities of ruining it.

Standing, she shoved the art pad into her large bag

and, tossing it over her shoulder, headed down the hall to the teacher's lounge. No longer willing to give up her originals, she made copies before driving home.

I'll give the drawings to Mitch. He can do with them whatever he wants. For a moment, she felt guilty that she was not going to give them to Bart, but they parted on such a peaceful note, she hated the idea of tearing down what they had built.

———

Faith sat across from Mitch in the coffee shop, watching his face as he scanned the copies of the drawings. She already explained where they came from and her reticence to share them with Ivan.

"Have you shown these to anyone else?" he asked, flipping through the pages.

"No, no one."

He looked up at her, flashing a smile, "Not even Bart?"

"No." She saw the doubt in his face, and she felt the need to explain, although, she did not want to. It felt too personal. Too raw. Sucking in a deep breath, she said, "At first, Bart didn't seem to want my assistance and, to be truthful, since I'm no longer working with him, it made more sense to call you."

Nodding, he said, "These are really interesting, Faith. Like you, I've got no idea if what you see in your mind has anything to do with Erik, but I'll share these with Krustas. Who knows? He may recognize something."

Releasing a breath, she had not realized she was holding, she nodded, "Good. Good. That'll be the right thing to do, I'm sure." Pausing for a moment, she then asked, "Mitch? What do you think? About Erik? I can't help but think of that poor child, away from his home and frightened."

"I honestly don't know," he answered. "It would be pure speculation to hazard a guess as to whether or not he's still alive." Seeing her wince, he added, "But the FBI is doing everything we can to find him, regardless of what Krustas thinks. Sure, we'd love to take down all the organized crime, but finding Erik is our priority."

She nodded slowly, allowing the idea that her drawings were proof he was still alive to chase away her doubts. Checking her watch, she stood, saying "I've got to get home. My cat will be ready to gnaw my ankles if I don't."

Mitch stood with her, placing his hand on her arm. "Are you sure you wouldn't like to grab dinner somewhere?"

Gazing up at the handsome agent, she shook her head. "Thanks, Mitch, but I'm..." her voice trailed off as she realized she had no idea how to answer him.

"You're taken?" he asked, his smile still in place. "Bart?"

"No, no, I'm not taken," she answered truthfully. But smiling as she walked out of the cafe, she admitted to herself, *But I'm hopeful.*

13

Bart lay awake, unable to sleep, thoughts of the unsolved mission and the beautiful Faith heavy on his mind. *Why did I imply to the guys I wouldn't be seeing her again when the only thing I want to do is call her?*

His phone vibrated on the nightstand next to his bed and, instantly alert, he grabbed it, seeing Jack's name identified. "Boss?"

"Looks like you and Ms. Romani will be working together once more. Mitch called and said the FBI would like you two to interview Sergio Krustas. They are digging into him, and he is rising to the top of their list. It seems as though he has a long reach outside of prison."

Instantly the idea of Faith being not only in a prison, but in the presence of more filth, made him grimace. "I can't go alone?"

"You got a problem with working with her?"

"No, it's just...I hate seeing her inside a prison and talking to one more crime lord asshole," he responded.

"If it were up to me, I'd say she doesn't need to be

involved at all, but this is actually coming from Ivan himself."

"I know he's desperate, but he's seriously grasping at straws with her." Sighing, he said, "Is the meeting set up for tomorrow?"

"Yeah. Krustas has already called her. You can pick her up about nine a.m. and you're to be at the prison at eleven."

Disconnecting, he lay back on the bed, throwing his arm over his head, sighing deeply. *I get this assignment over with, I'm asking her out on a proper date!*

Pulling up to Faith's apartment building several hours later, he saw her coming out of the door before he had a chance to jump out of his truck. He hurried around to open the door for her.

She smiled shyly at him, uncertainty filling her expression. "Hi," she said, offering him a travel mug of coffee.

"You're a lifesaver," he effused, taking a sip of the hot drink as he climbed into the driver's seat.

"How long will it take us to get to the prison?"

"About an hour and a half," he responded. Glancing to the side, he took her in. Her long hair was sleek and shiny, pulled back into a low ponytail. Her cheeks were rosy with the cool morning air. A navy coat cinched at the waist covered her clothes, but the grey pants with the heeled boots underneath caught his attention.

"I know you don't dress provocatively, but I gotta ask because of the prison visitation rules. Your blouse, under that," he nodded to her coat, "is it...um...does it cover everything?"

She saw the way he attempted to avert his eyes from her chest, and she could not hold back the grin. "I went on the internet and checked out the visitation procedures. I'm wearing a very boring blouse, I assure you."

The thought of any blouse on her was provocative to him and there was no way it was boring even covering the assets that he now could not keep his mind off of. "Good," he groused, adjusting himself in the driver's seat.

Several miles passed in silence. He hoped, after the kiss, they would fall into an easy camaraderie, but she appeared tongue-tied this morning. *I didn't contact her yesterday, and she probably thought I was never going to call.* The realization that this was his modus operandi hit him. He never called a woman back. Stealing another glance at her holding her coffee with both hands as she gazed out of the window, he knew she was different from other women. He had not only lied to his friends...he had lied to himself.

Faith sipped her drink nervously, not knowing what to say. She tried not to focus on the fact that he towered over her when he opened the door for her. Or that her hand still tingled from his touch when he assisted her up into the truck. For now, his hair was not sticking up, but she smiled knowing that after a few frustrated runnings of his hand through the thickness, his hair would be in all directions. *Did he want to see me again or was he forced into this trip?* Before she could ponder this anymore, he cleared his throat, drawing her attention over to him.

"You look very nice today—"

"Thank you," she replied a little too quickly, a nervous smile on her face.

"Um, I wasn't finished," he added.

"Oh," she mumbled.

"I was going to say you are beautiful, but you've got to remember where we'll be today. If you thought it was bad interviewing Miguel, Gavrill, or Luciano, they were nothing compared to what you'll face today."

"Oh," she replied again. This time, nervousness and a bit of disappointment that his compliment was more of a warning about the day's activities, had her clutching her coffee mug even tighter.

"I just want you to be confident I'll be right by your side the whole time. I promise."

A slow smile curved the edges of her lips at the thought. "I admit I've never been in a prison before...but I've seen lots on TV."

He chuckled, the tension broken, and spent a few minutes telling her about the check-in procedures. As he talked, he noticed her nibbling on her thumbnail again. "Still nervous?"

Her gaze jumped over in surprise. "Does it show? I'm trying hard to be cool."

He nodded toward her hand. "You bite your fingernail when you're nervous. Or deep in thought. Or irritated with me."

This time, it was her turn to chuckle as she moved her hand down to her lap.

"It's okay," he rushed to assure, not wanting her to be self-conscious. "Well, as long as you're not irritated with me."

"I'm not." Twisting her body to face him, she suddenly said, "Tell me something about yourself."

"Huh?"

"We've been in each other's constant company for two days now and there's a lot I gathered about you from observation. But...well, I'd like to know something about you that I haven't learned yet."

He looked askance at her, saying, "Now, I'm wondering what you think about me. That kind of makes me nervous."

Grinning as though she had a secret, she said, "Just things that I've picked up. It's easy if you really listen to people and watch them when they speak."

"Okay, I'm game, but first—you have to tell me what you've figured out."

"That's not how this game works," she laughed.

"My truck, my rules," Bart ordered easily.

"Humph," she groused. Licking her lips, she agreed. "Well, I know you're a very confident person by the way you speak and even the way you hold yourself. That can come from being a SEAL, but I think it's also just you. You have a great body, but I know you work at it by staying in shape."

He could not help but preen at that comment, knowing she had noticed his body. "Okay, keep going," he encouraged.

"I know you're loyal, not only to your family but to your friends. Um...let's see. I know you run your fingers through your hair when frustrated which, by the way, I've seen a lot since being on this case with you."

She discovered the corners of his eyes crinkled as he laughed just now, too.

"My mom used to bug me to cut my hair because it made her crazy when my hair was long and sticking out everywhere. She loved it when I was in the Navy." He looked over at her smile and wanted the expression to stay...and to be the one to keep it there. "Okay, what else?"

"Hmmm, well, I know you love country music, especially if it's a man singing and not a woman. We haven't talked about movies—and before you ask, no, I can't just tell what you like!"

"You really aren't psychic!" he exclaimed with false surprise, throwing his hand over his heart.

"Jerk," she laughed. "Okay, let's see what else do I know? Oh, yeah, you're an outrageous flirt—"

"Hey, no hitting below the belt," he complained.

"I didn't say you were an awful flirt or an insincere flirt!"

He stayed silent at that comment with the uncomfortable feeling that if she knew how much of an insincere flirt he really was, she probably would not be enjoying his company. He thought back to the times his buddies had commented on how he always leaves with the best-looking girl in a bar and he simply took that as some kind of right. Or how he would wink to grab a waitress' attention and then not look at her again when they brought his food or drink. Then his mind slid to the countless women whose bed he would leave with a wink and an insincere comment about how great it had been.

Suddenly, the air in the truck cab seemed thick and breathing was painful. He looked over at her concerned face, sure that she could see inside of him, knowing all his unflattering qualities. And, for the first time, he felt like he knew them, too. He was about to tell her he did not want to play her game anymore when she spoke softly.

"I know you love your big family. Your siblings, your cousins. I know your grandfather taught you about life and being a man. And your grandparents and parents have the kind of love most of us could only dream about."

Those words took his breath away. She was not psychic, but with just the simple, and yet complex, ability to really listen and observe people, she had garnered all this information.

The moment lay heavy between them, but the silence was not forced. Simply reflective. Warm. Even welcoming.

To lighten the mood, he joked, "You want to hear about my movie favorites, huh?"

Laughing, she leaned her head sideways on the headrest and said, "You can tell me anything you'd like."

He thought for a moment, realizing how hard it was to come up with something to say about himself when she had already peered into his soul.

"Tell me about how you got into investigations," she prompted.

That seems safe enough. "I loved being a SEAL. The missions, the camaraderie, hell, even the training. I hoped the Border Patrol would satisfy me, but the job didn't. I had a friend who was with them and thought it sounded interesting. I should have spent more time investigating them. Don't get me wrong, what they do is good and necessary."

"So...?"

He heaved a sigh, pondering the prompt. "It's weird, now that I think about it. In the SEALs, I had to follow orders exactly, but with Border Patrol, our hands were tied by regulations that made no sense. We would see what needed to be done but couldn't do it."

"You changed careers?"

"Yeah. I knew some guys that ran security companies

after getting out of the SEALs, but I was looking for something a little more..."

"Rule-breaking?" she grinned.

"Exactly!" he laughed. "I put out some feelers and found out about Jack Bryant's Saints."

"Why does he call his company the Saints?"

"That's a personal reason to Jack." Bart quietly reflected for a moment, and then added, "But the name means something to all of us as well."

Faith knew whatever it was he would share only when ready, so she turned the conversation to something more lighthearted. "What movies do you like?"

Laughing, he replied, "Probably nothing that you'd find interesting."

"Action flicks with lots of car chases and bombs going off?"

"Nope," he pronounced, then a faint blush appeared. "I like British comedies and mysteries."

She had already twisted in her seat to face him, but that had her looking up in amazement. "You're right. I wouldn't have guessed that." Smiling, she liked how he could surprise her. Make her laugh. Make her feel...less lonely. *Is that what I'm doing? Trying to force a friendship?* Her thumbnail managed to make its way back to her mouth, where her teeth began to nibble.

He glanced her way. *Is she nervous? Irritated?* Neither of those seemed right. Wanting to take the pensive look off her face, he said, "Well, I do like country music. I like the stories it tells. I don't mind female singers...I guess I just understand the male singer's perspectives more. Maybe the good-ole-boy feeling that comes with some songs...but mostly, I like the way they can tell a story about—" he halted suddenly, embarrassed.

"About love," she finished for him, smiling. "There is a romantic in there somewhere," she said, swirling her finger in his direction.

Looking over, he saw the light in her eyes as her smile lit up her face. Her dark eyes, shining, gazed into his. "Yeah, I guess there is."

They drove for several more miles, the comfortable silence blanketing them peacefully. Before they knew it, they turned off the main highway toward the prison. The air in the truck cab moved rapidly from content to anxious.

"What should I expect?" she asked.

Bart ran through the procedures with her, then said, "Take my lead with everything, Faith. If I decide we need to cut it short and get out of there, you go along with me. If I'm pushing, then you gather all the information you can as quickly as you can."

She watched as his hand passed over his head several times and realized her nervousness was in direct response to his. *He's worried about this one.* "Bart?"

"Yeah?"

"What makes this one different?"

He sucked in a deep breath before letting it out slowly, a slight hiss sounding as the air passed through his gritted teeth.

"The other guys, they were on the outside. They wanted to keep the Feds out of their business as much as possible, and they were willing to talk to us. They weren't happy about it, but they had a lot to lose if we got suspicious. But Sergio? He's got nothing to lose. He's already in prison and has publicly threatened his uncle. A man who's got nothing to lose can be unpredictable." Running his hand through his hair that was now standing on end, he added, "A prison's no place for a woman like you to be and Sergio is sure as hell not a man you should ever have to be around. I hate he'll even lay eyes on you."

"I'll be okay," she said softly, drawing his gaze back to hers. "I'll be with you."

Reaching across the console, he took her hand in his, giving it a reassuring squeeze. *Yes, you will, baby. Yes, you will.*

14

Faith could not explain her nervousness, considering she had recently been in the presence of three crime lords with no security around. She was fearful then, but somehow the looming structure of the prison set the sick feeling of nerves fluttering around her stomach.

She followed Bart's lead as they entered through the main doorway and showed identification. She removed her coat, handing it to the guard before moving through the metal detectors.

Bart glanced behind him to check on her. His eyes dropped to her outfit, and he noted she had indeed dressed with care. Her long-sleeved, dark blue blouse was buttoned to the top, showing virtually no skin. He realized a week ago, this woman would not have appeared on his radar at all as someone to be interested in. And now? He had to tear his eyes away as he wondered what delights lay underneath all those clothes. Giving himself a mental shake, he offered her a small smile of encouragement.

So far, the procedures reminded her of passing through security at an airport. *In fact, the guards appear friendlier than the airport security!* She expected everything to be grey in color but found flashes of light blue on the doorframes and chairs in the rooms.

Bart had explained that because they were there at not only Krustas' insistence, but the visit was sanctioned by the FBI, they would not be using the main family visitation room. "They'll place us in a smaller conference room, but don't worry—a guard will be there the whole time."

She nodded. They passed through another security checkpoint and this time, she noticed dark green covered the doorframes. *The different areas are color-coded.* She looked around at everything, nervous and yet fascinated at the same time. The sound of her boots tapping on the tile floors echoed as they continued down the long hall. Peering to the side, she slammed into Bart's back as he came to a stop.

Blushing a deep red, she looked up, mouthing *Sorry*, as he grinned down at her. Finally, they were shown into an interview room; this time, the grey table and chairs were what she expected. The windowless room had another door at the opposite end. Bart moved to a chair and pulled it out for her. Smiling her thanks, she settled in the seat, placing her shaking hands in her lap.

After about ten minutes, the door opened and a guard walked in, followed by Sergio, and another guard. They made sure Sergio was seated before one guard stood by the door and the other one moved back through.

Bart eyed him dispassionately. He had never met Sergio but had followed the investigation and trial since it occurred in his hometown, Virginia Beach. He wanted to glance to the side to see how Faith was doing but would not give Sergio the opportunity to think he was concerned about her...or to insinuate she needed protection.

Faith worked to keep her expression passive but felt her heart tap dancing in her chest and hoped no one else could hear it. Looking at Sergio, she recognized the familial relationship to Ivan. Bulky body frame, barrel chested, with dark hair neatly trimmed. His head was squarer than Ivan's, but his deep-set eyes—definitely Krustas eyes. And right now, they were staring straight at her.

Suddenly, his eyes jerked to Bart, and he sneered, "I figure my *dear* uncle sent you, but your time is limited so fire away. It's your nickel."

Bart held his eyes, never wavering, as he let another moment pass in silence before asking, "You hear about Erik's kidnapping?"

"Fuck, yeah. Even in here, I'm told the news."

Faith suddenly leaned forward in her seat and asked, "Tell me about Ivan?"

Sergio's gaze met hers and the silence was thick in the room. Bart watched him closely, allowing Faith to ask the questions.

Sergio snorted contemptuously before speaking. "My uncle? You want to know about him? Read the newspaper."

No one said anything, allowing the silence to begin sliding into all the empty crevices of the room. Finally, when it appeared that he was going to win the mute show-down, he shifted in his seat and said, "I loved him. Like a father. But he threw me over. And for what? He could become legitimate? That's like looking at a lion who's just eaten a kill and patting its head, saying 'nice kitty'."

Bart noticed Faith smiled slightly at Sergio's analogy, but it seemed to encourage him to keep talking. He realized how much more the men would talk with Faith around. *Is it because she's a woman...or non-threatening? Who knows, but it's working!*

Sergio's eyes moved away for a moment before he continued. "My father was not the oldest Krustas, but he was the mightiest. Fuckin' fearless." Sighing heavily, he said, "He got killed and Uncle Ivan could have ruled everything. With his, and then my dad's, share of things, there's nothing he couldn't have accomplished. Not even when Erik was born. Then, when his son, and then Anton's dad, both had heart attacks, Ivan changed. No longer wanted to expand. No longer wanted to take risks."

"What did you want him to do?" Faith prodded.

"He could have stepped down," Sergio bit out. "Me and Anton could've run things. Dmitry could have joined us when he got out of school. Or we could've split things up. But Ivan wouldn't hear of it. Decided that he wanted to clean things up so, one day, he could hand the reigns down to Erik."

Hurt, Faith realized. *Underneath all the bravado, piss, and fire, and anger, was a man who actually experienced hurt.*

Sergio's gaze lifted and slammed back into hers as though he could hear her thoughts and his sneer returned as he leaned forward, his forearms on the table. "I could have ruled. I could have taken the family business where my father would have taken it."

"And Erik?" Bart asked.

Sergio leaned back heavily in his chair. "Never had anything against the kid. But he was still a kid. Why would the family alter everything we'd ever done for a kid who wouldn't be old enough to take the reins for years? No fuckin' way."

"How do you feel about Ivan now?" Faith asked softly.

"Family should be everything. Every. Thing," he

growled. "But Ivan threw that away when he tossed me to the wolves. I don't care if he's outta his mind with worry."

Once more, silence fell over the people in the room, Faith fighting the desire to ask more questions while at the same time wanting to follow Bart's lead. Sparing a quick glance sideways, she noticed Bart's seemingly at ease posture. She adopted the same posture, her mind racing with images of a young man's anger. *That's what's different than the others. He has violence and anger just like them...but his is personal.*

After a moment, Sergio began speaking again. "I haven't got anything against Erik...he's just a kid. If you're looking for who took him, I can't do anything in here."

"You have associates. You have followers. You still wield power out there," Bart replied.

This time, Sergio's sneer was replaced with a smirk, as he said, "Yeah, man. I still got power."

"Is that what this is about? You using power to get back at Ivan? Strike him in the one place where you knew it would hurt the most?"

Sergio's face grew hard as he spat out, "You think I would mess with a kid to make a point? Then you don't know fuck about me! Yeah, I heard about Erik. And it made me sick." He shoved his metal chair back, the screeching as the legs scraped against the tile floor resounded in the small room. Twisting his body around to look at the guard, he snarled, "This shit's over."

One step away from the door he stopped and turned around, pinning Faith with a glare. "I know who you are, seer. I know what you're doing." Pointing to his head, he said, "You hope to see in here," then he lowered his hand to his chest, over his heart, and continued, "but you can't see in here." With that, he disappeared through the open door.

———————

The ride home began silently as both Bart and Faith were lost in their thoughts. Finally, he looked over, seeing her still expression staring out of the windshield.

"Whatcha thinking, Faith?"

Shaking her head slowly, she said, "Fear, anger, and mostly hurt is what poured from him. But if you're asking if I felt anything more, I didn't. Ivan wants me to be with someone and suddenly feel they are the one who took Erik, but it doesn't work that way. I'm afraid I'm very much a failure to him."

They were quiet for a few more miles before he spoke again. "How did he know you were a...?"

"Seer?" she provided.

"Yeah," he acknowledged, but then hastened to say, "I know you're not and never claimed to be, but still...why did he say that?"

"When I was a child, I was terrified someone would think I was a freak when I would have a dream about something or draw something that was going to happen. I cried my fears out to Babushka, but she would always hold me and tell me it would be a secret. She used to say that all people who believe in the old ways would know, but others wouldn't."

Shrugging, she continued, "I don't have any idea how he knew what I was doing. Maybe because I'm a psychologist he just called me a seer. Maybe he remembered my grandmother." Sighing heavily, she confessed, "I have no idea."

Bart, his heart pounding, realized he had done exactly what others had done to her as a child. Reaching out, he took her hand, wanting to erase his cruel words when he first met her. "I'm sorry for how I hurt you when we first met."

Squeezing his fingers, she said, "You've already apologized...and I've already forgiven you."

Continuing, he added, "But you've put yourself out there for possible ridicule in the hopes of helping others, including Erik. I...I'm not usually this judgmental."

She smiled as he linked his fingers with hers. "You can stop beating yourself up, Bart. It's okay, it really is." Seeing him about to protest, she continued, "After what happened to your grandmother last summer...I get it." Rubbing his hand, she added, "And if we're going to move forward, then you need to accept that I've forgiven you."

Lifting her hand up to his mouth, he held his lips for a moment against her soft skin, her words soothing. Pulling back, he nodded at her smile. "Okay, from now on...we move forward. And to start with, I've got to call Jack."

Placing the call, he was told Luke and Monty were already working on the video feed that was sent back to them from the interview.

"Grab some lunch on your way back," Jack ordered. "We've got this end covered."

Disconnecting, Bart turned to her and said, "Let's grab some lunch—boss' orders!"

A few miles down the road, he turned into the parking lot of a mom & pop diner. Looking over, he asked, "Is this okay?"

"Perfect," she replied, a huge grin on her face. "I was nervous this morning I couldn't eat breakfast."

Walking in, they found the lunch crowd almost over

and were easily seated in the back where they could relax. After ordering his usual huge lunch, Bart was surprised to see Faith order a diner-special burger, fries, and a milk-shake. Lifting his eyebrow at her, he smiled as she giggled.

"I'm hungry. What can I say?" she laughed, blushing.

"Hey, no worries on my part. I love that you're not afraid to eat in front of me."

"What? Most of your dates don't eat much?" she teased.

Bart looked down at his hands resting on the table between them, and answered, "I don't date very much."

This time, it was her turn to look amazed, but he continued before she had a chance to question. "I don't really have time to date. And never met anyone who seemed worth the bother." Running his hand through his hair, he said, "God, that makes me sound like a prick, even to myself. What I mean is, it takes time to get to know someone really well and that's if you find someone that you want to know. Until that time, I just usually go for hookups that are simple."

"Bart, what's so simple about no strings sex?" Seeing his expression, she held up her hand. "No, hear me out. Many people, not just men, say sex without any attach-ment is simple. Meet, share a drink and maybe a laugh, get naked and...um...well, you know."

Right now, listening to her unable to say the word *fuck,* she had never appeared more adorable to him.

"Bart, you can't tell me that you've never had a woman hope for more. It doesn't matter if they agreed to just have sex. Some walk away hurt...or hurt when you walk out the door. I mean, on one hand, you both get off and walk away sexually satisfied, I guess. But what about emotions?

Caring for someone? Talking to someone? Actually, being interested in someone?"

"I've just never found that," he said softly. *Until now,* he wanted to add.

"Then you've deprived yourself of a chance to find what your grandparents and parents have," she accused. "I agree sex doesn't have to equate to love, but to just have sex without the possibility of caring for that person seems...sad."

Saved from having to question more of his past, their food came, and they both dug in heartedly. He listened as she made little moans while eating and tried to keep his libido under control with every bite she took.

They ate in comfortable silence, the seriousness of the earlier conversation no longer between them. He ran her words through his mind. *I've always sought out the bar bimbos. They were easy. Little conversation. No expectations. Just sex and that was it.* Then his mind rolled back to the ones that were upset when he left their beds. Expressions of anger, frustration, or even hurt on their faces. *But there was not one that he had any desire to spend any time with.* Staring at the unassuming beauty in front of him, laying waste to her hamburger and fries, he realized he knew more about her than any other woman he had ever met. And then the reality hit him—*I like her more than any other woman I have ever met!*

"Hey, you know that game we were playing in the truck earlier?" he asked. "Where you told me what you knew about me and then asked me more questions about myself?"

She nodded, her mouth too full to answer.

"Well, we need to continue to play it on the way home."

Swallowing with difficulty, he handed her his soda, so she was able to speak again. "You want to tell me more about yourself?" she teased.

"No, no. Now it's your turn. I get to find out more about you."

Rolling her eyes, she finished her lunch and excused herself to the ladies' room. Paying the bill at the register, he grabbed a bag of Skittles. As he escorted her to the truck and assisted her into her seat, he tossed the bag into her lap. "Thought you'd like these."

Grinning, she ripped open the bag, thrilled he remembered. Popping a handful into her mouth, she rolled her eyes as she chewed the sugary goodness. He pulled back out onto the street, trying to ignore the sounds coming from her once more.

"So, more about you," he prompted.

"Hey, you have to play the game just like I did earlier —that means you have to say what you already know about me," she added nervously, wondering if she was opening herself up to painful criticism.

He caught her fear and inwardly winced, knowing he had brought that to her. Determined to make up for his previous behavior, he began. "Okay, I know you're smart— a double major and a master's degree. That's impressive." He saw her smile and desired to keep that look on her face.

"I know you care about people and were very close to your...um...Babushka?"

"Yes, my grandmother," she laughed.

"I know you're a hard worker and love what you do. I know you're selfless." He paused for a moment and continued, "And you like to eat, although where it goes, I have no idea," glancing at her perfect curves.

Loving the blush creeping from her neck upward, he continued, sure in his ability to keep her blushing. "Okay, I know you're beautiful, but you don't know it." Seeing her questioning expression, he continued, "You walk through a room and have no idea that most men are staring and many women glare."

"Glare? Why would a woman glare at me?" She shook her head, not understanding what he was implying.

"That's just exactly what I mean. You have no clue because another thing I know about you is you don't play games."

She leaned back in her seat, mind swirling in confusion. "I don't know what games you're talking about," she replied, a slight pout on her face, wondering if he was making fun of her.

Jesus, I'm messing this up because she's clueless, he realized despondently. "Okay, babe, here it is. Most women I meet are very aware of their looks. They add a bunch of shit to their faces and dress in ways that play up whatever assets they've got...legs, ass, boobs. They walk a certain way, talk a certain way, and act a certain way. And that's to grab the attention of every man they can. You don't do that, and it's...well, it's refreshing. I like it."

She grinned slowly as she realized he liked something about her, but then looked over sharply as the inference swept over her. "And just where have you gained your vast experience in how women walk, talk, and dress? 'Cause I'm here to tell you there are tons of women out there who don't give a hoot about trying to attract a man every time they go out!"

"Um...well, in college. And when I go out with my friends."

"To...?"

"Bars," he admitted.

"Right! Your knowledge of women is limited to those women who are looking for a hookup. Gotta tell you, Bart, not every woman you meet is trying to get you in bed!"

He rubbed his hand through his hair in frustration. *What the hell just happened? This game was supposed to let her know how much I've noticed her, and somehow, I've insulted all womanhood.*

Several miles of silence filled the truck. He spared a glance her way but, instead of appearing angry, her expression was pensive.

"Bart, I'm sor—"

"I didn't mean to—"

They both spoke at the same time, then halted, looking at each other and grinning. "You first," he said.

"You were giving me a compliment and I turned it around to something unpleasant, just because of my own insecurities," she replied.

"I didn't mean to insult women," he said honestly. "And you're right. In college, as a football player, I didn't have to look for women at all…they pretty much lined up outside the locker rooms and dorms to want to hang out with us. Then when I was a SEAL, there were bars outside the base where women would flock. They were either husband trolling or looking to bang…um…I mean…oh hell, Faith." He sighed heavily.

She nodded, a somber expression on her face.

"I suppose, now that I look back, I've only hung out with women who wanted the easy way, the easy night. I didn't have to work at a relationship because there was nothing to work at."

"You've never had anything more?" she asked, shaking her head. "That seems rather…"

"Selfish? Crude? Irresponsible?" he filled in, now hating the game he started.

"No. Honestly, I was going to say it seemed sad. After seeing the love you say your grandparents and parents had, I would think you would want that. Love. Marriage. Children."

"I guess I always figured it would happen someday, but never really looked beyond what was happening at the time."

Leaning over, she placed her small hand on the corded muscles of his forearm as he held the steering wheel tightly. "You'll find it someday...if you take the time to look for it. I don't think it's going to come out of nowhere and just hit you on the head!"

He glanced at her pensive smile and thought...*I think it already did.*

15

There was no sun peeking through the blinds when Faith awoke the next morning. As she twisted the handle allowing more light to enter, she saw dark rain clouds overhead, casting the gloom from the outside into her apartment...and her mood.

It had been almost a week since Erik was kidnapped and even with Ivan making two payments...nothing. Her dream had been vivid—a dark haired boy, sitting on a bed, this time playing some kind of game. The dream always ended at that point. No more clues as to where he was. Or who he was with. *But he's still alive, I just know it.*

She was glad for a day without teaching...*or interviewing the criminal underworld,* she thought ruefully. Stepping into the shower, she let the hot water pound the stress out of her body even if the images in her mind could not be easily removed.

Stepping into the kitchen, Smee made his obligatory figure-eights between her legs. "Hey sweetie," she cooed, putting the canned food in his dish. He immediately left her legs for the food, and she grinned. "I know. You only love me because I feed you," she teased. Fixing some toast and hot tea, she sat on the sofa, turning on her laptop.

Bills to pay, emails to check, and some online Christmas shopping to do. What to do first? Swallowing her last bite of toast, she paid her few bills first, determined to get that chore out of the way. Checking her bank statement, she winced. She would never take money from Ivan for helping, but she sighed deeply when seeing her balance. *I hate to wish for crime, but I need the police department to ask me to do some witness drawings!*

As she thought of Christmas, she grimaced at both the thought that she had little money for Christmas presents and the realization that she had almost no one to buy for. There were only two teachers at school that she had become friends with and the dispatcher at the police station. Her mind rolled to Bart, and she wondered if they were friends enough to exchange Christmas presents. *God, girl. Get over yourself! All he'd want for Christmas he can find in any bar on any night.* Sighing heavily, she checked her emails, deleting most of them.

Standing, she washed her few dishes and glanced down at the mail on her kitchen counter. Spending the last few days with Bart running around the state and then one day at school, she had not taken the time to go through her mail, all gathered in a pile. Credit card offers, newspapers, sales advertisements, general solicitations... all went into the trash.

A plain piece of paper fell off the stack and floated to the floor. Bending, she scooped it up and unfolded the missive.

Stop what you are doing.

What is this? Confused, she flipped the message over to the back, but it was blank. Her name was nowhere on the note, and she wondered if it had been meant for her. She heard a commotion outside in the alley behind her building. Walking over to the window, she saw two of her elderly neighbors yelling at each other. Cracking the window slightly, she could hear one accusing the other of putting their garbage in his can. The two men fussed and cussed for several minutes before moving back inside.

Grinning at their antics, she tossed the note onto the kitchen counter. *I guess this got mixed up in my newspapers by mistake. Seems like Mr. Carlotti is pissed once more at Mr. Giovanni and his note came to me by accident.* Downing the last of her tea, she headed to her room to get dressed. Wanting to hit the grocery store before the Saturday crowds set in was next on her list.

The Saints were piled up in Jack's living room, filling up the comfortable sofas and chairs around the fireplace. Bethany, Miriam, and Sabrina were getting ready to dish out the dessert. The men had ordered pizzas and the group had devoured several boxes. Each man, still frustrated by the lack of progress in Erik's case, had left their morning meeting, grimly accepting that there was little else they could do with the FBI in charge. Monty gave an update from Mitch, and all Bart's interview tapes had been forwarded, so there was nothing left for the Saints to do. Jack had distributed new assignments for everyone, and the group dismissed to move upstairs to share lunch.

Luke stretched his long legs toward the fire, mulling

over the facts. His methodical mind constantly worked on the puzzle of the case. Closing his tired eyes, he let the fire's warmth ease his mind, as his caffeine buzz slowly abated. Blaise came in from the deck, his dog bounding into the room ahead of him. Tired from his run, the dog flopped down in front of the fire, his owner not far behind.

Chad pulled out his phone and texted madly for a few minutes then slipped the phone into his back pocket before grabbing his dessert dish. Marc stared out of the window, the Blue Ridge Mountains in the vista. He had a new assignment and was going to be flying his plane the next day for a security escort. So far, the weather had been mild, and he hoped it continued that way. He loved the idea of being up in the air again looking down on the mountains.

Bethany moved to sit in the chair with Jack as Miriam snuggled up to Cam. Bart's cousin, Sabrina, sat on a cushion on the floor between Jude's knees as his hand rested on her shoulder. The conversation rolled back to the kidnapping, and Bethany shook her head sadly. "I can't imagine how that mother must feel. To have your child snatched away from you and to not know anything." Jack pulled her in tightly, kissing the top of her head as it rested on his chest.

Bart glanced over at the three couples among the Saints. He had been glad for Jack when he found Bethany, seeing it bring warmth to Jack's life that had been all business. Sliding his gaze to his best friend, Cam, and Miriam, he was happy for them also. Both from large, in-your-business families, they thrived in their new relationship and wedding planning. Sabrina was also planning her wedding to the newest Saint, Jude.

He thought of Faith, honestly admitting to himself that she was never far from his thoughts. *She sees me...the real me. She doesn't take any shit and lays the truth out.* He thought about the way they parted last night. He wanted to take her into his arms and kiss her again. The idea of the simple feel of her lips on his invaded his every thought. *Why didn't I?* She had seemed to hesitate before walking into her apartment and he let her. *Was I crazy? I've never let a woman get away.* He knew she was attracted to him, but their last conversation stayed with him. *What does she really think of me?* He acknowledged that, for the first time, he actually cared what a woman thought of him. And the realization that he came up lacking bothered him.

Coming back in from the store, Faith balanced her grocery sacks on her arm while fishing for the keys from her purse. Tipping one of the bags slightly, an orange rolled out of the top and landed on her welcome mat. *Damn it!* Finally setting the bags down, she managed to open her door and set the bags on the kitchen counter. Walking back to the door, she bent to pick up the errant orange when she saw the corner of a white piece of paper sticking out from under the mat. Pulling it out, she noted that it was folded in half, like the note from this morning.

Seer, stop meddling. You are not the only one who can see. You are being watched.

This time, she stood with shaking hands still holding the note. *Oh, my God, it was meant for me!* Her gaze jerked back and forth outside her apartment, but she saw no one. Backing into her apartment, she slammed the door shut and quickly bolted the locks. Heart pounding, she pushed her hair back from her face as her eyes darted around as though the person threatening her would suddenly appear. Sucking in a deep breath, she knew she needed to let someone know. *FBI? Mitch? Or Bart?* Without hesitation, she ran to her purse on the kitchen counter and dumped its contents trying to locate her phone.

Searching her contacts, she pressed the number.

Bart answered, his greeting warm, but she did not give him a chance to say anything else. "Someone's sent me a threat!" she blurted.

"Where are you?" he instantly demanded.

She was vaguely aware of hearing people's voices in the background as she told him she was at home.

"Stay there, stay locked in, do not go to the door for any reason unless you know it's me," he ordered.

"Okay," she breathed, heart still pounding. Moving away from the door, she walked over to her old sofa and perched on the edge. Her eyes darted to the side where her window blinds were always raised to let in as much natural light as possible. She jumped up, rushing over to pull the cord, lowering the blinds. The idea that perhaps someone was in the building across from her slid a shiver down her spine.

Time crawled until she finally heard the pounding of heavy footsteps coming up the stairs. She stood but did not go near the door until loud knocking was followed by Bart's voice calling her name. Running over, she threw back the deadbolt and barely stepped out of the way before he came slamming through.

Putting his hands on her shoulders, he leaned down to peer into her eyes. "Are you okay?"

She nodded but had no time to answer before he

pulled her into his broad chest, cradling her body against his. She was vaguely aware of someone else in her apartment and pushed her way back so that she could see.

Three other large men invaded her small space, and she jerked her gaze back to Bart for an explanation.

He looked down and saw her confusion. "Faith, these are my friends and fellow Saints. This is Monty, Chad, and Marc."

The three men smiled at her before quickly dispersing throughout her apartment. As small as it was, it did not take them long to check the area.

Leaning back, she looked up at Bart, she asked, "What are they looking for?"

"They each have various expert training and want to do a quick preliminary. Monty will take a look at the threats and call Mitch. Chad has explosive training—"

"Explosives?" she yelped.

Pulling her in once more, he said, "Babe, let me explain how this is going to work. I want to secure your safety and the only way I can do that is to have you with me. My friends are going to check out your place, contact the FBI, and then we'll plan what we need to do."

Monty saw the notes on the kitchen counter and, with gloved hands, bagged them to give to Mitch. Chad came back and said, "Preliminary sweep is negative." Marc swept for bugs, but also found none. The four men made eye contact, nodded, and then Bart turned his attention back to Faith.

"Faith, I need you to pack a bag so that we can get out of here. This place isn't secure, and I'll take you somewhere that is."

"I can't leave Smee!" she exclaimed, looking up, her dark eyes wide.

"Gather his stuff, too," Bart easily agreed.

Faith seemed stuck, and with his large hands on her shoulders, he turned her before giving her a gentle push toward her minuscule bedroom. Jolted out of her stupor, she grabbed her suitcase from under the bed and quickly began shoving in clothes before running to the bathroom to grab her toiletries.

Keeping their voices low, the four men conferred as they looked at the two printed threats. "Any ideas?" Bart bit out.

"If someone's watching her, there are no bugs inside this place," Marc said. He glanced toward the window, seeing the blinds slightly askew. Walking over to them, he saw the brick building right across the alley and shook his head at her crappy view. "If she kept her blinds open, it wouldn't be difficult for someone across the way to monitor her."

Monty's eyes were on the two notes, now securely in plastic evidence bags. "This isn't a very sophisticated method of threat, but very effective. FBI will try to pull prints, but chances are there won't be any except Faith's."

Chad looked at the group before settling his gaze on Bart. "You know what this means, don't you?"

The others looked at him as he answered his own question. "It means Ivan may have been on the right trail and it's made someone nervous. Someone who's been around Faith."

A small gasp came from the door of the bedroom and the men turned in unison, seeing the terrified expression on her face. Bart stalked over, his large body vibrating with anger. "Babe, we got this. You're coming with me right now. They're going to secure your place and install monitoring equipment in case someone comes here."

He peered at her face, seeing shock. Pulling her into his body for a moment, he willed his heat to seep into her. Stroking her back, attempting to massage her stiffness, he murmured soft sounds into her hair. As her shaking subsided, he leaned back. "Better?"

She nodded and left his embrace. Anger was beginning to replace shock. "I'm pissed that someone would do this to me. I'm nobody!" Bending down, she scooped Smee into his carrier and moved to the closet to get out a large tote bag. She stuffed the litter box and some extra litter and cat food in the tote before turning back around, hesitating.

"What is it?" Bart asked.

"I hate leaving my tree." She looked at the caring faces staring back. "I know it doesn't look like much, but those are my grandmother's antique Christmas ornaments."

Bart nodded to Monty before saying, "It'll be safe here, Faith. I can return to pack them up, if necessary."

"Okay," she said, resignation filling her voice.

Chad grabbed the tote and the suitcase, while Marc picked up her art portfolio that contained her pads and charcoals and headed out of the door. Monty stayed inside as Bart took the cat carrier from Faith's hand and led her down to his truck. Once she was buckled in safely, he turned to the others.

"Thanks, guys."

"No problem," Chad assured.

"Take her stuff to your place and then bring her directly to Jack's. He's still got everyone there and we'll meet as soon as you arrive," Marc reported. "We'll finish here and then head over."

"Will do," Bart agreed, wanting to get her to safety as soon as possible. Hopping into the driver's seat, the truck fired to life. Glancing to the side, he tried to joke, "We need to stop meeting like this. I'm beginning to think that something's wrong if you're not in the passenger side of my truck."

She gave a wan smile, her fingers still clutching Smee's carrier. He let out a long meow, and she tapped the side to distract him.

Bart wanted to ask about the notes but hated for her to have to repeat the story too many times. *It can wait until we get to Jack's.*

She stared out of the window, reality slowly sinking in as the miles rolled by. They turned into an older neighborhood on the outskirts of Charlestown. Mature trees dotted the large lawns, and she noticed that each house was different. *Unlike the modern neighborhoods where all the houses look like box images of each other.* When he finally pulled into a driveway at the end of a cul-de-sac, she was stunned at the home coming into view.

An old, large, two-story home, with a full front porch complete with columns, stood in front of her. The white porch, door, and shutters were in sharp contrast to the blue siding.

"This is...um...wow," she said, leaning down to look at it all.

"It's home," he shrugged, wondering what she thought of it.

"It's not what I expected you to have," she confessed. "I thought you'd be in one of those more modern apartment buildings, complete with a gym and a coffee shop."

Chuckling, he looked over at her face, eyes with dark circles underneath but shining nonetheless. "I lived in one for about six months when I first came into town but found that I kinda like my privacy. I bought a house that needed just a little TLC in an established neighborhood and have spent some time doing the small fix-it jobs that needed to be done."

Hopping out of the truck, he rounded the hood and opened her door. Taking the tote and suitcase from the back, he escorted her to the front. Once inside, he set her things down and said, "Let's get Smee settled."

She started to set the carrier down on the floor when a noise from the hall startled her. A large dog bounded toward them, tail wagging and tongue lolling. She stifled a scream as the huge animal jumped up as Bart knelt, rubbing its head.

"What's that?" she squeaked.

"Faith, meet Apollo," Bart introduced.

"Bart," she protested. "I can't leave Smee here with that...that..."

"Apollo is all heart, I assure you. He's completely harmless." He ruffled the dog's fur again, saying affectionately, "Aren't you, boy?" Looking at Faith, seeing her dubious expression, he said gently, "Come on, pet him."

She gingerly held out her hand allowing the dog to sniff her fingers before licking them. She smiled up at Bart. "He's a sweetheart, but there's no way Smee is going to get along with him."

He thought for a second, then said, "Let me crate Apollo until we come back from Jack's place."

The reminder of what she faced hit her and she grimaced as she thought of the poor dog locked up for hours. "No, let's not do that." Seeing Bart about to protest, she added, "Honestly, Smee is going to be freaked being in a new area. If you have a small room, I can get his litter box set up and he can easily be confined for a little while and will be perfectly happy."

He thought for a second and said, "Let's use the laundry room." Showing her the way, they placed the litter box, food, and water in there before she opened the carrier after Bart had left the room and closed the door. Petting Smee, she assured him she would return, before slipping out of the room.

Bart was standing at the kitchen bar when she came out. She glanced around in curiosity at the large, comfortable rooms. The living room, dining room, and kitchen appeared to have an old quality to them and yet were furnished beautifully. Definitely masculine, beautiful, but...empty.

"Something wrong?" he asked, watching the myriad of expressions cross her face.

"No...uh, well...you don't have a Christmas tree?" she asked in curiosity.

"It didn't seem to make any sense to decorate a house that just has me in it," he confessed.

He watched her gaze move around the rooms, and explained, "My cousin Sabrina helped me furnish the place. She's an interior designer."

"It's lovely, Bart. I admit that I never pictured you in a place like this."

"So..." he smirked, "you have been thinking about me?"

Swatting his hard arm, she shook her head. "Yep, just as cocky as always."

He inwardly groaned, *If only she knew what my cock thought about her being in my house!* As soon as he had that thought, it brought back to mind why they were there, and he became all business once more. "We'll get you settled in later but, for now, we need to head to Jack's."

"Maybe by the time we finish I'll be able to go back home tonight."

"We'll see," he said noncommittally, knowing there was no way he was letting her go back unprotected tonight. The idea of her staying at his house had him thinking, *And I'll work to make sure my house is where you want to be!*

Faith gawked with unabashed interest as Bart entered the security code into the panel by the tall, brick pillar next to the gate. Her fascination did not diminish as they drove through the woods and then into the clearing where Jack's house was located.

"Wow," was the only word she said.

Bart laughed, parking his truck next to the accumulation of other trucks and SUVs. Walking around to assist her down, he felt her hand tremble in his. Tucking her into his embrace, he enjoyed how her body fit into his.

"Who all is here?" she queried, her nerves betraying her.

"I think Jack has all the Saints here to process the threats to you."

"Do...do they all feel about me the way you did?"

Stopping on the front porch, he turned her around, still holding her close, but having her face him. Leaning down to make eye contact, he said, "Faith, I was a biased idiot. I made assumptions and I was wrong. They all know that." He watched carefully as she processed his words and nodded slightly. "And babe? I plan on making it up to you. Promise."

Before she could question him further, the heavy oak door flung open, and they were greeted enthusiastically by a beautiful, petite blonde woman smiling widely. "Come in, come in," she invited, stepping back. As they entered, the woman grabbed her and said, "You must be Faith. I'm Bethany, Jack's wife." Faith was engulfed in a warm hug.

Two other women stepped up, equally as friendly. Introduced to Miriam and Sabrina, Faith stood awkwardly, not knowing what was expected.

Bart's arm across her shoulders guided her toward the massive living room where she came to a sharp halt. The room was complete with a stone fireplace that continued up to the vaulted ceiling, floor to ceiling windows flanking the wall facing the mountains, and oversized furniture. But more than just the house caught her attention. The wall of testosterone facing her from the room caused her breath to catch in her throat. Eight men stood, three of them she recognized from her apartment.

A lumberjack of a man, complete with a full dark beard and intelligent blue eyes approached. Sticking out his hand, he shook hers gently. "Faith? Nice to meet you. I'm Jack Bryant. Welcome to my home."

She liked the way his eyes twinkled as he smiled and she responded, "Thank you." Her eyes wandered to the massive tree with Christmas ornaments on every limb. "Your home is beautiful. I'm...I'm really sorry to be so much trouble."

She saw his eyes darken to a stormy grey and he leaned in saying, "Nothing to be sorry for. You didn't bring this on. We're here to find the ones who did."

Jack turned to the group and pronounced, "Everyone settle in. We're meeting up here for now."

Bart understood Jack was not going to take Faith down to the command center and he appreciated that the other three women moved quietly into the kitchen. *Out of sight, but not out of hearing range,* he grinned.

Propelling Faith over, he settled them at the end of one of the sofas and waited as the other men made themselves comfortable as well. She looked around, noting each one had a tablet in front of them, several tapping away furiously.

Introductions were made quickly, but she knew she would never remember them later, except for Cam. The large Hispanic man was Bart's best friend, and his warm eyes stayed on her as they flicked back and forth between them.

Jack began easily, "Faith, let me explain how things are now." Seeing her nod nervously, he began, "My company was contracted to work for Ivan to check into his major enemies—those who would most likely profit from his business demise—while the FBI were investigating into the kidnapping. We work with the FBI, withholding nothing from them. My company was not directly hired to find Erik, but to discern what other information we could gather. Ivan told me that he had contacted someone else to assist, and of course, that was you."

She licked her lips, wondering what he would say about her involvement in the case. Bart leaned down and whispered, "Breathe," and the air left her lungs in a whoosh.

Jack continued, "Bart went to each meeting with the full acknowledgment of the FBI and was wired each time. The audio and video feed wasn't only analyzed by us but was immediately sent to the FBI. The two of you were never in any actual danger. Once the two of you finished with Sergio our contractual obligations were over, even though Erik has not been found." Seeing her furrowed brow, he reminded her, "Remember, we were only contracted to do some digging into Ivan's enemies to see if they would offer any info that would be withheld from the FBI."

She chanced a glance around the room, seeing all eyes focused on her and she shivered. She felt Bart's arm tighten against her shoulder, but wished she was closer to the roaring fire in the fireplace.

"And now?" Jack prompted. "Our focus has now changed. We are back into the investigation."

"To find Erik?" she asked, unsure what was happening.

"Not exactly. Our first priority now is keeping you safe and finding out who threatened you. Chances are that will bring us to the kidnappers."

The embarrassment of being poor slid over her, but she masked it with a steel will. Sitting up straight, pulling out from under Bart's arm, she looked Jack in the eye. "I'm afraid I cannot ask for your protection...or investigation." Seeing the question in the eyes of the men around, she plunged on, "I am quite able to pay my bills with the little I earn, but there are no discretionary funds, Mr. Bryant. I have absolutely nothing to pay you with. I want Erik to be found, and I will give you every bit of information I can, but I can't accept your security."

The silence in the room was deafening and Faith felt her nerves strung tight as a bow. Hating to be the object of anyone's attention, she now had nine pairs of eyes giving her their undivided attention. Refusing to look down at her clasped hands in her lap, she could feel Bart's fingers grazing her shoulder once more.

Suddenly, the mood in the room shifted and she noticed smiles all around. Unsure of the change, she stared at Jack, who was grinning as much as anyone.

"You misunderstand, Ms. Romani. You are..." he glanced at Bart, who tightened his grip on her shoulders and gently pulled her back into his chest, "one of us now, and we protect our own. You, are now our mission."

"I...um...I don't understand," she stammered.

"Quite simply, you are sitting in my house with one of my men's arms around you. He's offered his protection to you and that extends to us as well."

"But we're not..." she blushed deep red as she twisted around to look up into Bart's face.

"Faith, don't worry who we are or aren't right now. We're friends and that makes you mine to protect."

She nodded slowly, still noticing the grins from around the room. She hated taking charity but had to admit she was scared.

"Right," Jack proclaimed. "Let's get down to business."

She had a feeling that as welcoming as Jack had been, he was always about the business. *Except when he smiles at Bethany and then the big man showed his weakness.*

Monty began, "I've sent the original threatening notes over to the FBI for processing and told Mitch that I would be following up as soon as we finish here. He may need to meet with you depending on what information you can tell us." He smiled at her, "To start out, tell us exactly how the notes came to you."

She noted his smile, feeling it was not fake. He appeared relaxed, dressed for comfort, and yet a debonair man with an air of authority. Focusing on his face, she drew a shaky breath to steel her nerves, and answered calmly, "The first came sometime when I was gone with Bart. My mail had gathered for two days in my box, and I had three newspapers on my front stoop. When I went to get them, I almost threw them all into the recycle bin, and the note slipped out. It was folded in half and must have been slipped between the pages of one of the newspapers or between two of them. Because it fell to the floor, I have no way of knowing which day it was delivered. It just said to stop what I was doing. I actually didn't think it was for me."

At that, she noticed the stares of the Saints, and quickly explained with a little shrug, "I have two older neighbors who are always battling over which garbage can is theirs. In fact, this very morning they were in the alley arguing. I assumed one of them meant it for the other."

"Do they know where each one lives?" Marc asked.

"Oh, yeah," she smiled at the one who appeared to be more at home in the wilderness than a boardroom. "And their apartment numbers are printed on the garbage cans. That's part of the arguing. You know, like *You live in apartment 3B so stop putting your garbage in my 8B can*. Believe me, they can argue like that all day."

The silence slid into the room like a fog, leaving Faith unsure what they were thinking. Twisting to look at Bart, she realized he was frowning, too.

"If the two men know each other's apartment numbers, they're not going to leave a note at your door, which is clearly marked, 10A," Cam added, his expression sympathetic.

"Oh," she said, knowing the word sounded simplistic, even to her ears.

"What about the second one?" Monty prompted.

"I was taking care of my affairs since I had been gone for several days. You know, mail, email, that kind of thing. I needed to get groceries and walked to Mercer's, down the street."

"How far a walk is it?" Chad asked, then added, "I'm Chad, by the way."

Warmth exuded from Chad, and she suddenly had a vision of him rescuing others. *I wonder why it's stronger with him?* She gave a small smile, noticing the kind expression on his face. Of all the men in the room, he appeared to be the most easy-going, as though nothing would fluster him.

"Um, about three blocks away. I can walk it in ten minutes going and then about fifteen minutes coming back because my arms are full of bags." She heard a grumble coming from behind and looked at Bart once more.

"You shouldn't be walking in that neighborhood at all," he groused.

"Oh, yeah? And just how do you think I would be able to live if I stayed in my apartment all day long?"

"What about your car?" Bart continued to dig.

"It's not very reliable," she frowned, admitting more than she wanted.

Interrupting, Jack asked, "How long were you shopping?"

"About fifteen minutes."

"Someone must have been watching to see when she left," Chad surmised.

Her hand moved out to grip Bart's thigh, and he covered it with his own, wrapping his fingers around hers. "I don't understand," she said, looking around at all the faces, including the three women who had slipped unnoticed by her to the dining room. "Bart was with me the whole time we were talking to people. There's nothing that I know that he doesn't know. Why me? I'm nothing special," she protested.

"Babe," Bart started but, before he could stop her, she jumped up and walked over to the windows, her arms wrapped around her middle in a protective stance. He began to rise, but Jack put his hand out, shaking his head. Bart understood that sometimes victims needed time to process what they were thinking, but he hated that the victim was someone he cared about.

She looked out over the yard, seeing a white picket fence surrounding the side and back of the house. The woods behind, trees stark in the wintertime with only the relief of the green cedars and pines amongst them. And then the Blue Ridge Mountains rising in the background, sent peace inside that she had not known for a while. Breathing deeply, she brushed away a tear.

"I know Bart has spoken of me. About me," she began. "My grandmother lived with us and raised me since my mother died when I was twelve. She was from Russia but loved her American adopted country. She used to tell me stories that had been passed down for generations. According to her, our family were Russian gypsies." Snorting, she shook her head. "The stories of living in wagon houses and traveling to small villages sounded fascinating to a small girl living in a shoebox apartment with no view of trees. She never told me about any gifts, though, in case you are wondering about the power of suggestion. She just talked about our family history and made it come alive for me. My father left when I was a baby and my mother...well, she sort of mentally checked out, I guess is the best way to put it. When she died, when I was twelve, it was just Babushka and me."

The silence once more floated among the gathering, the men trained to let a victim speak in their own time, the women listening raptly, and Bart's eyes never leaving the lone woman staring out at the landscape, baring her soul in front of strangers. And it was the bravest thing he had ever seen.

She turned to face the group, not lowering her gaze, but keeping it firmly on their faces. "I will just say that there were incidents when I was younger where I drew pictures of images in my head, and they turned out to happen. The kids called me a freak and a few teachers avoided me after that. When I finally confessed to Babushka about what had happened, she told me about how there are women in our family with a gift. The gift to sometimes get an image of something that we can't see but is true."

Piercing the assembly with her firm stare, she added, "I've never called myself a seer. I'm not psychic, nor am I a medium. I simply sometimes have dreams and then draw them. I get strong feelings about people, and it comes out in my art." She released a held breath and relaxed slightly as she saw no signs of incrimination coming from any of the Saints.

"Ivan knew my grandmother. They were childhood neighbors before she moved away from Virginia Beach. He knew the gift was supposed to be handed down to daughters, but they skipped a generation. He called me the day after Erik was kidnapped and begged me to come. I told him I didn't think I could help, but he was insistent. He said he was desperate and even if I could just get a feeling as to what happened to him, it would be worth it.

He offered to pay, but I turned him down." Shaking her head slightly, she asked rhetorically, "What kind of person would I be to gain from someone else's pain?"

Once more the room was still, no sound heard at all. Squaring her shoulders, she walked back toward Bart and looked down at him as he stretched his long arms toward her. Hesitating for a moment, she placed her small hands in his and allowed him to pull her down into his embrace.

Jack allowed her a moment to pull herself together and then turned his gaze to his wife, giving her a small head jerk toward the back. Bethany nodded and moved over to Faith. "Sweetie, why don't you come with me for a few minutes. You've been cooped up in here with all these men for a while, let's take a little walk and it'll make you feel better."

Faith allowed herself to be propelled toward Bethany and the four women walked to the sunroom built on the back of the house. The room was filled with potted plants, wicker furniture covered in comfortable, floral pillows, and offered a phenomenal view of the backyard. Miriam brought hot tea for them, and the women sat, allowing the moment to relax them.

Jack immediately became all business. "Okay, what have we got? Any security cameras located anywhere close to her apartment building? Traffic lights? Building cameras?"

Luke called out, "On it," as he pounded away on his laptop.

"What about Sergio?" Cam offered. "Or Gavrill?"

"Why them?" Chad asked.

"They're both Russian and have a good chance of

having heard about her gift." Glancing over at Bart, he said, "Sorry man, I mean her supposed gift."

"You're good," Bart replied. "It's gotta be someone that thinks she's gaining more information than what we know."

"Like someone who's heard of her gift and thought she might have had some kind of vision when she was with them?" Marc clarified.

Blaise had been quiet, processing it all when, suddenly, he said, "What if this isn't about Erik?" All eyes cut over to him. "What if it's about her?" Seeing Bart about to explode, he continued, "What if whoever threatened her has something to hide and they're scared that she's going to reveal it?"

Bart exploded. "Every one of those assholes had shit to hide, that's why they met with us—to keep the Feds from looking too hard for anything other than to find Erik."

"Let's break this down, men, and look at everyone she was with," Jack ordered.

The group moved down to the compound's conference room where they could use all their computer resources, had the chance to video conference with Mitch, and the women would not hear their frustration.

Once there, they began a list of who had been in Faith and Bart's presence during the interviews.

"With this new possibility, that someone wants to hide something from her, we need to look at who was in the rooms," Luke said, ready to enter the information.

"With the Maldonis, there were the two sons, the children's nanny—"

"Nanny? Was she in the room long?" Jack asked.

Bart shook his head, "Nah, she honestly came running in after the kids, stayed maybe about two or three minutes and then left with them." He hesitated as he thought, before adding, "Also the manservant or butler, who let us in."

"Your report tells us about Miguel and Volkov's meetings. I wonder if we can find out anything about the men who met with you."

"I can tap into the FBI and see if we can, at least, determine who exactly was in the room," Luke said.

"What about Ivan's home?" Chad asked.

All eyes turned to him in question. "I'm just saying that we need to look at anyone who might want to threaten Faith."

Bart rattled off the family members who had been present, but added, "I still think this is tied into Erik."

"Keep working the intel, men," Jack ordered.

As the list grew, Bart became more tense thinking of the vulnerable woman upstairs that was becoming important to him. *Hell, she already is!*

The ladies sat in the sunroom, enjoying the beautiful December day. The blue, cloudless sky heated the room to a perfect temperature. Miriam and Faith shared a cushioned glider while Bethany and Sabrina sat opposite them in comfortable lounge chairs.

The quiet was not forced but allowed each woman to retreat into their own thoughts. Finally, Faith spoke, "I suppose you all think my story is crazy, don't you?"

The three shook their heads, but it was Miriam who spoke first. "When I was kidnapped in Mexico, each night I would dream of a rescuer. His face was dark, and I was unable to see any detail, but he was large. Sometimes, I woke up, looking around as though my avenging angel would actually be there. Of course, he never was. Until one day, Cam showed up in the camp and whispered the name of my brother. That one word let me know he was there to rescue me. And while I cannot say I ever saw his face in my dreams, if I could have drawn my dream rescuer...it would have been Cam."

"That must have been horrifying!" Faith exclaimed, shocked at Miriam's story.

Miriam reached over and took Faith's hand in her own, giving it a squeeze. "When I got home, my mama told me that she had prayed for my rescue every day and every night. And she once had a dream that a large, dark man swooped in to save me. She had no idea what the dream meant until she met Cam and said her prayers had been answered." Holding Faith's gaze, she continued, "There are things we cannot explain or understand. That does not make them less real. I believe you are a true seer."

Faith smiled, the emotion of acceptance was over-whelming. "Thank you," she choked out. As she gazed at the smiling faces of the three women, she realized how long it had been since she had someone to talk with. Sucking in a deep breath, she smiled. *Perhaps, I have just found some friends.*

"So..." Sabrina said, with a wink, "Tell me about being in love with my cousin!"

Furiously blushing, Faith stammered, "Oh, I...um... we're not...I mean..."

Sabrina laughed, saying, "Oh, I hope you don't break his heart because I definitely think he's met his match in you! He's been playing the field too long and I, for one, want to see him knocked on his ass by love!"

"I hate to disappoint you, but Bart is not falling for me," Faith said, trying not to show her disappointment. "I don't even know why he would be interested. From what I can tell, he's had pretty much any woman he's ever wanted. And honestly, that bothers me."

Miriam patted her arm and said, "I know exactly what you mean. Cam and I met under extreme circumstances and fell in love. It was much later when I heard about his reputation. I don't want to imagine how many women he had been with...before he was even eighteen years old!"

"How do you deal with that?" Faith asked. "All I can think of when I see him is that I'm not like the typical booty call he has."

"That's true," Bethany agreed. "You've got brains!"

At that, the women fell into giggles once more. Bethany, once sobered, explained, "I don't know about you, but I wasn't a virgin when I met Jack. Granted, he's had more partners than I have, but we agreed early on that our relationship began the moment we committed to each other. I don't ask about the decisions he made before me, and he doesn't ask either."

Sabrina nodded, "Totally agree." Looking at Faith, she added, "Bart always acted like the easy-going, laid-back guy, just out for a good time. But I always knew deep down he wanted what grandma and granddad had — a real, true love. And when he fell, he'd fall for life."

The easy conversation drifted to different topics, but Faith's mind stayed firmly on Bart. *Is he ready, like his cousin thinks, to find something more than a one-night stand? And with me?* The corners of her lips turned up in a small smile at the thought of sharing another kiss with him. And possibly more.

17

She and the other women had made their way back into the living room about the same time the Saints came up from their conference rooms. The conversation was polite, but stilted, once the men arrived, and she had been relieved when Bart said they needed to get home. Quick goodbyes were given, and they were soon in his truck.

Bart was uncharacteristically quiet on the drive back to his house. Faith stole glances over to him, but his stone face gave her no clues as to what he was thinking. Arriving at his house, Bart escorted Faith back inside, making sure to lock and set the alarm. She rushed to the laundry room, opening the door to find Smee curled up on a towel on top of the washing machine. "Oh my, you look just like you're at home," she cooed.

Apollo bounded into the room, causing Smee to arch his back and hiss before jumping to the top of the cabinets over the dryer. Looking up, she sighed.

"Don't worry. They'll make friends soon enough," Bart said, standing right behind her.

She jumped at his voice, her hand flying to her throat. "You scared me. Wow, for someone so big, you certainly can be sneaky."

He chuckled and led her back to the living room. "I ordered Chinese. Is that okay? I kind of figured neither of us felt like cooking tonight."

She eyed him carefully. "Are you all right? You were quiet on the ride here."

He wrapped his arms around her, pulling her in to kiss the top of her head. "I'm sorry, princess." She was startled, leaning back to look at him, her expression unreadable. "What's wrong?" he asked.

She looked away, her eyes blinking rapidly. He lifted her chin with his fingers, peering deeply into her eyes.

"It's...the name you called me," she admitted, battling tears.

"Princess? I promise I've never called another woman that in my life," he vowed, assuming that was the reason for her discomfort.

"No, it's not that." She searched his face before admitting, "But that's nice to know. Something that's just mine."

"What is it?"

"Printsessa. It was Babushka's nickname for me. She called me the Russian name for princess."

Sighing, he maneuvered her toward the living room sofa and settled them. "I won't call you that if it upsets yo—"

"No, no," she assured. Blinking away the tears, she smiled over at him. "I like it. It...feels right."

"I'm glad," he said, holding her face in his hands. "We need to talk. I've got your safety on my mind."

"Hmm, that sounds ominous."

"I want to fill you in on what the Saints talked about.

Do you understand you're our new mission? Now, we hope to hell that finding who has been watching and threatening you will lead us to Erik, but you are my number one priority."

She nodded slowly, biting the corner of her lip in thought. He brushed her hair back away from her face and noticed the dark circles underneath her eyes.

"It's been a rough week. You're tired and stressed, but I promise you can rest here. You're completely safe." He watched as she lifted her eyes to his as her mouth curved into a sweet smile. "Come on, I'll show you where the bathroom is, and you can take a hot bath."

Her eyes widened at the suggestion. "A bath? I only have a shower in my apartment, and a bath would be amazing. Thank you so much!"

They stood together as he once more realized how hard life had been for her. "It's little enough, princess," he said, leading her up the stairs, with her suitcase in tow, to the guest bathroom down the hall. Making sure she had her toiletries and the fluffiest towel he could find, he moved back downstairs, leaving her to luxuriate. Once he was out of earshot, he made a quick call.

Faith ran the large, garden tub as full as she dared with warm water. She snooped just to see if he had any women's bath oil or shampoo in his cabinets and was pleased to find he did not. The generic body wash he had offered smelled wonderful, and she gratefully sank into the depths, leaning her head back and, for the first time in several days, cleared her mind.

Downstairs, Bart picked up her laptop case and art pad from where she had placed them near the front door and set them on the coffee table. Throwing himself down on the sofa, he flipped on the TV. Finding a British comedy, he settled in trying to keep his mind off of the beautiful, naked woman in his guest bathroom.

Apollo bounded into the room, eagerly jumping on his master's legs. Leaning down to ruffle the dog's thick coat, he said, "What do you think, boy? Can you put up with the cat so that the beauty can stay here...as long as she wants?"

Apollo, enjoying the rub, moved away to grab his rubber ball in his mouth, bringing it back to Bart. Tossing the ball gently down the hall, Apollo ran to retrieve it before rushing back into the living room. His bushy tail swept the coffee table, sending the art pad flying into the floor.

At a quick command, Apollo sat obediently as Bart picked up the pad, his eyes immediately moving to the opened picture. He was amazed at the meticulous drawing. *This is so much more than what the typical police artist draws!* Knowing he should ask before looking, he continued to turn the pages, each picture exquisite in its detail with a documenting note and date at the bottom. Some were of individual people, others of scenes from a park or playground. She had even drawn the two feuding neighbors; the angle appeared to be from her window overlooking the alley. *She has talent!* Their faces were true to life as though he were looking at a photograph instead of a drawing.

He came to the image of Miguel, seeing the cruel visage staring back at him. It was not just a portrait of a staid figure, but rather he could feel the danger rising from the man on the page. The next one was Gavrill. This time, his picture was accompanied by details of the men who sat next to him and then, those around the room.

Bart stared, mesmerized at the precision with which she captured the cold-blooded men.

Next came pictures from the Maldoni home. How different these pictures looked—more like a family gathering instead of an interview with a crime lord. She had even captured the children playing. Bart's gaze landed on Luciano's youngest son sitting to the side. Faith had meticulously drawn the evasive expression on the man's face.

Flipping the pages once more, he was startled at the sight of Sergio's deep-set, dark eyes glaring forward. Bart had to admit that rage, anger, and cruel violence poured forth from the page.

His mind raced with the possible implications, trying to discern if there was anything to gain from her insight. Leaning back, he tried to combine her intuition with his own observations. It seemed as though the two of them reached the same conclusions about the players, but no obvious evidence was forthcoming.

Running his hand over his face, Bart continued his perusal of her pad, no longer feeling guilty about his curiosity. His heart skipped a beat as he turned to a drawing of himself. It was easy to see he was angry in the image; his facial angles were hard, and his lips were tight in a grimace. *Jesus, is that how I looked to her?* His mind rolled back to the first days they were together, and he remembered how much of an ass he had been. Running his hand through his hair, he heaved a sigh. *No wonder she drew me like this—I was such a prick to her!*

Flipping the page, he saw another drawing of himself, this one much easier on the eyes. She had drawn him smiling, with a flirty wink. While happier with this image, he could not help but remember her accusation of him being a notorious flirt. Staring at the picture, he wondered if this was the practiced expression he had perfected over the years, used liberally on women everywhere.

One more flip of the page and, this time, he was surprised when another drawing of himself stared back. This time, his face was relaxed, eyes twinkled, and his hair was tousled. Smiling, he felt the air rush out in relief, knowing he was now showing his real side to her—and she understood. His heart much lighter, he wondered if she had any more drawings of him.

Continuing to flip through the pages, he stilled as his eyes landed on the drawing of a boy's face. *Erik Krustas.* Looking at the date at the bottom of the page, Bart noted it was drawn the night of Erik's kidnapping. *How did she know?* Flipping the pages, he found two more detailed drawings of the same boy, each one with seemingly more detail. In the last one, he was sitting cross-legged on a bed, the comforter scrunched around his body as a light came from the side, illuminating the book he was reading. Anger slowly crept in with the realization she had been having visions and not sharing them with him.

When her body had finally pruned, Faith stepped out of the bathtub and toweled herself off with the fluffy towel Bart left for her. Her towels at home resembled the course ones found in bargain hotels, but this one was soft and large enough to wrap around her body twice. Stepping to the mirror, she wiped the steam from the glass and saw the escaped, wet tendrils of dark hair framing her pink cheeks.

Friends...he said we were friends. She smoothed her hair

back from her face. *What does he see when he looks at me? He seems to be attracted, but...*

Her thoughts trailed to the handsome man waiting for her downstairs. Quickly moisturizing and then dressing in her pajamas, she was glad to have brought a robe. Slipping her feet into her warm, fuzzy socks, she headed down the stairs.

Rounding the bottom, she said, "I can't thank you enough for the bath! It was amazi—"

She halted seeing his angry face before glancing down at what he was holding in his hand. *My art pad!* The thoughts of the pictures she had drawn of him rushed through her mind, embarrassment flooding her face.

"You want to tell me what the hell these are?" Bart bellowed.

"You shouldn't snoop at things that don't belong to you," she retorted, reaching forward to snatch the pad from his hands.

He held it away, his expression still hard. "You didn't tell me you've been drawing these," he accused.

"I told you that I draw whatever comes into my mind. We've spent a lot of time together in the past couple of days, so naturally I've drawn you," she said, her voice rising in frustration.

He blinked, rearing back, a look of surprise crossing his face. "I'm not talking about the pictures of me," he said. "I'm talking about these!" With that, he turned the art pad around, showing the latest drawing of a boy, sitting on a bed.

She looked at the image and then back to Bart's face, her expression questioning. "What on earth are you yelling about? Those are images I've had in my head but have no idea if they have any bearing on Erik."

"You could have told me! You could have shown these to me!" he retorted.

"Why? You would berate me again for my images, which you don't believe in anyway? Why the hell would I want to put myself through that again?"

Tossing the pad on the dining room table, he dragged his hand through his hair in frustration. "You don't have to throw that in my face. I know I was a prick at the beginning, but I thought we were over that! We're supposed to work together, and I had no idea that you were drawing pictures of Erik."

"I don't even know if it is Erik! I can't see anything clearly," she huffed.

Standing almost toe to toe, he continued to rant. "I would have taken them to Krustas to see if there was anything to gain."

"I gave copies to the FBI," she said, righteous indignation coursing through her blood. Along with the desire to kick him in the shins.

Bart reared back at her proclamation. "Who'd you give them to?"

"Mitch," she replied. "I called him and gave them to him earlier. He said he'd take care of everything."

The jolt of jealousy Bart felt when he saw Faith with Mitch before now slammed into him. "Why would you give them to him instead of me?"

Lifting her hands to her head, she rubbed her temples, the raging headache now returning after the calming bath had abated. Sighing, she forced her words to soften. "Bart, you made it clear from the beginning you had no belief in my ability to see anything." Seeing him about to retort once more, she raised her hand in defiance. "No, listen to me. I get it, Bart. I really do. I've had to face people's disbelief and scorn my whole life. But Ivan asked me to see if there was anything I could do to help, and it's been a huge disappointment to me that I haven't. I have had some images of a boy, in a room, but I have no idea if it's Erik. I don't feel fear with these pictures. These images don't scare me and, quite frankly, with the men we have been interviewing lately, I'm surprised."

Her shoulders lifted and fell with another deep breath. "I kept them from you at first because you didn't believe, and I wasn't about to give you another reason to discredit me. I continued to keep them from you because they don't tell us anything. A boy sitting on a bed reading a book is hardly newsworthy. I have no details of the room or the boy. They don't offer any clues." She stepped forward, leaning her head back and added, "Bart, I know you apologized for your harshness when we first met, and I forgave you. But that doesn't mean that you believe me now. I just thought Mitch might be more open to seeing if they had any value in the case."

The air in the room became less chilly as Bart stepped back and hung his head for a moment. He felt her small hand on his arm and peered into her face, seeing nothing but honesty.

"I gave them to Mitch on the very off-chance that perhaps Ivan might identify the boy as Erik, but I hated to do even that. After all, how cruel is it to taunt him with the idea Erik could be alive when we don't know if he is."

Her gentle voice of reason broke through Bart's irritation and, once more, he was embarrassed at his inability to say the right thing to her. *She's trying to do the right thing,* he conceded. Placing his hand over hers, still resting on his arm, he said, "You're right, Faith. I'm sorry."

Her delectable mouth curved in a small smile as she

threw her hand over her heart. "Why, as I live and breathe, Mr. Taggart. You can be a gentleman!"

Rolling his eyes at her gentle sarcasm, he glanced over at the Chinese takeout boxes on the counter. "I'm also sorry because I'm afraid our dinner is cold now." He felt bad, knowing she must be tired and hungry, and he had just made her stress worse. As she moved away from him, he immediately missed her hand in his.

"No worries," she replied. "A quick microwave and they'll be hot enough."

As she heated the food, he pulled out the plates. Watching her in secret, he compared her to the women of his past. *She's not demanding even when we argue. She's not screaming about food getting cold.* Her hair was still piled on top of her head from her bath, but the escaped tendrils had now dried and curled gently over her ears. Her face, devoid of all makeup, appeared fresh and unblemished, the porcelain complexion glowing. His eyes skimmed down the figure that even her fleece robe could not hide. A pink camisole top peeked from the V-neck opening of her robe. Her toned legs encased in pink, flannel pajama bottoms ended in green, fluffy socks. Altogether...*enchanting. And cute as hell!*

Just then there was a knock at the door. She looked up in surprise, but noticed Bart seemed to be expecting someone. Chad walked in carrying her small, table-top Christmas tree with the antique ornaments still hanging perfectly.

Squealing, she bounded over, clapping her hands. Bart carried the tree over to the end table next to his sofa. Placing the tree on top, he then scooted the table near a window so the lights could be seen. Plugging it in, the small tree twinkled as it illuminated the corner of the room.

She hugged Chad and invited him to dinner. He laughed, catching Bart's head shaking behind her back. "It was no problem. This Scrooge needed a little cheer anyway," he joked, nodding at Bart. Accepting their thanks, Chad headed back out into the night as she walked over, lovingly touching her ornaments.

Bart wanted to pull her into his arms and cradle her close to his warmth. *But I can't. Not yet, at least.*

She saw his gaze on her and cocked her head to the side. "Are you okay?"

Startled out of his musings, he grinned. "Yeah, princess. I'm great."

They sat down to the meal, and for the first time all day, she began to relax. The warm bath combined with the warm food gave her more comfort than she had had in a while. The argument forgotten, they conversed easily.

After dinner, Bart settled back on his sofa hoping she would join him. *Since when did I get almost shy around a woman?* Glancing over at the table where she was still sitting as she pulled out her art pad and other papers, she seemed engrossed in her work. Firing up his laptop, he reviewed the latest information from Luke. So far, they had no idea who would be threatening Faith. *Great, just great.*

At the table, she flipped the pages Bart had studied earlier, comparing them to notes she had jotted down after their interviews. She closed her eyes, trying to still her mind, but nothing came to her. No more visions of the boy and no inspiration from the criminals they interviewed.

Suddenly a hand came down on the table next to the drawings and a voice at her ear, said, "How's it going?"

Jumping, she replied, "Jesus, Bart! How do you move with such stealth?"

"Sorry, princess. I wasn't trying to sneak up on you," he said, resting his other hand on her shoulder. "You're concentrating hard over here, and I thought I'd see if you were coming up with anything."

She twisted around, looking at him suspiciously. Seeing nothing but sincerity, she shook her head. "No. Not at all. The images of the boy are completely gone and when I look at all of these...these...horrible people," pointing to the other pictures, "I get nothing."

Sliding down into the chair next to hers, he asked, "I know you've explained how you work and, seeing these pictures, I can now understand why you are so good at what you do. These are not anything like the typical police artist renderings. You can see the emotion in the details."

"I do like helping the police, but I really like working with the children."

"If I'd had an art teacher that looked like you, I woulda never skipped art," he joked, hoping to lighten the mood.

She smiled at his words, allowing the warmth of them to slide over her. Turning back to the pictures of the boy on the bed, she sighed. "Bart, I have no idea if this is Erik. Or, even if it is, is it where he is now, or could this just be his room?"

Staring at the picture, Bart said, "Faith, if it is Erik, it can't be his room—you drew a wall behind his bed, but his actual room has a window."

Sucking in a deep breath, she jerked her head to the side, her wide-eyed gaze finding his. "You're right!"

18

"I'm telling you to look harder," Bart ordered into the phone.

"And I'm telling you that I did," Mitch argued back. "We've gone over her drawings, and there's nothing to suggest the boy is actually Erik and, if it is, there's nothing in the details to give us any information at all."

"Damn!" Bart bit out, his hair already sticking out at strange angles.

"Listen, man. No one wants to have her help more than me. She's special, but she can't help if she can't see anything. I know you don't want to hear this, but you just take care of Faith, keep her safe, and let us worry about Erik. We're at the end of a week, and the Bureau is on it...I swear."

Bart disconnected, but his frustration had him on edge as he looked across the room at the dark, soulful eyes of Faith. "I'm sorry, princess, but he says there's nothing to go on."

She nodded, her face sad as she walked over to him. Stopping short of his body, she placed her hands on his broad chest, the feel of taut muscles underneath her fingertips. A bold move for her, but she desperately wanted human contact. "I had hoped I could help," she said, the loneliness creeping through her words. "I've never seemed to understand the visions like my grandmother did. What purpose is it to have a gift if it can't be used for good?"

A tear hung on her lashes and before he could stop himself, he lifted his hand, wiping the escaping drop from her cheek. Pulling her in, he lowered his head.

She watched as his lips moved slowly, the excruciating wait sending her rising on her toes to meet him.

The kiss began as the barest touch—just a whisper of lips brushing lips. Even with only a few shared kisses, the taste of him was already familiar, already something she craved. As his mouth moved over hers, a warmth spread through her, making her draw a steadying breath. She shifted closer, needing the contact, wanting to close the space between them.

Bart felt her press against him and nearly lost his grip on restraint. He wanted her—more than he had ever wanted anyone, but something in him held back. *She's not just anyone.*

Trying to find the right way forward, the right way to make this mean something, he hesitated. When she pulled back slightly, uncertainty flickering across her face, his chest tightened.

As she tried to step away, a blush rose along her cheeks. "I'm sorry," she murmured. "I...thought—"

"Oh no, princess," he said quickly. "I want you more than I've ever wanted another woman. It's just that—"

Before he could finish, she rose onto her toes and

kissed him again. This time, the kiss answered everything. No hesitation. No uncertainty.

Heat flared between them, immediate and undeniable, as their mouths moved together. His arms wrapped around her, lifting her easily, holding her close as if he couldn't bear even an inch between them.

He broke away just long enough to brush his lips near her ear. "Give it over, princess," he murmured. "Let it go."

With a soft sound, she did just that, letting the tension of the night slip away as she melted into him, her fingers tangling in his hair as he kissed her again, deeper this time, more certain.

For a moment, nothing else existed. Then doubt flickered. He pulled back slightly, searching her face, something uncertain in his eyes. *What does she need?*

Seeing it, Faith smiled softly, lifting her hands to rest behind his neck as she leaned in again, her lips hovering just shy of his.

"I want you," she whispered. "I want this."

That was all it took. With a low sound, he kissed her again and carried her toward the stairs, not breaking contact. This time, he bypassed the guest room, heading straight to his bedroom. When they reached the bed, he set her gently on her feet.

He paused. For perhaps the first time in his life, he looked unsure.

"Princess... you've got to know I want this. I want you. But only if it's what you want. You say the word, and we stop."

"No, don't stop. Please, Bart." Her voice softened. "I'm tired of being lonely."

The words hit him like cold water. He stepped back slightly, his gaze sharpening as he searched her face.

"Oh no, babe," he said, his tone firm but gentle. "This... this has to mean something. I don't want it to be something you use to forget."

She pulled away fully now, frustration flashing across her face as she wrapped her arms around herself. "What?" she demanded. "You've never lost yourself in someone else just to forget something?"

"Dammit, Faith," he exhaled. "That's not fair, and you know that's not what this is."

"I don't know what this is," she shot back. "Your reputation doesn't exactly suggest emotional involvement."

"I told you—it was always clear before. Always just physical." He ran a hand through his hair, frustration and something deeper threading through him. "With you, I never said that... because it's not just physical."

Silence stretched between them. He drew in a deep breath, forcing himself to slow down. *How did this get so tangled?*

Stepping forward, he cupped her cheek gently. "You're right," he admitted. "I never said it out loud. So how could you know?" His voice softened. "Hell... this is new for me, too."

Sliding his hand down, he took hers and guided her to sit on the edge of the bed. Pulling a chair close, he sat in front of her, his knees bracketing hers.

"Right now... this?" he said, gesturing between them. "This is real."

He held her gaze, making sure she understood.

"You need to know something. I've never brought another woman into this house. Not like that. This place... it's mine. It means something."

Her eyes widened slightly, and he nodded.

"And if this were only physical, I would've said so." His hands closed gently over hers. "But it's not."

He traced his thumb lightly over her fingers. "In less than a week, you know me better than anyone ever has. And I know you." His voice dropped, steady and certain. "And I love what I know."

She lowered her gaze to their clasped hands, watching how gently he held hers. When she lifted her eyes again, she found only sincerity in his deep blue gaze.

"I...I didn't mean to make this seem like something it's not," she admitted softly. "I've just been alone for a long time, and... if all you wanted was something physical, I think I would've taken it." She huffed out a small, self-conscious breath. "Even knowing it wouldn't be enough."

"This isn't just physical to me," he said, his voice steady. "Not with you. This... this is real. I don't even know what to call it yet, but I want to find out." He leaned closer, his heart clearly in his eyes. "If you'll let me."

Her smile was soft, certain. "Yes. I want you."

This time, he didn't rush.

He took his time, as though memorizing her... every look, every breath, every quiet response. More than anything, he wanted her to feel how much she mattered.

They rose together, standing close once more, before he lifted her easily into his arms. Her world narrowed to the feel of him. The warmth of his body, the steady strength in his hold, and the way his lips found hers again.

The kiss deepened, stealing her breath.

She pulled back just long enough to slip out of her robe and shirt, letting them fall away before returning to him. He didn't rush to follow, his gaze lingering, appreciating rather than consuming.

When he lowered his mouth to her neck, then to her

shoulder, she shivered at the slow trail of his lips. His hands followed, gentle and unhurried, as though discovering her rather than claiming her.

She wrapped her legs around his waist, drawing closer, needing the connection, her hands framing his face as she kissed him again.

A quiet sound escaped him as he moved with her, lowering her carefully onto the bed. He paused above her, his weight braced on his arms, his expression filled with something deeper than desire.

"I've got you, princess," he murmured.

Her answering smile was soft, trusting.

He continued slowly, his touch deliberate, his focus entirely on her, watching her reactions, learning what made her breath catch, what made her hold onto him just a little tighter.

"Bart..." she whispered, her voice unsteady. "I need you."

"I'm right here," he answered gently.

And he was. Every movement, every touch centered on her, on making sure she felt safe... wanted... cherished.

The moment built gradually, the tension rising until she could no longer hold it back. Her body arched, her breath catching as she clung to him, his name slipping from her lips as the wave of sensation carried her away.

He stayed with her through it, steady and sure, until the trembling eased and she settled back against the bed.

When she opened her eyes, she found him watching her—soft, pleased, and something more.

He rose then, pulling his shirt over his head, his movements quick but controlled.

Her gaze followed him, taking him in... not with boldness, but with quiet curiosity. The strength in his shoulders, the lines of his chest, the story written in the ink on his skin... it all drew her in.

She had never expected to feel this way. Not about him. Not about anyone. And yet... here she was... watching and wanting him. And realizing, all at once, just how much this meant.

He saw her expression shift from desire to uncertainty. Leaning over her, he placed his hands on either side of her shoulders, surrounding her with his presence. "What are you thinking? If you're unsure about this, we can stop."

Her eyes dropped as she searched for the right words. "I know you... have had a lot of... experience..."

"I promise, you're safe with me," he said gently. "I take care of that. You don't have to worry."

"No, that's not what I meant," she said quickly, her cheeks flushing as she kept her gaze lowered.

He lifted her chin, encouraging her to look at him. "We're not starting this with you holding back. Tell me."

She nodded, drawing in a breath. "You've been with women who... know what they're doing. I just... I don't want to feel like I don't measure up."

His heart clenched at the vulnerability in her voice. Lowering himself beside her, he propped his head on his hand, his other resting lightly at her hip as he turned her toward him. "Faith, there's nothing I can say that erases who I was before you. But that was *before* you."

"Bart, we've only known each other a week. And half that time, we didn't even like each other."

"I know," he admitted with a small huff of breath. "But what's happening here? This isn't like anything I've had before. I'm not comparing you to anyone. There is no comparison." His voice softened. "You're already... everything."

Her fingers lifted, brushing along his jaw before slipping into his hair. "We always seem to get tangled up, don't we?" she murmured.

"No," he said quietly. "We're figuring it out. And we move forward. That's what matters. You and me... right here."

His words filled the empty places she'd been carrying for too long. Smiling faintly, she leaned in and kissed him soft and unhurried. For now... this was enough.

Lying together, he began to explore her slowly, with care rather than urgency, as though he had all the time in the world. She traced the lines of his chest, feeling the steady rhythm of his breathing beneath her fingertips.

When his touch deepened, she drew in a soft breath, her body responding instinctively as warmth spread through her.

He followed her reactions, attentive, adjusting, making sure she felt every bit of his focus.

She pulled him back to her mouth, needing the connection, and he didn't resist—meeting her kiss fully, completely, before letting the moment guide them forward.

Still, he paused, hovering slightly above her. "Has it been a while?" he asked quietly. "I don't want to rush you."

Her gaze lowered again. "About a year."

He nodded, something protective settling in his chest. "Then we take this slow," he said.

And they did. Careful. Intentional. Together.

She held onto him as the moment built, her breath catching, her voice soft as she whispered his name.

He stayed with her, focused only on her, on the way she responded, on the way she trusted him.

And when the intensity finally crested, it carried them both with it, leaving everything else behind.

Afterward, he rolled slightly, bringing her with him so she rested against his chest. His arms wrapped around her instinctively, holding her close as their breathing slowly steadied.

For a long moment, neither of them spoke.

Her head rested against his shoulder, her body still tucked into his, their legs tangled together as their heartbeats gradually slowed.

He stared at the ceiling, still trying to understand what had just happened.

Never... never like this. His arms tightened slightly around her. If he had anything to say about it... she'd never feel alone again.

As their breathing slowed, she lifted her head and looked down at him, her dark eyes shining. "Wow," she whispered.

His head nodded slowly as his gaze wandered over her face, wanting to make sure she was all right. *I meant to go slow. I meant to go easy, but once I got inside of her sweetness, I just—*

"Hey, where'd you go?" she asked, praying he was not beginning to have regrets.

"I'm sorry, Faith," he began, then quickly realized his mistake when he saw the shadow pass over her eyes. "No, no," he amended in a rush. "I'm not sorry about what we did, just how I did it. I meant to take it slow but, once I started with your sweet body, I got a little crazy."

She smiled, her fingers tracing patterns on his tattoo.

"I didn't know it could be like that," she said honestly. Her hand moved down to the pendant on the silver chain around his neck. Holding the medallion, she saw it was of St. Bartholomew.

He caught her curious expression and simply answered, "A gift from my grandfather."

She let the pendant slip through her fingers before patting it against his chest, right over his heart. "Then I know it's special and next to your heart is where it should be," she murmured.

He watched her expression for a moment, tucking her hair behind her ear to see her face clearly. *I've never met anyone as honest as her. No pretense. No faking. Just real. How could I have ever accused her of being false?*

He tightened his huge arms around her, enveloping. Protecting. Needing. They may have started out on the wrong foot, but he now vowed to move forward with this woman.

"Princess, I may be many things, but I'll always lay it right out there. I was wrong about you from the beginning and I'm sorry for being such a prick to you at first. But I want you here with me and to work to see where this can go."

Her eyes searched his, finding truth, but hers were filled with uncertainty.

"What is it?" he asked, running his knuckles over her cheek.

"I don't know, Bart," she said hesitantly. "I mean, this was great but, from what you've told me, I don't know that you're cut out to be relationship material. And I can't do casual and share you—"

He rolled over, pinning her underneath his body, holding his weight off her. "I know what you're trying to say, but Babe, I promise you that I'm ready for a relation-ship—I was just waiting for the right woman. I told you that I've always wanted what my parents and grandpar-ents have. If I'm with you, there's no one else. We're solid, and we're together."

A gentle smile rolled off her lips. "Together? That sounds good." She watched as his handsome face broke into a grin. *I've never seen anyone so heart-stopping gorgeous in my whole life.* She ran her fingers over his strong jaw, loving the feel of the rough stubble underneath her fingertips.

He pulled her head down to his and kissed her once more. This time soft. Gentle. Full of the promise of a future. "Yeah, princess. Together."

19

The next morning, Bart headed to the Saints after dropping Faith off at the elementary school. "I'll be back at three p.m. to pick you up," he said.

"Are you sure it's necessary?"

"Absolutely. Until we determine what's going on, I want you safe." Touching her lips with his in a chaste kiss that had him wanting to take it deeper, he leaned back. "I'll be in touch with Mitch this morning to check on what's happening. I think another money drop from Ivan may be happening today."

At the thought of how frightened Erik must be, she nodded sadly before walking through the school doors.

Four hours later, just as she was rolling her art supply cart to her closet office, she heard the bell ring as school dismissed. *It's only noon!* Looking over at one of the teachers, she asked, "Was this a half day?"

"Oh yeah, thank goodness. The kids go home early today so the teachers can enter the grades. Did you forget?"

"Yep," she answered, feeling foolish. *With everything going on in my life, it's no surprise I can't keep anything straight.*

Since most of the teachers were eating with their grade levels, she decided to treat herself by going across the street to grab lunch at a nearby deli. As she stepped off the curb, the hairs on the back of her neck began to prickle but, when she turned to look around, she saw nothing suspicious.

The lunch crowd had already passed, and she was pleased to find an empty stool at the counter. She usually packed a peanut butter and jelly sandwich when she was working, so a deli lunch was a rarity. Enjoying the warm turkey, swiss, and cranberry croissant, she was munching on her sandwich when the same feeling of being watched crept over her. Casually looking around, she still found no suspicious eyes on her. Giving her head a shake, she finished quickly, determined to get back into the school building where she could feel safe.

Moving through the doors, she made her way to the sidewalk, where the cold air slapped her in the face. *Good,* she thought. *I needed to get out of my head!* With her head down to protect her face against the biting wind, she walked to the intersection.

Stepping off the curb, she began walking across the street glad to have taken the time to have a nice lunch instead of her homemade sandwich. Lost in thought, she barely felt the tingling again over the roar of an engine. Jerking her head around she saw a black sedan, its dark-tinted windows hiding any humanity, speeding toward her. She darted toward the other side of the street but saw the sedan move to the next lane, continuing straight for her. As its tires squealed to keep from running into a parked car, she jumped at the last second, sprawling on the far sidewalk. Pain exploded in her arms and shoulders as she tried to protect her head, which hit the pavement anyway.

Heart pounding, she heard the car as it sped away down the street. With the wind knocked out of her, she was aware of several people crowding around offering assistance. The tingling had stopped, but the ringing in her ears grew louder. She tried to stand, but eager hands insisted she sit. A man held a handkerchief against her forehead to stem the flow of blood as others called 911. As the blood continued to trickle down her face, she felt the world grow smaller and darker. The faraway sound of a siren was the last thing she heard before slipping into unconsciousness.

———

Bethany was in the kitchen of the home she shared with Jack, working on the programs for Cam and Miriam's wedding, when her phone rang. Looking at it, she did not recognize the number.

"Hello?"

"Bethany? It's Faith," came the soft voice.

"Faith? Hey, girl. What's up?"

"Um, I was wondering if you knew where Bart was? He was going to come pick me up at school at three, but I... uh—"

"He's here. Do you need him to come now?"

"I tried to call his phone, but it just went to voicemail and I didn't want to interrupt something important." She took a ragged breath but, before she could say anything else, Bethany jumped in.

"Faith, are you okay? You don't sound good. What's going on?"

"I'm...well, I'm at the hospital. University Hospital, downtown."

"Oh, my God! What happened?" Bethany shrieked, already running for the door leading down to the compound conference room.

Before she could take a step, Jack appeared at the bottom of the stairs questioningly, having heard her exclamation.

"Someone tried to run me down," Faith's voice cracked as the exhausted, frightened tears began to flow.

"I'm getting him. We're coming now," Bethany promised. Barely disconnecting, she yelled, "Bart!" as Jack was already heading toward her.

Bart came around the corner, looking up, as she yelled again, "It's Faith. Someone tried to run her down. She's at University Hospital."

"Damn!" he barked, running up the steps right behind Jack, followed quickly by the rest of the Saints.

Jack, always in control of his men, barked out, "Cam, you drive. Monty, get with Mitch and find out what they know. Jude, work with him. Luke, get the info from the CPD and find out where she was and look at any of the street cameras. The rest of you know what to do. Bethany, babe," he gentled his voice at the top of the stairs, and said, "you're coming with me."

Nodding, she grabbed her purse and quickly followed him, Bart, and Cam out to their vehicles.

Faith sat on the narrow, hard mattress in the ER, fiddling with the sheet covering her legs. Glancing down at her battered body, she sighed. Her head pounded, and she closed her eyes, trying to block out the glare of the harsh lights in the room.

A noise down the hall had her jerking her eyes open, then immediately wincing at the movement. Before she could discern the voices, Bart bounded into the room, coming to an abrupt halt at the sight of her.

Attempting a smile, she said, "Hi," not knowing what else to say.

Cam came into the small room, right on Bart's heels, followed by Jack and Bethany. The men stood speechless for a second as Bethany rushed forward. "Oh, Faith, you poor dear." Bethany pushed Faith's long, dark hair back away from her face, clearly showing the stitches on her forehead. A growl from the other side of the room had the two women looking up at Bart's face.

He stalked to the other side of Faith's bed and bent to take her hand, but halted when he saw it was bandaged. Reaching for the other, he saw the same treatment. His face, tight with anger, tried to force a smile for her, but rage had him seeing red. "What's the status, princess?"

Before she could answer, the doctor squeezed into the room, shock on her face at the three huge men taking up all the space. She looked over at her patient and grinned. "Well, Ms. Romani, if most of my patients had these kinds of friends waiting for them, they would probably recover quicker," she joked.

Faith smiled, first at the doctor and then Saints filling the room. Her eyes swept over to Bethany as she offered her thanks.

"Doc?" Bart asked curtly, not willing to wait for one more second to see what was happening with his girl.

"We treated the cuts and abrasions on her hands and knees. Even though she used her hands to catch her fall, the force of her movement caused her forehead to hit the pavement anyway, therefore, we have stitched the more severe cut. We had a plastic surgeon on site and he was the one to do the stitches, which will greatly reduce the size of a scar. We did order x-rays to make sure there were no further injuries, and I was just coming in with those results." Turning back to Faith, she reported, "I'm pleased to tell you there are no broken bones."

Looking up at the group, the doctor focused her gaze on the large, blond man hovering by the side of the bed, noting his hand caressing Faith's shoulders. "With the force with which she hit her head, I'm concerned about a concussion. She'll need to be watched tonight and brought back if there are any problems. I assume that won't be a problem?"

"No, ma'am," he vowed. "She's coming with me."

Closing her laptop, the doctor smiled. "Good." Walking over to Faith, she touched her arm, saying, "It was a pleasure to meet you, Ms. Romani. The nurse will be back in with the discharge instructions."

Bart focused his attention back on Faith, leaning over her bed, placing his hands on either side of her hips. As his face came to within a breath of hers, he said, "I want to know everything princess, but first, I want to be sure you're going to be okay."

Mesmerized, her gaze never wandered from his as she nodded slowly as in a trance. "I'm okay," she whispered.

"No, you're not okay now, but I'm sure as hell going to make sure that you will be."

Jack interrupted, saying, "Bart, let Bethany help Faith get dressed and we'll talk outside. I've got a Charlestown PD detective outside to fill us in on what happened."

Leaning down the rest of the way, Bart settled his lips onto hers in a barely there, gentle kiss that left no doubt in her mind that it was a kiss of promise.

By the time she opened her eyes, he had moved silently out of the room with Jack and Cam, leaving a smiling Bethany in their wake.

It did not take long for the two women to get Faith's skirt and blouse back on. Her tights were shredded and ended up in the trash. Bethany squatted to slip Faith's sensible flats onto her feet. "It's cold outside, but Cam will bring Bart's truck around to the entrance. Then Cam'll ride back with us while Bart takes you home."

The simple act of dressing had Faith's head pounding once more and her abrasions stung. By the time the nurse came in with the discharge forms and instructions, she would have signed a pact with the devil to get out of the hospital and back into her own bed. *Oh yeah, I can't go home yet.* She quickly decided Bart's bed was even better.

The ride home was silent, but not uncomfortable. Bart shucked his jacket, making a pillow for Faith's head before they pulled out of the hospital parking lot. She knew she should not doze off, but it felt nice to rest her eyes from the glaring lights.

He cut his eyes over to her often, making sure she was not asleep. He wanted to talk but did not trust his temper. *Someone's going to pay for hurting her,* he vowed.

Later that afternoon, he tucked her into his bed telling

her to rest, but that he would be waking her often. She smiled wanly up at him, touching his heart.

Walking back downstairs, he called Jack. "Tell me you got something, boss." A sigh on the other end of the phone had Bart's blood boiling.

"Nothing yet, but we need to meet. I'm sending everyone to your place unless you have an objection."

"No, come on over. Someone's after Faith and it's gotta be because of the Krustas case."

Disconnecting, he checked on her before waiting back downstairs for the rest of the Saints to arrive.

Within thirty minutes, all of the Saints were settled around Bart's large dining room table. Cam's fiancé, Miriam, came also. As a nurse, she assured Bart that she would sit upstairs with Faith. Offering her a genuine hug, he kissed the top of her head. "Owe you, darlin'," he said.

"Oh, please, Bart," she said, rolling her eyes. "After all you did to help Cam rescue me, I hardly think you owe me anything." Giving him a squeeze before winking at her fiancé, she headed upstairs.

Turning back to the group, he asked, "What have we got?"

"The witnesses told the PD that the sedan was black with dark-tinted windows, and they corroborated Faith's story that it changed lanes to go straight for her. There're no cameras at that light. There are cameras around the block focusing on the elementary school, but not on the intersection."

"Damnit," Bart cursed. "There's no way she can get run down in broad daylight and no one can figure out shit!"

"And the news gets worse. I talked to Mitch," Monty added. "Ivan made another transfer of money this morning, but no word on Erik yet. Over a week now. Jesus, this sucks."

Luke said, "I've been working around the clock to try to follow the money trail. I know my skills are better than what the FBI has, but it's like someone is a step ahead of me. There's some kind of blocking system that I've never seen."

"While the field of suspects could be huge, it seems if someone is after Faith, then the culprit has to be someone that you two interviewed. Someone who feels that she's on to something," Jude said.

"Are the FBI focusing on the Maldonis, Miguel, or the Volkovs?" Blaise asked, looking at Monty.

"My money's on Sergio," Bart said, his voice cold and hard.

The Saints looked at him, waiting to see what he would say.

"The other three want Krustas out of business, but Faith didn't get a definite feeling about any of them, other than the criminals they are. But Sergio? She felt anger, betrayal, and even hurt over Ivan turning him over to the Feds. And this kidnapping bullshit? It's personal. It's goddamn personal."

The others nodded in agreement while Luke's fingers were tapping quickly on his keyboard.

Bart leaned forward, piercing them with his stare. "Ivan's worth a shit ton of money. Yeah, these constant payments are hurting him, but it's not going to take his business down completely. Someone wants his money, they demand a couple of million right off the bat. But this? This is wanting to gut the man where it hurts. And that, to me, leaves Sergio."

"Who were his cohorts before he was sent to prison?" Blaise asked.

Quickly sending the information out to their tablets, Luke said, "He had no one else in the family that was working on the takeover, but he had his own large crew of men, with a possible tie to Volkov."

"What are they doing now that their leader is in prison?" Chad asked. "Or could Volkov be doing it for Sergio?"

Blaise spoke up. "I don't see Volkov doing anything for Sergio. Sergio may still have power, but he's got a long prison stay. They're both ruthless leaders. I don't see one wanting to work for the other."

"According to Mitch, most of Sergio's men integrated into other, smaller gangs, but the FBI is sure Sergio has sway on the outside with them...or others," Cam added.

"Who's had contact with him in prison?" Chad wondered as Luke pulled up the prison records.

"His lawyer is the only one who has visited. His mail and email are monitored, but it is assumed that anyone contacting him with that method has codes they use and hidden identity."

"FBI follow up on any of it?" Marc prompted.

Monty shook his head. "Nah, it's too much work and not enough manpower for the FBI to do that. They wanted Sergio, not his underlings. Ivan handed them what they wanted, so as long as he's in prison, they're satisfied."

Bart exploded again, shoving his chair back in frustration. "I've got my girl upstairs, bruised and concussed, and I've got no fuckin' clue who did this to her!"

The men around the table shared a smile as they looked at the big, blond amongst them.

"Your girl?" Cam asked, his white teeth gleaming against his tan skin as he looked at his best friend.

Bart's gaze moved around the table as he slowly nodded his head. "Yeah. My girl."

"Then I should go back and visit Sergio to see what feeling I get now," came Faith's soft voice from the middle of the stairs as she walked gingerly down with Miriam's assistance, her eyes on Bart.

20

As the Saints erupted in *Hell, no* and *Fuck that*, Faith stopped short of the bottom of the stairs, Miriam's arm still around her waist.

Bart jumped up from the table, his chair scraping against the floor, and stalked over to where she was standing.

"Princess," he forced his voice to gentle, "Why are you up?"

"Miriam had to wake me up and then I needed to... uh..." she blushed, leaning in to whisper, "go to the bathroom. We heard voices and I asked her to bring me down."

Miriam had moved over to Cam, looking up apologetically. "I'm sorry, sweetie. I shouldn't have let her come down."

Cam hugged his fiancé, saying, "It's okay, babe. Bart was going to have a hard time keeping her from knowing what we're looking into."

Jack came over to where Bart was standing with Faith tucked into his embrace. His eyes moved over her forehead, a bandage covering the stitches. "Faith," he said softly, "you don't need to go meet that piece of trash again."

She met his gaze before slowly looking at the other men in the room. "I'm sure you don't believe in the feelings that I get, but I'd like to keep working on this." She twisted her head around to stare into Bart's eyes, wincing in the process, and said, "Maybe this time I'll be able to get us closer to finding Erik."

"We'll talk about it later, princess, but not now. Right now, you need to rest and heal," Bart said, brushing her hair back from her face, seeing the dark circles underneath her eyes and the bruising showing at the edges of the bandage on her forehead.

Too tired to argue, she nodded and allowed him to sweep her off her feet as he carried her back to bed. Miriam followed, stepping out into the hall after he tucked the covers around Faith.

"Miriam, I need you to stay with her. Jack's going to obtain special permission to go to the prison tonight even though it'll be late when I arrive. I'm going to talk to Sergio myself."

"I'll stay with her," Miriam promised.

"I'm asking Cam to stay with you two for protection while I'm gone. I'll be back in the middle of the night. You two can stay in the guest room."

"We'll be fine," she assured once more, patting him on the arm. "I'll check her and make sure she's well."

Bart quietly entered his bedroom again, seeing Faith already in the large bed. Kneeling by the bed, he whispered, "I'm going out, but I promise to come back to our bed as soon as I can. Holding you through the night is the only thing I want to do."

Bending over to kiss her lips in a feather-light touch, he admitted in a whisper, "I'm falling, princess. Falling hard for you."

He stole out of the room and back down the stairs to the Saints.

Faith drifted off to sleep, a smile on her face.

This time, as Bart sat at the grey table in the prison conference room, he had Jude sitting with him. Jude's eyes darted around, trying to take in everything, until the guard entered the room with Sergio following behind. Glancing to the side, he adopted Bart's nonchalant attitude, keeping his eyes on the prisoner.

Sergio shifted his eyes between the two large men before he sat down in the plastic chair across from them. His lips curved into a slow grin. "I see you brought someone else with you this time, big man. What happened to the pretty seer?"

Bart saw red but refused to fall for Sergio's dig. "You got something to hide from a seer?"

"Everybody's got something to hide," Sergio sneered.

The room was silent for a moment that uncomfortably stretched among the players. Jude said nothing, keeping his dark eyes on the prisoner. Bart was willing to let the silence continue until Sergio spoke, but the man sitting across from them appeared to have all the time in the world. *He does have all the time to wait us out.*

"I think you've got more than you told us," Bart said. "I think you know exactly where Erik is and that's why you're afraid."

Sergio laughed at that, throwing his head back. "You

are searching, aren't you, big man." His face taking on a serious expression, he shook his head. "I'll tell you this, but only because I've got nothing against the kid. You want to find him? Don't look at me, 'cause I got nothing to do with it. You want to know...look closer." The metal chair scraping against the tile floor screeched as Sergio pushed his seat back and stood. "Got nothing else for you, big man."

The images seemed to float among black, rolling clouds. *A storm's coming.* Faces, mostly filled with anger, swept by. Her chest hurt, heart pounding in fear, as the faces from the past week continued to haunt her.

One final image burst through the inky darkness, causing her to gasp as she jerked awake, her mouth open trying to breathe. As her eyes darted around in panic, recognizing Bart's bedroom, Faith leaned back against the pillows, willing her fluttering pulse to slow. Swinging her legs over the side of the bed, she padded into the bathroom. Staring at herself in the mirror, she was horrified at what looked back. The dark bruise escaped the bandage over the stitches crossing her forehead.

With shaking hands, she drank a glass of water before returning back to the bedroom and crawling under the covers. *What woke me? What was that last image?* Unable to hold a pencil with the wrappings on her hands, she could not even let her mind wander to her fingers to create an image on paper.

Willing her thoughts to slow, she brought the last image back to the forefront. *A smile. It was a smile. Innocent.*

Gentle. Unafraid. But whose smile? This time, the night held no answers.

Jude reported in to Jack as Bart drove back to Charlestown. Disconnecting, he looked over at Bart. "Jack says we're upping the protection on Faith, but I know you won't let her out of your sight."

"Damn straight," Bart agreed, his hand tightening on the steering wheel. After another minute of silence, he heaved a sigh. "This case is so frustrating. It's not what we normally do."

Jude, new to the Saints, turned his full attention to Bart, willing to give him the time to explain more fully.

"We're usually given a specific assignment and we go in and do whatever we have to do to make it happen. This? Hell, the FBI is in charge of investigating the kidnapping—we're not even supposed to be working on that. The bureau chief never called us in on the kidnapping case."

"It's all Krustas this time?" Jude said, more of a query than a statement.

"Yeah. Just investigate his enemies and take Faith along to see if she can help. And now, she's right in the middle of this mess."

The silence filled the truck cab once more, for several more miles, before Bart added, "I never expected this, you know?"

Jude looked over, unsure as to what Bart was referring to.

"Faith," Bart said, admitting everything in that one word.

Jude grinned, remembering the first couple of times he met Sabrina's cousin. In fact, the first time he laid eyes on her, she was on the arm of Bart. Jude had assumed she was his date and was relieved to find out the beauty was his cousin, allowing him to make his move on her before anyone else did. Bart was known for his easy-going manner and cavalier attitude toward no-strings-attached sex. To meet someone like Faith—*totally threw the man for a loop.*

"You're going to keep her safe, Bart."

"Or die trying," Bart added, with a slow grin. A few more miles down the road, he asked, "Where are you and Sabrina celebrating Christmas?"

"We thought about going to Nonnie's house but, with everything going on, we'll probably just stay here and celebrate it together. My mom might visit to help with some of the wedding planning. What about you?"

"I planned on heading to Virginia Beach to visit my parents and Nonnie, but I don't want to leave now. I could ask Faith if she would like to go, but it's too soon."

Jude laughed heartedly. "Nonnie would be planning your wedding, not caring that you've only known her for a week!"

"Seriously!" Bart was thoughtful for a moment, then added, "But maybe it would be good to get her away from here. We could spend Christmas with my parents."

"Don't think the danger would follow her?"

"I don't know. I'd like to think that it wouldn't, but whoever is threatened by what they think she can see would probably follow her anywhere."

An hour later, after dropping Jude off and giving his cousin a quick kiss, he hurried back to his house. Walking in, he was not surprised to see Cam and Miriam already awake. While Cam let him know the night was uneventful, Miriam filled him in on Faith's condition.

"She was restless, and I think had nightmares a few times. I checked on her once and she was sitting in bed, frustrated because she couldn't use her hands to draw. But she's out of the danger zone for the concussion, and I have given her some pain medicine. She's sleeping right now."

Thanking his friends, he walked them to the door, saying goodbye, before taking the stairs two at a time.

Stripping down to his boxers as soon as he got to the bedroom, he slipped underneath the covers, pulling her close to his body. She was warm and soft, dark hair spilling over his pillows and face peaceful in sleep. Tucking her in closely, he fell asleep with her in his arms, the surprising realization hitting him—*I want this every night.*

An hour later, he came instantly awake as her body jerked against his. "Faith? Faith?" he gently shook her.

Her eyes flew open, breath coming in pants. "Bart?" she rasped. "You're back!"

"Yeah, princess. I've been with you for about an hour."

"Oh, I'm sorry I woke you," she said, her dark, haunted eyes turned toward him.

His large hand cupped her face as his eyes roved over her forehead. "How are you doing? Headache?"

"No, not really," she said, more glad than she could express that he was back from his trip and holding her closely in his bed. "Just dreams," she added softly.

"Miriam said you were upset that you couldn't draw earlier."

"Yeah, but hopefully today I can fix the bandage so that I can hold my pencils," she said. "I...I'm having visions, Bart."

His heart hurt at the hesitancy of her voice, as though she were afraid to tell him. Rubbing his rough thumb over her soft cheek, he leaned it to whisper, "Princess, don't ever be afraid to tell me what you're feeling. I...I don't know what it is that you can do, but I know something special happens. And I believe in that something special." He watched for a moment as the insecurity left her expression, replaced with a small smile. "Can you tell me what you're seeing?"

She shook her head sadly, admitting, "No, not really. I see the images of those we have been dealing with and then it ends with just a smile. I don't know whose smile... just a little smile and then it goes away."

Tucking her back into his mighty embrace, he kissed her lips softly before watching her slip back into slumber. *A smile? Whose smile?* Wondering if her gifts—and he finally had to admit he believed in her special somethings as gifts— were going to help them move in the right direction, he knew that placed her in more danger. Vowing to keep her safe, he fell asleep once more.

21

F aith had Miriam come over later the next morning to re-wrap her right hand. "I've got to draw and, the way the bandage is now, I can't move my fingers."

Miriam saw that her palm was the injured area, and her fingers were undamaged in the fall. "I should be able to make this work so that your fingers are exposed, and you can move them." She lifted her gaze back to Faith, saying, "But you realize that, as you bend your fingers, it will cause your palm to move, which will cause pain."

"I can deal with some pain," Faith assured, "but I need to be able to try to make sense of the images from my dreams."

A knock on the door interrupted the two, as Sabrina came in. "Jude got in late and left early. I assumed that Bart did too."

Bart walked in from the kitchen, a spatula in his hand as he kissed his cousin on the cheek. "You'd assume wrong, little cuz."

"Well, don't you appear domesticated," Sabrina teased. Turning to see Miriam re-wrapping Faith's hand, she rushed over. "Oh, Faith, I'm sorry this happened to you! What can I help with?"

Before Bart could tell her that he had everything under control, another knock on the door produced Bethany walking in with a freshly baked coffee cake. Rolling his eyes, he looked over their heads, seeing Faith's eyes on his, a little smile gracing her face. Knowing she had suddenly gone from being a loner to having good friends, he grinned as he headed back to finish the eggs.

Faith enjoyed the conversation among the women while Bart quickly whipped up breakfast, easily including Bethany's treat. A few minutes later, another knock on the door sounded and she wondered who was left to visit. This time, an unfamiliar man walked into the hallway, greeting Bart. She watched as Miriam's eyes lit up.

"Jobe! Hey, big brother," Miriam exclaimed, rushing over to hug the newcomer.

Bart introduced Jobe Delaro, a friend working for a different security agency—and her babysitter for the day.

Bart interrupted her. "I've got to go to Jack's and there's no way I'm leaving you unprotected. We've contracted with Alvarez Security to keep an eye on you when I'm not here."

Jobe, a tall man, fit and muscular, although, not quite as large as Bart, strolled over. His sharp eyes quickly assessed her inability to shake his hand, so he gently put his hand on her shoulder in greeting. "Nice to meet you, Faith. I'll be in the car out in Bart's driveway today if you need me. For anything," he added pointedly.

"It's too cold outside," Faith protested. "Please stay inside where it will be warmer."

"Thanks, but I'll want to keep a check on the perimeter," Jobe explained. "But I'll come in periodically to check on you in here."

The two men walked out onto the porch for a moment, while the women finished their visit. As they left, Bart stalked back to Faith, scooping her up from the couch, twisting to sit, and placing her on his lap.

"Jobe's a good guy, princess. Let him do his job of keeping an eye on things and I want you to rest as much as you can. The Saints are still working the case and I'll be home as soon as I can. When I come home, I've got something I want to discuss."

"That sounds ominous," she said, anxiety in her expression. Using her free fingers to push her hair behind her ears, she held his gaze.

He watched the silky strands slide through her fingers and wanted to feel that himself again. "Nope, not ominous. In fact, I hope you'll be happy."

Cocking her head to the side, she continued to stare, hoping that he would spill his surprise early.

"Not happening," he laughed as he stood and settled her back on the sofa. He looked down at the coffee table holding her pencils and art pad. "You got everything you need?"

"Yeah," she said softly, only looking at him and not glancing at the table.

The double meaning was not lost on him as he grinned. Leaning down to kiss her full lips, he whispered, "As soon as you're able, I want to get lost in your sweet body again. But, until then, I've got something for you." He pulled his St. Bartholomew from around his neck and placed the chain over her head, settling the medallion on her breast.

She touched the esteemed pendant reverently as her eyes lifted to his.

"There's a tracer on the back of it. I want you to wear this at all times, to keep you safe. The other women have one...I can't believe how it has helped each one of them. Hopefully, you'll never need it as they did, but I want you to have this part of me anyway."

"I don't know what to say..." she began, her lips curving in a delectable smile.

He chuckled, shaking his head. "I swear, when Jack named his company the Saints, he never knew how far reaching that would be." Leaning down he kissed her once more, losing himself in her luscious lips, wishing he did not have to leave.

Reveling in his kiss, she finally gave him a little shove. "Go save the world, Bart. I'll still be here when you come back."

Laughing, he left, reluctantly closing the door before waving at Jobe on his way out of the driveway.

A few minutes later, with a pencil in hand, she tried to work out the stiffness in her fingers as she began to draw. Closing her eyes for a moment, she allowed the images of the night to drift through her mind once more. The tingling that usually accompanied her thoughts traveled down her arm to her fingers.

Sharp, piercing, they assaulted as she drew what slammed into her. The evil, gold-toothed grin of Miguel. The deep set, hard eyes of Gavrill. The fierce, protective expression of Luciano, as well as the evasive expression of his youngest son. The pure hate pouring off Sergio.

Her hand ached by the time she had finished the drawings, but still an image clung to the corners of her mind. Leaning backward, her head resting on the back of the sofa, she tried to still her mind. *A smile. A simple smile.*

Putting pencil to pad again, she allowed the lines and curves to shape what was in her mind. A few minutes later, a slight smile stared back at her from the page. No face. No background. Just a smile. *But whose?*

Bart sat at the conference table, listening to the reports from the other Saints who had been working diligently trying to investigate all the players.

Luke, his mind racing, began with the banking aspect. "Not one of the people in the list we created have had any significant changes in their financial records in the past month." He grinned, "But when I dug a little deeper, especially looking for any offshore or overseas accounts, I found a few interesting items."

Taking a large slurp of his ever-present coffee, he continued. "It appears that James Maldoni, the youngest son of Luciano, has been moving some of his money around. He has been investing and the last month has shown interesting growth, considering the market. And he is on his accounts, moving money around almost daily."

"Anything in the past week?" Blaise asked, his fingers drumming on the table.

"That wouldn't really matter," Chad threw out. "If he's involved in the kidnapping then he'd be setting things up before actually having someone take Erik."

"What else?" Jack asked.

"Sergio's money is still very much alive and well. He has holdings that weren't stopped by the Feds when he was convicted. He still has a private banker and investor who manages his money. If he ever gets out of prison, he'll be doing well."

"Enough to pay off someone to take and hold Erik?"

"Absolutely," Luke answered. "And if he's the one who's getting the payoffs, then he's in good shape."

"Bastard," Bart growled, remembering his previous night's conversation. "That prick is too confident."

Monty added, "Unless Luke's uncovered something else about Miguel's group, I just don't see them as having the money, or brains, to execute this kind of operation. They are too reactionary. Their planning only extends to the foresight of drugs, guns, and pimps."

Jack nodded, "I agree, but we're not taking anyone off the list yet."

Monty added, "Gavrill's still topping my list. That bastard is ruthless in his dealings."

"Yeah, but it's not his MO," Chad argued. "He's a ruthless killer, but kidnapper? And then keeping Erik alive for a week? If he wanted to gut Krustas, he'd just take the kill and sit back to watch what happened."

Bart scrubbed his hand over his head, ruffling his hair, in frustration. "Damnit, we're getting nowhere. It's like we're spinning our goddamn wheels here while Erik's still missing, and Faith's still threatened."

"Bart, you're too close to the case," Jack warned. "Luke and Jude will focus in on the money trail that's being uncovered. Monty will work with Mitch, getting every scrap of info from the FBI. Why don't you take Faith away for a day or so? Get away. Go celebrate Christmas with your family."

Bart's usual easy-going gaze glared at his boss. "You kicking me off the assignment, boss?"

"Bart, listen to yourself. You're in the middle of the

goddamn assignment. You take care of her and let us work on the threats."

Cam placed his hand on his best friend's shoulder. "He's right, bro. Focus on Faith."

Blaise nodded his agreement. "You're too close, man. Let us help while you make things easier for her. My folks are coming into town, so I'll be here. I'll come by and take care of Apollo."

Bart looked over and grinned. "Faith's cat is at my place. Its name is Smee."

Blaise answered his grin with one of his own. "All right. A woman after my own heart!"

Bart hung his head for a moment. Looking up, he glanced around the table at the men he trusted as much as he had his SEAL team. "I've done it, haven't I?" Seeing their uncertain faces, he clarified, "Fallen."

The others grinned, while Chad proclaimed, "It's 'bout time."

Several hours later, Bart and Faith were back in his pick-up truck, heading to Virginia Beach. Faith huffed nervously, twisting to look at Bart. "Tell me once again why we're doing this? It seems as though we have spent the last week riding up and down Hwy 64 between Virginia Beach, Richmond, and Charlestown. I feel like I am living in this truck!"

"I know," Bart admitted. "But I always go and see my family for a day or so at Christmas and...well...I want to keep you safe." *I want her with me and can't even say it to her.*

"I could have stayed with someone else," she

protested, the idea of meeting his family making her want to hurl. "Sabrina—"

"She and Jude will probably be in Virginia Beach also."

"Okay, then Miriam and Ca—"

"This is their first Christmas together and they'll be with family."

Huffing, she asked, "Do you have an answer for all of my suggestions?"

"Yes," he answered while grinning. "And before you say anything, this is Bethany and Jack's first Christmas together. I'm not about to have you stay with any of the single saints, even if they are like brothers to me. I don't know any of your friends, so that's out of the question."

Turning back to the front, she pouted. "I'll bet Mitch—"

Bart bellowed, causing her to jump. Glancing guiltily at her, he quickly said, "I'm sorry, princess. I understand you have no idea what games people play, but Mitch would like nothing more than to move onto you."

"Oh, Bart. Don't be ridiculous," she admonished. "He's just friendly."

"Friendly, my ass. That guy wants you, and I'm not about to let him have a chance!"

Laughing, Faith replied, "Well, you're safe. You're the only one I want."

"Damn girl, that makes me want you even more."

Still grinning, she shrugged. "Serves you right for dragging me off to meet your family."

Bart reached across the console, taking her hand and giving it a light squeeze. "What's really on your mind?"

Sighing deeply, she said, "I feel weird, Bart. You and I have known each other for a week. We've slept together and you say it means something. Something that we're going to explore. It just seems...I don't know...weird to be meeting your parents this soon. What are you going to tell them? Here's my friend? My lover? My investigating partner? My—"

"I was planning on introducing you as my girlfriend," he answered, his voice calm while his insides cringed at what her response would be. *I should have thought of this before now!*

The silence in the truck cab was deafening. Bart's façade of confidence began to crumble as he turned his head to glance at Faith's profile. His heart pounded as he saw her lips curve into a smile before she cast her gaze over to him, surprise etched on her face.

"Girlfriend?" she asked.

"Yeah, girlfriend," he assured. Sighing, he thought about what she must be thinking. "Look, Faith, I admit our relationship got off to a rocky start and has been a whirlwind ever since. But I told you that I want to explore this. I know you more than any woman I have ever met, and I really like what I've discovered. And you certainly know more about me than anyone else."

"But girlfriend? Are you sure that you want to put a label on us?" she prodded, hopeful, but afraid he was speaking too quickly.

"I know we haven't talked about it, but...but...," he stuttered. After a moment, he asked, "Are you going to be seeing anyone else while you're with me?"

"No, of course not."

"Well, I'm certainly not either." Sucking a deep breath in, he pulled off at an exit and came to a stop on a little side road. Popping his seat belt, he twisted his body around and faced her full on. "Princess, you're right. I know this is a messed-up time to be telling you this 'cause I should have said something earlier. What we have discovered, I want to keep going. I want to take you on a proper date—and not just grabbing food when we're on the road. I want to keep learning more about you and I love the way you make me feel. I've never done this before, so that's probably why I'm screwing this up. But, Faith, I want you to meet my family, and I'd like to introduce you to them as my girlfriend." He gave her a boyish grin, hoping the sparkle in her eye meant what he wanted to see.

"Well, allrighty then," she said with a laugh.

Holding her face with his palms, he gently kissed her. She wanted more, so with a lick of his lips, she dove in. He allowed her to take over the kiss for a moment and then, angling his head, he owned her mouth. Plunging his tongue deep inside, sweeping the delicious taste of her, he moved within her warmth.

She captured his moan, continuing to tangle her tongue with his. She knew he was aroused and tried to stifle a giggle.

Pulling back, he tried to offer a stern look. "Woman, what the hell are you laughing at?"

"I want you and just wish we could do something about this."

With a final kiss, he slid her back across the console and leaned over to buckle her in. plPulling back out onto the highway, they smiled at each other, the air in the truck much lighter. "All right, princess. Let's get going."

22

L uke leaned back in his chair, stretching his arms over his head as he heard his back pop and crack. He had no idea what time it was but, glancing at the last dregs of coffee in his cup, he realized he had been at it for hours. Hearing a noise behind him, he turned around.

Jack stepped into the command center, piercing him with a glare. "How long you been here?"

Rubbing his hand over his eyes, Luke admitted ruefully, "Haven't left since we had our last meeting."

"You're no good to me if you can't function," Jack admonished, walking over and taking a seat next to him.

"I can't figure out the codes to breaking down how to follow the money trail," Luke confessed, "and it's driving me crazy. I keep thinking that if I can just find this piece of the puzzle, then we'll know who took Erik and can sic the FBI onto his ass."

"You're the best Luke, but that doesn't mean that you can crack everything. What you need to do is go home and sleep."

"Yeah," he agreed. His secure email notice sounded. "Let me check my emails and then I'll head out of here."

"All right," Jack said, shaking his head. He knew Luke would spend the night in that chair if he thought there was a possibility of cracking the code.

Luke turned back to his email, his tired eyes focusing on a new one. Clicking on it, his heart pounded as he read,

I know what you are seeking. I can help.

Who the hell is this? Trying to get a read on the IP address, he found he was unable to ascertain their identity. *Whoever this is, they know their shit!*

Forgoing trying to see who was emailing him, he let his curiosity override and sent a reply.

How can you help me?

He sat nervously waiting to check what the response would be. *Is this some kind of joke? No way. Someone with skills can see what I'm trying to do. A hacker? It has to be. But what do they know?*

I wrote the code to block what you are trying to find. It's not used for what I want. But I'm not alone. I have to be careful.

Jesus, what the hell is this person doing? His mind rushed over the possibilities. *Not just a hacker, but someone who actually writes the secure codes for financial transfers.* He realized if this person was involved in organized crime, then their life could be in danger.

I can keep you safe. Tell me what I need to know, and I can protect you.

He had no idea if he could actually do that, but the desire to find Erik overrode any other thought at the moment.

No one can protect me. But I will help you anyway. I

will send you what you need as soon as I can. Not right now – too dangerous. But soon.

No, no! He tried to get them to respond back, but the emails stopped coming. *Damn!* Trying to trace the origin of the emails, he came up empty. Thirty minutes later, he leaned back in his chair once more, this time the adrenaline pumping through his body. Standing, he moved over to his coffee maker, pouring another cup of the strong brew. Unwilling to leave, he settled in for a long night.

Pulling into a long driveway leading to a large, brick Colonial home, Bart parked the truck behind several other vehicles.

Faith looked out nervously at the decorated, picture-perfect home. *Bart grew up here?*

Picking up on her anxiety, he leaned over to take her hand, diverting her attention to his face. "Princess, it's just a house. That's all. It's the people inside that make the difference. Those people love me and will be excited to meet you."

Sucking in a deep breath before letting it out slowly, she pushed her long, dark hair behind her ears and moved her hands over her pants. "Okay," she smiled. "Let's do this."

Bart jumped out and rounded his truck. Assisting her down, he linked his fingers with hers as they walked to the front door holding a huge wreath. Before they made it to the doorbell, the door swung open and a beautiful woman stood there, her face bathed in happiness. Her silver-blonde hair was trimmed in a chin length bob. Her red turtleneck was paired with an outlandish Christmas vest, covered in tinsel and a string of lights that actually twinkled.

"Bart! You came!" she shouted, rushing forward to pull him into a hug.

"Hey, Mom," he greeted as his arms wrapped around her. "I see you're wearing the traditional Christmas vest." As she pulled back, he quickly introduced Faith. "Mom, I'd like you to meet Faith Romani. My girlfriend," he stated proudly. He watched his mother's eyes widen in shock and prayed she would not frighten Faith.

"Oh, my goodness," his mom said, her hand over her heart as her eyes moved to Faith. Instantly moving in, she enveloped Faith in a hug as well. "Welcome, welcome to our home!"

Stunned to find herself in an embrace, she answered, "Thank you for having me, Mrs. Taggart."

"Oh, forget the Mrs. Taggart! Call me Paula," she begged. She looked down at her appearance and explained, "The children gave me this vest about twenty years ago and I pull it out every Christmas Eve."

"It's lovely," Faith replied truthfully, glad to see that his mother was dressed for comfort.

"Mom, we're kind of freezing here," Bart reminded as he pulled Faith back into his embrace.

"Yes, yes, please come in," Paula said, leading the way into the tall entryway, complete with Christmas ball wreaths and evergreens on the side tables.

Faith looked around curiously as they made their way past a formal living room and dining room, both equally warm, as well as beautifully decorated. Moving into the large kitchen that included another eating area opening into the family room, she found the space filled with people and her heart began to pound once more.

A large man, resembling an older version of Bart that had to be his father, quickly stood and walked over to hug his son. His eyes immediately found Faith and he stepped over taking her hand in his. "Son, this is the first time you've ever brought a friend to celebrate with us. And such a pretty one, at that."

"Dad, this is my girlfriend, Faith Romani," Bart said, pulling her next to him again. He felt her body quiver and hoped his warmth would provide her with the support she craved when nervous.

"Girlfriend!" shouted a young girl, trying to get to Faith while tugging on another woman's hand.

"Faith, this is my sister Sandra and her little monkey, Julia," Bart introduced.

Faith once more found herself in an embrace, this time with his sister and her little girl, hanging onto her legs.

"What happened to your face?" Julia asked in innocence.

"Um...I was out running and fell down a hill," she lied as her fingers lightly touched her bandage.

The child was mollified, but Bart noticed his parents looking at him in question. Mouthing, *tell you later,* he then moved her farther into the room. He continued the rounds of introductions, including Sandra's husband, Roger, and Bart's brother, Will, and his wife, Tessa.

"My cousins are at their other grandmother's house and won't be over until later," Julia announced.

More? Faith felt overwhelmed with the number of people in the house already and could not imagine having more to meet.

"Faith, can you help us in the kitchen?" Paula asked as Sandra, Tessa, and Julia began to move into the adjacent room. Her eyes glanced up at Bart and noticed his worried expression. Gifting him with a smile and a wink, she moved out of his embrace to follow the other women.

Bart stood nervously for a second, hoping that she was not about to be grilled by the others. *Or, God forbid, told embarrassing stories.* He was startled when a hand clamped on his shoulder.

"She'll be fine," his father said, a huge smile on his face. "Your mother'll have a care with her." Then, propelling his son into the den, he said, "Girlfriend? We've got some catching up to do, son!"

An hour later, after Bart had explained how he met Faith and she had been politely questioned in the kitchen about their relationship, the family sat down to dinner. He kept his eye on her, but she laughed and smiled during the meal. He finally relaxed, knowing his family had welcomed her just like he knew they would.

"Will you two be staying with us?" Paula asked hopefully.

"Sorry, Mom. I figured the house would be full and I've made reservations somewhere for Faith and me for the night."

Faith turned quickly, her eyes searching his in question. His face only returned a grin, and she could not help but grin as well.

Will and Tessa's two tow-headed boys came in as dessert was being served, bounding in with energy, greeting Faith and Bart enthusiastically.

"Uncle Bart, look what I got!" the oldest shouted. In his hands was the newest popular children's series book.

"Wow," he said. "I didn't think it was out yet."

"It came out yesterday and dad waited in a long line at the bookstore to get it."

"Do you like to read?" Faith asked softly.

He turned his enthusiastic face toward her and replied, "Oh yeah. I've got every one of these books as soon as they came out. I read lots, but these are my favorite."

After dinner, Bart and Faith said their heartfelt good-byes with promises to visit the next day. Steering her to his truck, he quickly turned on the heat as he pulled out of the driveway.

"Where are we going?" Faith asked, unable to contain her curiosity.

"It's a surprise, princess," he replied, a grin on his face.

About twenty minutes later, they pulled up to what she now considered to be their B&B, a squeal escaping her. "Oh, Bart. This is wonderful!"

After he assisted her down from his truck, he leaned back and grabbed their overnight bags. Escorting her inside, they were greeted enthusiastically by Mrs. Carswell.

"How lovely to see you two again! I have you all registered from the last time. Please follow me," she said.

Walking up the stairs, Faith wondered if she would have the same room. She was beginning to feel an affinity for the quaint blue and yellow room with the window toward the ocean. She was surprised when they bypassed the second floor and continued up the stairs toward the third.

At the top of the stairs was only one door. Swinging it open, Mrs. Carswell stepped through, flipping on the light to a large, delightful, attic bedroom. The room held a white, distressed chest of drawers and matching dresser with a mirror over the center. A king-sized bed was in the center of the back wall and a door opening to a large, private bathroom was to the side. A sliding glass door opened onto a small deck overlooking the ocean, containing two comfortable lounging chairs.

Faith looked around, her thoughts racing. *Is this room for Bart? Or me? Or—*

"I was happy when you called to say that you wanted this room," Mrs. Carswell said. Leaning forward, she whispered loudly, "Many a happy couple have stayed here, I assure you."

Faith's gaze jerked first to the happy woman showing them the bathroom and deck and then up to Bart's smiling face. Her face flamed, both with embarrassment... and anticipation.

Mrs. Carswell paused at the door, saying, "Remember, breakfast is at eight," before walking back down the stairs.

Faith stood in the middle of the room, her wide eyes locked onto Bart's. He stalked toward her, a nervous expression on his face. Reaching her, he instinctively wrapped his arms around her, pulling her into his body.

Resting his chin on the top of her head, he wondered what she thought. *Too much? Too soon? Too forward?* The entire afternoon and evening flew through his head in a flash. Taking her to meet his family. Having his brother and father grill him about her since he had never introduced them to a woman before. His mother's delighted expression as she warmly talked to Faith. He had never made special reservations anywhere for a woman before either and hoped this surprise was welcome. Unable to wait any longer, he asked, "Princess? Are you all right with this?"

Hearing the nervousness in his voice endeared him to her even more. Smiling as her cheek rested against his strong heartbeat, she nodded. "Yes. It's been a wonderful day." Lifting her face so that she was looking up into his eyes, she continued. "I was nervous, but I really like your family."

His arms tightened more, and he admitted, "Well, you'll meet Nonnie tomorrow. I'll warn you, she'll latch onto you and have you picking out china before you can blink."

Laughing, she replied, "I think I can hold her off."

Bart grinned but found himself thinking that he would not mind if Nonnie went overboard. He lifted his right hand and cupped her cheek, bringing his mouth down to hers. *Jesus, have I only known this woman for a week?*

Before he could deepen the kiss, she pulled back slightly. "Do you mind if I take a shower before we...uh..."

Bart's grin spread slowly as he brushed his nose against hers, then down to her neck. "Not at all, Princess. Mind if I join you?"

Her lips curved as she shook her head, a soft laugh escaping as his mouth lingered briefly at her neck.

He didn't hesitate. Scooping her into his arms, earning a surprised squeal as she wrapped herself around him. Carrying her into the bathroom, he set her gently on her feet before reaching past her to turn on the water. Steam began to rise as the spray warmed.

His hands moved to the hem of her sweater, lifting it slowly as his gaze followed. He paused, taking her in. Not with hunger alone, but with appreciation that made her breath catch.

She answered in kind, slipping out of the rest of her clothes, her movements a little bolder now, a little more certain. When she reached for him, her fingers brushing the edge of his shirt, her voice softened.

"Don't you want to join me?"

"Always," he murmured.

For a moment, they simply stood there, close, the air thick with anticipation. Then he guided her toward the shower.

Warm water cascaded over them, washing away the last of the day's tension. She tipped her head back as he reached for her hair, his fingers gentle as he worked through it, massaging slowly.

Her eyes drifted closed, a soft sigh escaping as she leaned into his touch.

When she turned, her gaze traveled over him... not hurried, not shy, but curious. Appreciative.

His answering smile was quiet, almost reverent as he dipped his head, brushing a kiss along her forehead. "I take it you like what you see?" he asked softly.

"Very much," she admitted.

"Well," he said, his voice lowering, "I don't think I've ever seen anything more beautiful."

She searched his eyes, finding only truth there. Rising onto her toes, she kissed him slow at first, exploratory, before the kiss deepened naturally. The water continued to fall around them, but neither seemed to notice.

He drew her closer, his hands steady at her waist as the kiss grew more intense. For a moment, the world narrowed again to just the two of them... the warmth, the closeness, the quiet trust building between them.

She pressed closer, her hands moving over him as though memorizing, and his breath caught at the contact.

"Princess..." he murmured, a warning and a promise all at once.

But she only smiled.

And whatever restraint he'd been holding onto slipped.

He lifted her easily, turning so the spray fell against his back, shielding her from the water as he pressed her gently against the tile. Their foreheads brushed, breaths mingling, the moment stretching, deepening.

"Bart..." she whispered.

"I've got you," he answered.

Later, the sound of the water softened around them, steam curling through the air as they stood wrapped in each other.

Her head rested against his shoulder, her breathing slowly evening out, while his arms held her steady, as though he had no intention of letting go.

Neither of them spoke. They didn't need to.

Lifting his forehead from the wall he gazed into her eyes, seeing warmth in their depths. Smiling, he slid his lips over hers again, kissing her gently. His hand slowly lowered her feet to the tub as he made sure she was steady. After washing her lovingly, he reached around, turning off the water. Smoothing her wet hair back from her face, he noticed the deep blush.

"What's wrong?"

"Do you think Mrs. Carswell could hear us? I kind of... yelled."

Chuckling as he stepped out of the tub before turning to lift her onto the thick bathmat, he wrapped a fluffy towel around her body not wanting it to chill. "Yeah, you did yell and, I gotta tell you, it was hot!"

Pretending to slap his arm, she blushed deeper. Before she could dry off, Bart took the thick towel and patted her dry then quickly dried himself.

"Come on, princess."

Linking his fingers with hers, he led her into the bedroom, settling them between the soft flannel sheets under the thick comforter.

Tucking her into his embrace, he kissed her once more. Their eyes locked onto each other's as the moonlight streamed through the window, casting a glow on their faces.

She reveled in his arms, feeling warm, safe...*loved?* Before she pondered that emotion further, he kissed her forehead, pulling her into his body.

"Sleep, baby. We'll enjoy Christmas Eve tomorrow with more of my family. And I promise it'll be a great day."

Closing her eyes, she remembered how happy his family was as she was introduced as his girlfriend. Hoping his grandmother felt the same, she drifted off to sleep, secure in the knowledge that Bart would take care of her.

She awoke, heart pounding, as the early morning light was beginning to peek through the windows. Her dream... so vivid...so detailed. Turning her head slightly, she could see Bart's face peaceful in slumber. Slipping from the bed, she moved to one of the chairs in the room, wrapping herself in a soft blanket and grabbed her art pad from her bag. Trying to keep from waking him, she closed her eyes, allowing the image to form clearly in her mind once more.

Her fingers automatically held the pencil and began their work. Lines, curves, shapes—all began to blend together as she felt light-headed, hoping to re-create the vision. Her nerves were taut, and the air in the room seemed thick, making it difficult for her to breathe.

Her fingers stopped their movements, and she stared

at the pad held in her arms. Once more, the dark-haired boy, who was looking more and more like Erik, looked up from the book on his lap. He was sitting on rumpled bed covers, a blank wall behind him, but with the corner of a bookcase on the side. He was smiling in this image—the same smile that she had seen the previous day but had been unable to connect to him. It was directed at someone out of her sight. Her eyes moved to the book on his lap, this time, closed instead of open. She peered closely, looking at the cover. As realization washed over her, she gasped. The cover was the same as the book Bart's nephew held in his hand from the night before. The new book. The one that had just been published.

Heart pounding, she tried to rationalize her image. *Am I simply putting two different scenes together? Am I imposing the idea of what he's reading to having seen the book last night? Oh, Babushka, what am I seeing?*

23

Luke stayed long into the night, sleeping fitfully on the sofa that was in the compound's main room. A small room to the side held bunk beds in case any of the Saints had to spend the night, but Luke was unwilling to be in a different room from his computers. He wanted to be close to the tenuous connection he had to someone that seemed to be able, and willing, to help unravel the complex financial trail from Ivan's extortion money to whoever it was going to.

An alert dinged in the silent room, jolting him awake instantly. Rushing over, he quickly recognized another email had come in. Clicking, he read the message.

Look to the beginning.

What the hell? Beginning of what?

He typed, **I need more than that.**

No, you don't. You're smart. This is all I can give you. It's not safe. I'm sorry.

His heart pounded as his fingers flew over the keyboard fast and furiously, trying to follow the email trail to discover who was sending the cryptic message. *Nothing!*

He looked at the clock. Three a.m. He hated to call up to Jack but had no choice. Picking up the phone that connected to the house phone upstairs, he dialed. Jack's sleep rough voice answered, "What've you got?"

"Boss, you gotta call everyone in."

"Right. On it." Within three minutes, Jack came downstairs into the room. He had not asked Luke why he needed everyone—he trusted his men completely.

Luke met him and showed him the emails. "I can't get a trail of who is sending these but, I'm telling you, they have to be from someone who knows what the hell is going on."

Jack nodded his agreement and said, "ETA for the others is about twenty minutes. We'll wait and go over it all when they arrive."

A half hour later, all of the Saints except Bart were around the table. Jack quickly thanked them for coming and had Luke take over.

"I'm sending the emails to your tablets, and you can read what came in." He gave them a minute to read through the notes, listening to their mummers of surprise.

"Before you ask, I can't tell you who sent them because I can't track it." Looking around, he saw their amazement. "I'm telling you that whoever is sending these, has a sophisticated encryption system rivaling anything I've ever seen."

"You think it came from one of the camps trying to cast suspicion on someone else?" Blaise asked.

"No way," Luke answered. "Whoever has these elaborate computer programs and systems has top notch equipment and education. No way does Miguel or Gavrill have this kind of power."

"What about Maldoni or Sergio?" Chad queried.

"I don't see them having the money or the intel. I think it's someone from the outside. Someone not involved in the case at all." He once again saw their incredulous expressions. "There are tons of computer geeks around, usually getting their start in college dorm rooms of some of the best computer software engineering programs. Many learn some added hacking skills and most go on to jobs where they can make some serious money with gaming, business, software development, whatever. But a few—true geniuses—are able to take their knowledge to a different level. They can be sought after by companies or the government because of their ability to develop secure...super secure programs. I gotta tell you most are snapped up by companies who pay them a shit-ton of money—more money than the government can pay."

"You think this is someone private, who may have developed software to hide the various money laundering transactions and now have found out that you're trying to crack it?" Jack asked.

"If that's the case, wouldn't they want to keep someone from getting the information? Why contact you to offer to help?" Monty asked, knowing the FBI had no system as elaborate as what he was hearing about. "Why wouldn't someone want to work for an agency instead of using it to help criminals?"

Chad said, "They're scared. They admit they're in danger. Could be they started working for someone, not knowing what the software would be used for. Now they understand and want to help."

Jack pierced Luke with his stare. "Luke, you're in this. What do you think?"

"I don't know, but we've got no reason not to trust this person right now. We've got nothing else to go on. The FBI hasn't been able to find Erik and we're no closer to finding out who might be threatening Faith."

"All right," Jack acknowledged. "What does it mean to look to the beginning?"

"The only beginning I can think of is Krustas," Luke admitted, "but that doesn't make any sense."

"Let's focus on someone from Krustas' organization," Jack ordered.

Monty sent the dossiers from Ivan's businesses to Luke, who forwarded them to the others. Looking over Ivan's contacts, it was evident there were not many. "He holds the reigns tight with his company. Other than family, there are only a couple of men who help run his dealings."

"Looking at these men, I don't see anything different," Luke commented. "They've been with him for many years and there's nothing to suggest their money is from anything other than him."

"Check out the ones closest to Ivan. Hell, check out Ivan himself. Maybe this is some kind of perverse way to get attention or... damnit!" Marc said sharply, getting the consideration of the other Saints. "What if Ivan's doing this to put the heat on his competitors?"

"I'm on it," Luke confirmed.

"While you're doing that, check out the nephews as well. I've got a feeling we're staring at the solution and just can't quite see it," Jack said as the rest of the men poured over the information.

Bart stirred in the bed, reaching his hand out to caress Faith, finding her side cold. Lifting his head quickly, he blinked as the sunlight peeked in the windows and heard the water running in the bathroom. Standing, he moved to the door and was about to knock as Faith walked out. His warm greeting halted in his throat at the expression on her face.

"What's wrong?" he asked, pulling her into his arms.

"I...dreamed," she said haltingly, before lifting her head to peer into his eyes.

"Faith, you don't have to be afraid of what I'm going to say," he admonished, leading her over to the bed, pulling her down beside him. Holding her cold hands in his, he rubbed them. "What did you dream?"

She sat for a moment, then stood and walked over to her art pad. "I got up early this morning to capture what I was feeling...seeing." She turned it around, showing the latest drawing to him.

Bart searched the pictures, seeing the same child as before, this time his smiling face raised up as though looking up at someone else in the room. The bed appeared the same, but the corner of a bookshelf was added to the drawing. Try as he might, he could not fathom what had Faith so upset.

"Princess, I know there's something here that bothers you...I need you to point it out because I'm not following you."

She pointed a shaky finger to the book in the boy's lap. "Look at the title."

He followed her gaze and saw the book that was the same as his nephew's from the night before. *What does she think it means? Is she just dreaming and mixing up the details from my family to Erik?* Even with the questions running through his mind, he found himself trusting her. Completely.

"You see something here," he said, "and I want you to know I trust you totally." He saw the doubt pass over her face and hated that his words from a week ago put that look on her face now. "I'm being honest, Faith. I totally trust you. Tell me what you see."

Licking her lips, she said, "It's Erik. I feel it. I know it."

"Okay?" he said slowly, drawing the word out in a question, prompting her for more.

"Bart, he's smiling. He's not scared. Whoever he's looking at is someone he trusts. Someone who does not frighten him. And the book? Your nephew said it only came out yesterday, so if someone has given it to him, he's still alive. And well. And being looked after, by someone who cares for him."

Bart's eyes moved back to the drawing. He could see what she had seen in her dream, but was it real? *Was it the imaginings of an overactive dream? Or the visions from a woman who has a special gift. One in which he had never believed.* The idea of his grandfather standing with him filled his mind. *Search for truth, Bartholomew. Always search for truth.*

Bart suddenly realized his grandfather never immediately dismissed something without first searching for the truth. His gaze lifted to her doubtful one and, before he could stop them, words flew from his mouth. "I believe you. I believe in you, and I believe you."

Her face glowed as she rushed into his arms. "What does it mean?" she asked, her words muffled by his chest.

His fingers found their way through his hair and slid down to clinch his neck as his mind raced. Pulling her back, he said, "We need to go to Ivan's. You need to be back in his presence and the presence of some of the family. Maybe...maybe...oh hell, Faith, I don't know. Maybe you'll get a better idea then."

Just then his phone vibrated, and he snagged if off the nightstand. "Yeah, boss?"

Jack quickly filled him in on what Luke had uncovered...or what had been revealed to him. Bart, in return, told Jack about the revelation Faith had. He looked up as she nervously twisted her fingers in the bottom of his large T-shirt she was wearing. Winking, he tried to reassure her Jack would not be judging her.

Disconnecting, he said, "Get dressed, princess. We've got to head back to Charlestown. I'll explain as we're getting ready."

She jerked his shirt over her head and knelt at her overnight bag, pulling out her bra and a clean sweater. Bart's mind, normally focused on a mission, short-wired as his gaze perused her gorgeous, panty-clad body.

"Damn, girl," he growled.

Lifting her gaze to him, she blushed. "Get your mind back on the case, Bart. You can ogle me later!"

Grumbling while he pulled on his jeans, he began to explain Jack's news.

She looked askance. "Bart, if Ivan was engineering this, why would he take a chance in calling me in?"

"Hell if I know," came Bart's reply, his mind working overtime trying to process the intel. "Maybe he was sure you wouldn't be able to see anything. Or maybe he thought he was too smart. Or may—"

"Or maybe he's not guilty," she replied.

Bart walked over, placing his hands on her shoulders, saying, "Look Faith. We don't know who's guilty, but we're following a hunch that it's someone in Ivan's camp. Associate or family member or him. I don't really want you involved in this at all, but I need you. I need your insight."

Nodding, she realized what a leap of trust he was making. "Okay. What do you need me to do?"

Leaning down to grab the closed bags, he stood and said, "Let's go make our excuses to Mrs. Carswell and we'll plan in the truck."

Several minutes later, after compromising with the proprietress and taking travel mugs full of her coffee and a pastry bag filled with some breakfast treats, they were on their way.

Bart had been planning and, as soon as they pulled onto the road, he said, "Okay, here's what I've got so far. We're going to go back to Constance's house. Ivan is with her for Christmas Eve. We'll stick to the truth, which is, we came out to meet up with my family and since we were passing them on our way back home, we didn't want to leave without seeing how they're doing. You ask questions...or not. Um...I guess I'll leave it up to you to do... uh...whatever you do."

"Don't worry, I've got this."

He turned to peer into her serious face. "I know you do, princess. I trust you."

"But what if I don't get any feelings with him?"

"If we're lucky, the rest of the family will be there too. Jack didn't say it was confirmed to be Ivan. They just think it might be someone close."

"What were the words that person used to Luke?"

"They said to look to the beginning."

"Beginning." She thought for a moment but could not come up with another meaning. Pushing her hair back from her face, she sighed heavily. "I really don't want to think he could have done this," she admitted softly.

Bart glanced at her, nodding his head. "I know you don't, but you've got to remember he's not just a grandfather, but also a ruthless man who's run the Russian Mafia for years in this area. We have no real idea what he's capable of."

Less than four hours later, they pulled into the circular driveway at Constance's house. Several cars were there, and Bart recognized the presence of the FBI as well.

A sense of déjà vu moved over Faith as she thought about their visit here a week ago. *Was it only a week?* Watching Bart as he alighted from the truck and stalked around the front to her door, she also realized how much they had changed in that time. *I met him last week...it seems like much longer.*

It was no surprise to be greeted by Mrs. Dukakas at the door and she explained that Constance had the rest of the family here to support each other during Christmas. She escorted them into the living room, where they found Ivan, Anton, Dmitry, and Constance.

Ivan walked over, shaking Bart's hand and kissing Faith's. "To what do we owe this pleasure of your visit?" he asked smoothly.

Bart noticed Ivan's face still appeared ravaged and at, a quick glance, so did Constance's. Anton and Dmitry were harder to get a feel for, but the entire room appeared subdued.

"We were coming back from a visit with my parents and we both wanted to come by to offer our continued support for your situation."

"And to find out if there is anything we can do for you," Faith added softly.

"Oh, you are a dear," Ivan said, leading her over to the sofa where Constance sat. The two women greeted each other, but then Constance sat with her head down, twisting a tissue in her hands.

Anton and Dmitry greeted them as well and the men moved to the side of the room. Mrs. Dukakas brought homemade eggnog in for the group, as well as a tray of pastries. Faith helped serve and then sat back on the sofa next to Constance, hoping to draw her into a conversation.

"Have you heard anything else?" Bart asked Ivan. "I saw the agents on the outside and wondered if you had any news?"

"Nothing new," Ivan reported. "I've made two payments, but both were accompanied with a note saying Erik would stay safe as long as I keep paying."

"Bastards!" Anton groused quietly, looking over to see that Constance was not listening.

"I don't understand who would do this," Dmitry added, his eyes shifting over to Constance as well.

"How's she holding up?" Bart asked softly, his head nodding in the direction of the sofa.

"She stays to herself mostly," Ivan added. "Dmitry has tried to see her more since he's in graduate school at the university in Charleston. And of course, Mrs. Dukakas has been keeping an eye on her."

"She has lots of visitors—friends who want to check on her—but she mostly turns them away according to Mrs. Dukakas," Dmitry added. "She'll go out occasionally to visit close friends, trying to keep up some routine."

"I'm sure the holidays don't help," Bart noted.

"We were sure we would have him back by Christmas," Ivan said, his voice laced with pain.

The men continued to talk for a few minutes while Faith tried unsuccessfully to draw Constance into a conversation. Erik's mother spoke little, keeping her eyes on her lap.

Faith looked around the room at the Christmas decorations. She closed her eyes for a moment, feeling fear pouring off Constance. Her neck tingled as the emotions in the room began swirling around. *Fear, pain, uncertainty, guilt. Guilt? Of course...survivor's guilt.* Faith opened her eyes and glanced at the woman next to her.

Bart moved away with Ivan, to the side of the room, as they discussed the case in more depth. Faith walked over to them, taking the opportunity to be closer to Ivan. "I'm afraid there's little I can say to make Constance feel better. I can only image her anguish."

Ivan nodded his agreement. "Yes, I find I'm tongue-tied around her as well."

As Bart and Ivan continued to talk softly, she lowered her head, closing her eyes, allowing the feelings to wash over her again. *Fear, sadness, anger.* A vision of Ivan and his grandson playing in the yard filled her mind. Laughter. Sunshine. She jerked her gaze up to him, seeing Ivan staring at her carefully, as though he knew what she was doing.

Bart drew Ivan's attention back to him as Faith moved away. She tried to still her breathing, clearing her mind, but the images crowded into her mind.

She noted Anton and Dmitry had moved to the fireplace as they sipped their drinks. Walking on unsteady legs, she made her way to them, hoping the expression on her face was one of concern and not scrutiny.

"I haven't had a chance to offer my sympathies to the two of you. When we first met, everything was crazy and well...I wanted to make sure you knew that I'm very sorry about Erik. I pray that the FBI will be able to locate him soon."

Anton nodded politely, thanking her. Dmitry smiled at her, offering his appreciation as well.

"I wasn't able to offer much to Constance. I can't image what she's going through. It must be a comfort for her to have you nearby, Dmitry."

"I'm afraid I'm not here much, with my studies and work during the day, but at least I'm here as much as I can be."

She nodded and moved to the mantle, pretending to study the ornate Christmas decorations placed there. She recognized some as antiques, similar to her grandmother's. Closing her eyes, she once again tried to allow the emotions to flood through her. Her neck tingled once more as she let images run freely through her mind.

Anton, playing with Erik. Dmitry, teaching him to ride a bike. Family gatherings...a previous Christmas in this very room. The images poured through her, then began to be crowded out as emotions moved into her consciousness. Many, the same as the others. *Fear...anger...hurt...anguish... guilt. Guilt again? Survivor's guilt?*

Once more, she tried to steady her pounding heartbeat, hoping no one was paying attention to her. Before she opened her eyes, she was unaware someone was staring at her. Dark eyes focused on her. Knowing eyes. Guilty eyes.

24

——————

The room began to close in on Faith as the assault of emotions swirled around her. Unable to discern where they were all coming from, she hurried over to the nearest chair and sat quickly. Catching Bart's concerned eye, she gave a silent plea.

Bart casually disengaged and walked over to where she was, placing his hand comfortably on her shoulder. "We really need to get going, Faith." Giving her the excuse needed, she smiled gratefully and stood, leaning her weight slightly into him. Offering their goodbyes, they made their way out of the room, following Mrs. Dukakas to the door. Faith felt the prickles of needles in her back the entire way out of the house.

Once inside the truck, she blurted, "I know you may not believe me, but Bart, I swear there was something wrong in that room. I didn't feel it last week, or maybe it was just buried underneath all the grief, but there is something now. Something real."

"I believe you, princess," he vowed. "What do you need to do? Is there something I can do?"

Shaking her head, she replied, "No, no. I just...I..." Her voice trailed off as the images filled her mind. "I need to draw."

Bart thought for a second, then said, "What about we go back to my place? Can you work there?"

Nodding, she agreed. "I know it's Christmas Eve but, for the first time, things are so strong."

Reaching across the console, Bart grabbed her hand giving it a squeeze. "You don't have to explain. We'll go there. I'll leave you alone to allow you to do your drawings and then we'll discover what you can come up with."

Sucking in a deep breath, she let it out slowly. Closing her eyes, she felt the images of the dark-haired boy coming into her mind, strong and steady.

Faith allowed Bart to take charge once they arrived at his house. She rushed in to see Smee, glad to see that he and Apollo had achieved a civil détente.

Once settled, Bart turned to see Faith's pale face, the faraway expression worrying him. Unsure, he stood awkwardly for a moment before finally pulling her body into his, offering his warmth. She wrapped her arms around his waist, pressing her cheek against his chest, feeling his steady heartbeat against her face.

Surrounded by all that Bart was, the calm descended. Looking up, searching his eyes, she saw acceptance, concern, trust.

"What do you need me to do, Faith?" he asked.

Pulling away from him slightly, she answered, "I really need some quiet time. I just need to let the feelings, emotions, and images flow through my drawings."

"How about if I order some lunch? We can have take-out, and I'll stay out of your way."

"You're right. We need to eat, and I'll work where it'll be quiet."

Leaning down, he kissed her gently. Moving back slightly, he smiled, thinking how much he loved her kisses. Deep, long, and passionate. Or just a touch of her intoxicating lips. One of promise or one of a quick good-bye. *I thought I was falling...but I've already fallen in love with her.* Even with everything swirling around them, he could not keep the smile off his face. *When this is over, I'll tell her...and hope to hell she feels the same.*

He placed the call for Chinese delivery and was stunned when they said it would take almost forty-five minutes to deliver. After they explained they were short-handed today, he considered going out to get it. *No, I need to be here in case she remembers something as she's drawing.* He agreed, then moved to the study that overlooked the front yard. Faith walked into the room, her coat and scarf on. He looked up questioningly but, before he could ask, she said, "I'm going to sit on the back deck. I know it's chilly, but the deck is in the sun right now and I feel the need to have fresh air."

Nodding, he agreed, "Whatever you need to work best."

After a few minutes, he slipped into the kitchen and looked out of the sliding glass door to see her sitting in a deck chair, her art pad in her lap and her fingers flying over the paper. Smiling, he walked back to the study and pulled out his phone, calling Jack. Leaning back in his chair, he spent the next thirty minutes going over the case, along with the new information, with the Saints.

Sitting on the deck, Faith found the fresh air cleared her mind of everything except the images that were flying onto the page from her fingertips. She quickly drew a picture of Ivan playing with Erik. An image of Anton playing games with him. Dmitry teaching him to ride his bike. Page after page of images.

Come on, Faith. Do it. Let it flow. Please, Babushka, let me get those evil emotions down onto the paper. She began to draw once more, the electricity moving through her, the tingling at her neck and down her arms. Her breath came in pants as her heartbeat pounded a staccato rhythm.

The form of Erik sitting on his bed, this time dressed in clothes instead of his pajamas, filled the page. The new book was still on his lap. The bookcase against the wall. A light coming from the ceiling was now clearly visible.

Her vision was blurry, and a rushing filled her ears as she immersed herself in the world of her drawing. Her fingers continued to create as though a will that was beyond her own was taking over. Erik's face, relaxed in a smile, looking up at...*oh my God!*

She stared, shocked at her drawing, her heart pounding. *What if this isn't real? What if this is just my imagination? Babushka, what do I do?* Feeling faint, she closed her eyes against the swirling images fearfully swarming at her. She worked to still her breathing—*in, out, in, out.* Slowly, sucking in enough oxygen, she opened her eyes and gazed at the picture once more. And she knew. It was real.

The doorbell finally rang, and Bart disconnected. Opening the door, he gratefully accepted the food bags and tipped the driver handsomely for working on

Christmas Eve. He moved to the dining room table where he set the food out, admonishing Smee to move off the table, and shouting at Apollo to stop barking.

Walking into the kitchen to see what Apollo was barking at, he headed to the sliding glass door, sure that Faith must be frozen by this time and wanting to hustle her inside.

Apollo continued to jump on the glass, growling and barking incessantly. Bart stopped short, seeing her sitting motionless in the chair and the art pad lying on her lap. Rushing to the door, he jerked it open, flying onto the deck.

At the same instance, Faith startled from her trance at the noise behind her. Before she could rise, Bart reached her and knelt down beside the chair.

"Princess, it's freezing out here." He bent to scoop her up when she grabbed the front of his shirt.

"Bart, I know. I know where Erik is."

Bart halted in mid-squat, his eyes searching hers before dropping to the art pad in her lap. He stared dumbly for an instant before lifting his eyes back to hers. He scooped her up in his arms as she grabbed the pad and said, "We gotta call Jack and Mitch."

Marching inside, he ordered Apollo to sit before gently placing Faith in a dining room chair. The smell of their meal would normally have been tantalizing, but all she felt was nausea.

Placing a call to Jack, he told him what Faith had drawn. "I'm calling Mitch, but I'm heading there now. I may need backup so send whoever is available on Christmas Eve."

He continued to talk for another minute as Faith watched, stunned. *He never asked if I was sure. He never questioned. Neither did Jack. They believe me.* Taking another deep, shuddering breath, she cleared her mind, readying herself for what was to come.

By the time she stood, Bart was already on the phone to Mitch, coordinating the meeting place. His heart hardened as he called Jack back with the rendezvous point. Stalking to his hall closet, she watched as he armed himself quickly with the Kevlar and weapons he had a license to carry.

As he approached her to say goodbye, he noticed she still had her coat on and was waiting by the front door. Cocking his head to the side he glared down but, before he could speak, she beat him to it.

"I have to go with you. While I know the drawing is right, there could be something else I'm not seeing right now. We can't afford to waste time with me here when I could possibly help there."

He sputtered, wanting to deny her, but stopped for a second sucking in a deep breath, held it, and then let it out slowly. *Focus. Plan the mission. She's right. She could be of use.* Nodding reluctantly, he agreed. *Now execute the mission.*

Stepping into her space, he gazed deeply into her eyes. "You do what I say, when I say it, princess. No exceptions."

She nodded, adding, "Don't worry, Bart. I've got no desire to be a hero."

He grabbed her hand as he ran to his truck, roaring it to life, and backed out of his driveway to race down the street. Glancing to the side, seeing her pale face, he thought, *You already are a hero.*

Sitting in the truck cab, Faith watched as Jack, Chad, Blaise, Cam, and Monty met in a local parking lot. She saw another SUV pull up, seeing Mitch arrive. The men grouped, talking in hushed tones. As tense as the situation was, she could not help but admire the men giving up their Christmas Eve on nothing more than her hunch. Watching them, a circle of controlled testosterone, she also admired their form. As her gaze roved over the gathering, she smiled as her eyes landed on Bart, the tallest and largest of the group. *Well, maybe Cam's a little taller.* But Bart was the only one holding her attention. *How far we've come in a week.*

The driver's door opened, jerking Faith out of her musings. Her eyes sought his for instructions.

"We're going to the location and parking nearby. Don't come into Constance's house," he added with emphasis, "Mitch and Monty will go in the front, and I'll go around the back. Got that?"

She nodded. "Got it," she replied.

Within a few minutes, they parked down the street from the location. She watched as the men spread out, moving steadily. She sat back, looking around, her nerves needing something else to focus on. A tingling began at the back of her neck as her eyes stayed on one place. Nerves taut, she jerked her gaze back to where the men had disappeared, before looking to the opposite side of the street again. *It's there, I'm sure of it.* Her stomach clenched with anxiety. *But who's there? What if I'm wrong? What if I lead them to a neighbor's house and it's wrong?* Closing her eyes for a moment, she allowed the images to form and solidify in her mind. Opening her eyes as she stared at the new location, she knew. Grabbing her phone from her purse, she sent a text to Bart.

Across the street. Basement. I'm sure.

She waited a few minutes, but no response came back from Bart. *If I check it out, then I won't take a chance on sending the cavalry in falsely.* Sliding out of the truck, she saw no one around as she crept around toward the back of the neighbor's house. Seeing several low, rectangle windows that would indicate they belonged to the basement, she moved to the back of the house where she hid behind shrubs before approaching the windows. Trying one, she found what she expected. *Locked.* Looking around, she did not see anyone, so she checked her phone again. No response to her text. *Jesus, what do I do? What if I'm wrong?* Sending Bart another text, she waited an anxious minute. No response. Butterflies warred in her stomach as her restlessness had her trying another window.

This time, the window jiggled, and the latch slid out of its catch. Wide-eyed, she stared. Leaning around the bush, she tried to see if Bart or one of the others was coming. *Damnit! Do I go back or go in?* Her fingers moved the glass window back and forth a couple of times, noting it made no noise.

Follow your instincts, Printsessa. Faith startled as her grandmother's voice came to her as though she were next to her. Sucking in a deep breath, she fired off another text.

Going in.

Pulling the window open all the way and propping it with a stick, she peeked her head in. All was quiet. It appeared to be a small room in what must be the basement. She noticed a few plastic storage containers along the wall. Pulling her head back out, she twisted her body around and slid her legs in first. Slowly, on her stomach, she scooted backward until her feet found the boxes underneath her. Testing them gently, she continued to hold onto the windowsill until she was entirely in the basement. Moving her feet until they felt steady, she squatted before attempting to hop down to the floor.

The top box shifted as she jumped, falling off the stack and crashing to the concrete floor. *Damnit!* She stood, statue-like, until she was sure there were no other noises to be heard. Instantly filled with the realization she was breaking and entering, she placed her hand on her stomach, pressing in to still the nerves. Fighting the desire to throw up, she glanced around the room.

The walls were painted cinderblock. Metal shelves lined one side, holding empty plastic tubs labeled Christmas. A door on the opposite side of her was the only exit. She moved on rubbery legs, carefully making her way to the door. Locked. *Of course,* she thought ruefully. *I would break into a closet with a locked door. Bart, where are you?*

Taking a moment to gather her wits, she looked back down at the doorknob. It appeared to be a simple, push-button type of doorknob lock with nothing but a hole in the middle on her side. *It's not a deadbolt!* She reached up to her hair, pulling out a bobby-pin and wondered if she would be able to pick the lock. *It doesn't look difficult on TV...but what do I know?*

She inserted one end into the hole and jiggled it around. In a few seconds, she felt something inside that the bobby pin was hitting against. Continuing to move it around, pressing against the obstruction, she heard a click. She winced in fear as the noise echoed in the concrete room. She held her breath waiting to see if someone had been alerted. Licking her dry lips, she finally let the air rush out of her lungs in relief.

Pressing her ear against the door for several minutes,

she heard nothing. No talking. No movement. Taking the knob in her hand, she turned it slowly, her heart pounding in her chest. When the doorknob reached its limit, she pulled the door open an inch at a time once more holding her breath. Still no sounds.

When the door opened enough for her to peek out, she realized she was in a larger basement room. A few pieces of furniture, some paintings, and odds and ends lined the walls. On the other side of the room were stairs that she assumed led to the main level of the house.

Tiptoeing up the steps she hesitated at the top, leaning her ear close to the door, hearing voices on the other side. Voices raised in anger.

"What are we going to do now?" a voice spoke, soft, but vibrating with anger. "I'm telling you, I think she knows."

"I don't know what to do now," a deeper voice answered. "But we have to do something. We need to get him out of here."

"We've got a good thing going, and I'm not about to have it fucked up because of some seer," the first voice said.

"You believe she can really tell what's going on? What we've done?"

"I've got no idea if she can or not, but I saw the look on her face. I know she knows something."

"What if she finds out what's downstairs?"

"Well, tomorrow it won't matter. We're leaving."

"Shh. Look, there's that FBI guy's SUV across the road. Fuck, I'd better get over there."

Faith heard retreating footsteps but felt no safer. Not able to see what was happening on the other side of the door, she was too afraid to try to escape that way. Turning their words over in her mind, she glanced around the room as she quietly went back down the steps. *What's downstairs?* Looking around, she saw nothing out of the ordinary for a basement. Boxes, metal shelves with plastic tubs. An old table and a few chairs in one corner. A treadmill covered in dust that looked like it had not been used in ages.

Sighing deeply, she rubbed her temples, trying to keep the threatening headache from overtaking her. Walking to one wall, she began slowly perusing the area. Nothing. The hairs on the back of her neck began to stand on end and she felt her vision blur.

Unsure if what was happening was nerves or—

A sudden vision filled her mind as she passed by one of the shelving units. She closed her eyes tightly as her hands reached out to steady her shaking body. Knuckles white against the grey metal shelves, she pulled involuntarily. They moved.

Her eyes flew open as she looked at the area that had shifted. Instead of just metal shelves moving away from the wall, it was evident they hid another door. Her breath came in pants as she walked on unsteady feet to the edge and peeked around. Her hand reached out to the doorknob of its own volition. The rushing of blood roared in her ears as she turned the knob and slowly opened the door.

It swung open and a gasp escaped her lips.

———

25

Mrs. Dukakas opened the door, her eyes registering surprise at seeing Monty and Mitch standing on the front stoop. Without waiting for her to welcome them, they stepped inside the house, Mitch immediately headed for the family room where he heard voices.

Ivan, Anton, and Dmitry were sitting, the pall of a devastating Christmas Eve hanging over the room. The three men's eyes furtively looked up as the two stalked in.

"We have new information that indicates we need to search your basement," Mitch stated.

Ivan stood immediately, expression uncertain as he queried, "What are you looking for?" Instinctively, Anton and Dmitry stood, flanking their uncle in support.

Constance walked into the room, her eyes tearful as she looked up at the visitors. "Do you have any news? Anything about Erik?" she begged.

Anton stepped toward Monty, his face a mask of anger. "What the hell are you trying to pull here, Lytton?"

Before he could respond, a call came through on his and Mitch's earpieces. "Basement. All clear. No one here."

Anton stepped forward to intervene when Mitch put his hand on his gun holster. "Easy men."

Ivan's jaw was set, eyes blazing, voice like gravel. "You two better explain what the hell you're doing in my daughter-in-law's house, making demands."

While Mitch was inside talking to the building's inhabitants, Bart circled back around to his truck, seeing it empty. His head swiveled around quickly, looking for Faith. *Where the hell did she go?*

Monty and Mitch left their target, unhappy expressions on their faces. They walked back toward the others who were appearing as ghosts from the back.

He already heard through his earpiece that the location checked out clean and the occupants were furious. Before the others could get to him, Bart growled loudly, "Faith's gone."

While the others looked stunned, Jack pulled out his phone, speaking to Luke.

"What'd Luke find? Does he know where she is? She can't be far and no matter what you all think, she was right about what she saw!" Bart's jaw was set, his teeth grinding together in anger. "I swear if they've—"

"We've got this," Jack said, walking up to Bart, and quickly joined by Monty, Blaise, Cam, Chad and Mitch.

Shaking his head, Mitch looked at Bart. "I believe her, but I gotta tell you," he said, jerking his head to where he came from, "I'll be lucky to not have disciplinary action over that."

"Not waiting," Bart warned. "Not waiting."

Jack pierced him with a long look. "Understood. Been there myself. But we want them to go down? We do this by the book."

Locking his jaw, Bart nodded as Luke gave him her new coordinates. They all stared for a second at each other before turning around to look right behind them. Feeling his pocket vibrate, Bart pulled out his phone.

2 missed text messages

"Damnit!" he shouted. "She's there!"

Faith stood numbly, looking into the room that closely resembled her drawings. A room equipped to look like a boy's bedroom. Comfortable bed covered with a dark blue comforter. A bookcase on the side, filled with books and games. An overhead light plus a floor lamp provided excellent illumination. What had been outside of her vision included two chairs at a table still containing a tray with lunch leftovers. A thick rug covered the concrete floor giving the space warmth and comfort. A door on the opposite wall stood open, showing a full bathroom.

And in the middle of the bed, sat a boy playing a video game. Dressed in a clean shirt and jeans, socks on his feet. He looked up, his smile halting in place. Erik Krustas.

"Who are you?" he asked, his head cocked to the side. "Is the surprise ready?"

She stepped closer, standing at the foot of his bed, her heart beating a staccato pattern as she willed the light-headedness to pass. "Su...surprise?"

"Our trip. I only had to stay in this room for a week, while the secret trip was planned, and then we're leaving on Christmas. That's tomorrow, you know. Did you come here to help me get ready?"

"Is...is that what you were told?"

His face scrunched up in confusion. "Yeah. But honestly, I'm getting bored. That's why I'm glad we're leaving tomorrow."

Licking her lips, she knew she had to get him out of there. Her eyes darted around, landing on his shoes on the floor. "Erik, there's been a change of plans. You need to put your shoes on now. Do you have a coat?"

He giggled as he pulled his shoes on. "I don't need a coat here in my hiding room." He looked up at her, saying, "You never told me what your name was."

"Faith. I'm Faith. Lots of people have been looking for you all week."

His nose wrinkled adorably as he peered at her. "But why?"

Pulling in her lips, afraid to tell him too much, she simply said, "Well, no one knew where you were. They were scared."

Laughing, he replied, "That's silly! I was right here!"

She could not help but grin at his animated face. "Yes, yes. You were." Looking behind her, she turned back quickly and said, "We need to go. We need to try to sneak out of here and find some friends of mine, okay?"

"Like another game?"

She hesitated for a moment, before nodding. "Absolutely. A game we're going to win!"

Hearing a noise coming from the stairs, she hurried to close the door. *Dammit!* Looking at the confused expression on Erik's face, she said, "I need you to go into the bathroom for a few minutes and close the door. I'll surprise whoever comes in."

Laughing, he did as she asked while her eyes glanced around for anything to use as a weapon. The large book on the bed was the only thing she could grab before she heard a sound at the door. Slipping behind the door with the book grasped over her head, she held her breath, hoping whoever came in could not hear her hammering heartbeat.

Slowly the door opened. "Erik?" a voice whispered, as a body came into the room.

Slamming the book down on top of their head, she saw the body pitch forward as they cried out moaning on the floor. *Shit, in movies it knocks them out!* Not knowing what else to do, she kicked the man in the groin, turning his moan into cries of agony.

Rushing to the bathroom door, she threw it open. "Come on, Erik. We've got to go now!"

Grabbing his hand, she rushed him through the bedroom toward the open door. Erik pulled on her hand when he saw the man on the floor.

"What's wrong with him?" Erik asked.

She pulled him through the door into the basement. "He's just feeling sick," she said and continued toward the stairs in the back.

With Erik tucked safely behind her, Faith continued slowly toward the second set of stairs she hoped led to the garage. As she was about to reach the bottom, the door above opened and a dark figure appeared. Scurrying backward, still protecting Erik, she moved into the shadows of the basement corner.

Several huge men came quietly down the stairs, weapons drawn. As one turned toward her, she gasped.

"Cam!" she cried out.

The men immediately whirled around, and Cam barely had time to lower his weapon before she rushed into his arms.

"Where's Bart? I have to let him know I'm okay," she said, her words coming in a rush.

Bart rushed from the closet she had initially entered, grabbing her from Cam's arms and crushing her body to his.

She felt his arms quivering as they held her while he whispered over and over, "I've got you, princess. I've got you."

Jack and Chad quickly looked into the room where Erik had been kept, seeing the still writhing man on the floor. Hauling him up, Chad used zip-ties to restrain the groaning man.

Jack kneeled to the floor in front of the small boy whose eyes were large with fright. "You must be Erik? I'm Jack and we're here to help."

"Who's down there?" Anton asked.

Without answering him, Mitch escorted Constance down the stairs, handing her off as his eyes landed on Faith.

Bart noticed a young, dark-haired boy standing with Jack. Just then Ivan, Anton, and Dmitry noticed him as well. Gasping his name, Ivan rushed over before his legs gave out as he came to his grandson. Clasping Erik to his chest, his heart-wrenching sobs filled the crowded room. Anton and Dmitry rushed over as well, engulfing the two in their embrace.

After a minute Ivan stood, his hands firmly holding Erik's shoulders, and turned toward the assembly. Before he could speak, Erik called out, "Mom? Is our game over? Roger's in the room, but Faith said he was sick."

Constance tried to move out of Mitch's grasp, but his grip was equally unyielding. Blaise came from inside the room, a staggering Roger in his custody.

Ivan, finally finding his voice, roared, "Somebody better tell me what the hell is going on!"

Mitch, handing Constance over to Chad, walked over to peer into the room before looking back at Ivan. "If you look here, you'll see where your grandson has been all along."

Walking on stiff legs, Ivan moved to the hidden room, his eyes disbelieving, with Anton and Dmitry on his heels. The noise of other FBI agents coming into the room was disregarded as the three men stared into the holding room that Erik had been in for over a week. Ivan, head shaking, turned back to the group. First piercing Mitch, and then Bart, with a stare, he finally landed his gaze on Constance.

"You? You?" his voice was deathly cold. "You held my grandson in this prison for over a week? What kind of monster are you?"

"He's my son and he was never in danger!" Constance bit back, her face twisted in anger.

"For what?" Anton asked, his expression still one of shock.

Her eyes shifted over to Roger, who was not making

eye contact with her anymore. Pursing her lips, she glared at the men in the room. "For the money, what else?"

"Money?" Ivan repeated incredulously. "You want for nothing here. I pay for everything for you and Erik."

"I wanted out from under you," she growled. "By the time you finish going legitimate, there may be nothing left of Erik's inheritance. I decided to take you for what I could get and then leave. Roger and I have been planning this for over a year. We built this safe room, just waiting for the right time."

Constance smiled, cocking her eyebrow as she looked over at Mitch. "As you can see, my son was perfectly safe and comfortable in this room. After all, it's not a crime to have your child sleep in a different bedroom in a neighbor's house. He had food, water, a lovely room and bathroom, plenty of toys and books, and I saw him every day." Leaning in a little closer, she smirked. "I didn't send any demands. I've come in no contact with any money. I didn't commit a crime, Agent Evans."

Mitch smiled an equally cocky grin as he moved directly in front of her. "You should have done your homework, Mrs. Krustas. Extortion, filing a false police report, actual knowledge of a crime, aiding and abetting, aiding in a felony, assaulting Ms. Romani, accessory, conspiracy—"

"But, but" she interrupted, looking between Mitch and Roger. Lifting her hand, she cried, "It was his idea! He's got the money. He sent the notes—"

"Shut up!" Roger, finally coming to life, roared at her.

Having listened quietly, Faith's gentle, but firm, voice called out, "We need to take care of Erik and leave this for a later time." Walking out of Bart's embrace she moved to Erik, kneeling in front of the boy whose confused expression concerned her. "How about you and I go upstairs for a little while?"

Offering her his hand, he took it as she walked to the bottom of the stairs. Constance broke loose, running over to him. "Baby, please tell them you were safe. We had fun down here in our little pretend castle, didn't we?"

He threw his arms around his mother, saying, "Don't cry mom. As soon as you talk to them, we can pack for our trip, right?"

Constance glanced up at Faith, her eyes filled with tears. "Oh baby, we might have to wait on that trip for just a bit."

The FBI agents allowed Faith to lead Erik upstairs first, before handcuffing Constance and Roger. Ivan glanced at his two nephews, his face torn between emotions. Mitch gave orders to the other agents to take Constance and Roger up the stairs leading to the garage. "I'll finish here and then meet you at the police station." Giving more orders to the other agents to begin processing the scene, he then nodded to Ivan to proceed up the stairs. The group ascended into Roger's kitchen, finding Faith already speaking to a sobbing Mrs. Dukakas, who had followed the group over and now held Erik to her expansive bosom.

Bart moved over to Faith seeing tears in her eyes as well. "Come on, princess. Let's go." He began to lead her toward the front door when Ivan called out to her.

"Faith, when did you know?"

She turned and looked at the group. For a moment she froze, seeing all the faces. *How do I explain this to them?* The Saints...several FBI agents...the Krustas family. She felt a strong hand on her shoulder and twisted to look up into Bart's face. The face that only a week ago, with these very people, denounced her. And now that face gazed down at her in acceptance...understanding...concern. Offering him a tiny smile, she turned her face toward the group seeing encouragement—not condemnation.

Sucking in a deep breath, she said, "I didn't have a clue until this morning." Her eyes met Ivan's. "Last week, all I felt was hurt and anger and fear from all of you. I didn't feel any fear in Erik's room but didn't understand that at the time. With your...uh...competitors, I felt overwhelming violence, but nothing that tied them to Erik."

"What about your drawings?" Dmitry asked as he moved to stand with his uncle.

"I finally had an image of Erik, but he was smiling. He would only do that if he were comfortable with where he was and who he was with."

"And this morning? Did you know it was her?" Anton asked.

Shaking her head, she admitted, "No. I felt sadness from everyone, but then began to feel the presence of something else. A little guilt...but...more like contentment." Her eyes moved from Dmitry to Anton to Ivan. "I honestly moved around the room, hoping that I could pinpoint my feelings. It wasn't until I went back home and began to draw."

She hesitated, searching the gazes once more, but seeing nothing but interest. "I saw images of the three of you playing with Erik, but it wasn't until I drew the last picture of him sitting on the bed that I knew. This time, I saw his mom in the room with him and he was smiling." Giving a little shrug, she admitted, "I mistakenly assumed that it meant he was at her house. When I was in the truck waiting, I began to feel that he was close, but not there."

Dmitry nodded, saying, "I saw her immediately leave

the room after you left this morning. She must have told Roger she suspected you knew."

Ivan walked over, his red-rimmed eyes pinning her as he reached out to clasp her hands in his. "Thank you, my dear."

"I'm sorry that I couldn't have helped sooner." Her shoulder lifted and fell with a sigh. "I can't turn it on or off. Sometimes, things just have to come to me."

He leaned over, kissing both cheeks before whispering in her ear. Moving back, he turned swiftly, once more the man in charge. "Agent Evans, I'm sure you'll want to interview Erik. I'm calling my private doctor to examine him first. Anton, Dmitry—we need to find out how to get the money back. Mrs. Dukakas, let's get Erik comfortable back in his own room."

Jack and the Saints grinned as they trooped out of the house, Bart and Faith surrounded by them. Monty conferred with Mitch for a moment before following the rest of the Saints out as well. Bart led her to the passenger side of his truck, but halted before lifting her in. Leaning over, he placed a kiss on her lips. Tender.

"Gotta tell you, I was scared when I couldn't find you," he confessed. "You and I need to have a little talk about staying where I put you."

Arching her eyebrow while cocking her head, she said, "That discussion may not turn out as you desire. I'm not a dog—"

She was shushed as his lips hit hers, this time scorching. Melting underneath his ministrations, she kissed back with equal ardor.

Finally moving an inch back, but still breathing her in, he touched the St. Bartholomew pendant hanging between her breasts, adding, "Never been scared on a mission before."

"What made this one different?" she boldly asked, lifting her hands to his shoulders before sliding them around his neck.

"Never been in love before," he grinned the panty-melting smile that was now only hers.

Having received word that Faith was safe, and Erik had been found, safe as well, Luke sent a message.

All is well. You were right.

He waited just a moment before the reply came back.

I'm glad.

He sat staring at the screen, his fingers dancing across the keyboard, begging to be told the identity of the person on the other end. His forefinger hovered over the enter key, but he knew. *This person will let me know what I need to know...when they want me to know it.*

He deleted his entire response and added a new one.

Thank you.

26

ONE WEEK LATER

E ntering Chuck's Bar and Grille, Bart linked fingers with Faith as they made their way toward the tables pushed together, holding the Saints and several women. Bethany, Miriam, and Sabrina made up the core women —those with lasting power. Faith moved over to greet them as Bart signaled Trudi, the longtime waitress, for more beer. Faith looked up in surprise as the tall, middle-aged blonde with big curves and even bigger hair walked over, setting their beer on the table.

"Well, as I live and breathe," Trudi said, looking Faith up and down.

Faith, nervous under the woman's scrutiny, smiled as the woman slapped Bart on the arm.

"Looks like the big dog finally settled down," Trudi cackled. "There'll be hearts breaking all over the county!"

Having the good graces to blush, Bart pulled Faith into his embrace, pretending to glare at Trudi over Faith's head.

After throwing her head back in laughter, Trudi gazed fondly at the other men gathered. "Hmm, that makes four of you now hitched." She waggled her finger around to the others. "And I'll wager it won't be long for the rest of you!"

Blaise, Marc, and Luke pretended to be horrified while Monty just shook his head and Chad looked thoughtful. Mitch had joined the celebration of another successful case closed and grinned at seeing his friends squirming.

"And for you, gentlemen, tonight's beer is on the house!"

The Saints cheered while Chuck grumbled behind the bar. Faith looked around the old establishment. The well-worn, mismatched bar stools along with the tables were filled tonight and she saw a few women looking over at the Saints speculatively. Suddenly nervous, she bit her bottom lip, wondering how many of them were wanting to be in her place.

"Stop," came the whispered order at her ear.

Glancing up, she blushed as she saw Bart's eyes on her.

"I know what you're thinking," he admitted, regret in his eyes. "You're it for me now, princess. Only you. What-ever I was before, is gone. That part of my life is over." Leaning down, his lips a whisper away from hers, he added, "I only see you. Forever."

Her lips curved into a smile as her eyes met his.

———

Later that night, after a fun evening filled with good friends that ended with Bart worshiping her body long into the night, they fell asleep with their legs tangled together in the sheets. In the wee hours, Faith woke, her mind filled with images. Slipping silently into the living room, she sat on the sofa tucking her legs underneath her. Holding her art pad on her lap, she began to draw, the light of the full moon providing the only illumination.

Lines, shapes, curves, shadows. Figures began to emerge. Finally, she held the pad away from her, seeing what she had drawn. It was another drawing of Bart, this time in his backyard. She was there as well. Holding a baby. A toddler played at Bart's feet. Apollo sat nearby.

Grinning, she closed the pad and moved back to the bedroom. As she slipped under the covers, she found her body pulled in tightly to Bart's as his arms curved around her, one hand settling on her breast and the other on her hip.

"You okay?" he mumbled into her ear, nuzzling her neck.

Her answer was to snuggle closer into his warmth, her lips curved in a soft smile.

Four Years Later

Faith stepped out onto the back deck, her baby girl fresh from her nap resting in her arms, Smee curled up in a deck chair sleeping in the afternoon sun. She looked out at the commotion coming from the backyard. Apollo was charging around, barking as he jumped after the ball. Bart trotted around the dog, their toddler son on his shoulders. The glee on her son's face matched the beauty of her husband as he laughed, tossing the ball once more.

Bart's gaze moved to the deck, seeing Faith and their daughter. He smiled again, this time just for her. He held her eyes for a moment, communicating his love for her as he then looked around. His house. His yard. Their pets. Their children. The woman he loved. *I never saw it coming...but this is the image I love.*

Walking up to the deck, he swung their son down to the ground before taking Faith into his arms. First kissing the top of his baby girl's head, he then leaned into a breath away from Faith's lips. "What do you see for us, princess?"

Smiling, Faith leaned in for a whisper soft kiss. Peering into his eyes, she admitted, "I see forever."

Don't miss the next Saint!
Honor Love

ALSO BY MARYANN JORDAN

Don't miss other Maryann Jordan books!

Baytown Boys (small town, military romantic suspense)

Coming Home

Just One More Chance

Clues of the Heart

Finding Peace

Picking Up the Pieces

Sunset Flames

Waiting for Sunrise

Hear My Heart

Guarding Your Heart

Sweet Rose

Our Time

Count On Me

Shielding You

To Love Someone

Sea Glass Hearts

Protecting Her Heart

Sunset Kiss

Baytown Heroes - A Baytown Boys subseries

A Hero's Chance

Finding a Hero

A Hero for Her

Needing A Hero

Hopeful Hero

Always a Hero

In the Arms of Hero

Holding Out for a Hero

Heart of a a Hero

Hidden Hero

More Than a Hero

Falling For a Hero

Baytown Legacies - A Baytown Next Generation Series

Jack's Legacy

Trevor's Legacy

Jeremy's Legacy

For all of Miss Ethel's boys:

Heroes at Heart (Military Romance)

Zander

Rafe

Cael

Jaxon

Jayden

Asher

Zeke

Cas

Holiday for a Hero (Miss Ethel's love story)

Lighthouse Security Investigations

Mace

Rank

Walker

Drew

Blake

Tate

Levi

Clay

Cobb

Bray

Josh

Knox

Lighthouse Security Investigations West Coast

Carson

Leo

Rick

Hop

Dolby

Bennett

Poole

Adam

Jeb

Chris's story: Home Port (an LSI West Coast crossover novel)

Ian's story: Thinking of Home (LSIWC crossover novel)

Oliver's story: Time for Home (LSIWC crossover novel)

Lighthouse Security Investigations Montana

Logan

Sisco

Landon

Devlin

Home for Justice (LSIMT crossover novel) Tyler's story

Todd

Casper

Bert

Hope City (romantic suspense series co-developed

with Kris Michaels

Brock book 1

Sean book 2

Carter book 3

Brody book 4

Kyle book 5

Ryker book 6

Rory book 7

Killian book 8

Torin book 9

Blayze book 10

Griffin book 11

Saints Protection & Investigations

(an elite group, assigned to the cases no one else wants...or can
solve)

Serial Love

Healing Love

Revealing Love

Seeing Love

Honor Love

Sacrifice Love

Protecting Love

Remember Love

Discover Love

Surviving Love

Celebrating Love

Searching Love

Follow the exciting spin-off series:

Alvarez Security (military romantic suspense)

Gabe

Tony

Vinny

Jobe

SEALs

SEAL Together (Silver SEAL)

Undercover Groom (Hot SEAL)

Also for a Hope City Crossover Novel / Hot SEAL...

A Forever Dad

Long Road Home

Military Romantic Suspense

Home to Stay (a Lighthouse Security Investigation crossover novel)

Home Port (an LSI West Coast crossover novel)

Thinking of Home (LSIWC crossover novel)

Time for Home (LSIWC crossover novel)

Home for Justice (LSIMT crossover novel)

Letters From Home (military romance)

Class of Love

Freedom of Love

Bond of Love

The Love's Series (detectives)

Love's Taming

Love's Tempting

Love's Trusting

The Fairfield Series (small town detectives)

Emma's Home

Laurie's Time

Carol's Image

Fireworks Over Fairfield

Please take the time to leave a review of this book. Feel free to contact me, especially if you enjoyed my book. I love to hear from readers!

Facebook

Email

Website